Succulent

Zane Presents

Succulent

Chocolate Flava II

The Eroticanoir.com Anthology

ATRIA BOOKS

New York   London   Toronto   Sydney

A Division of Simon & Schuster, Inc.
1230 Avenue of the Americas
New York, NY 10020

This book is a work of fiction. Names, characters, places, and
incidents either are products of the author's imagination or are used
fictitiously. Any resemblance to actual events or locales or persons,
living or dead, is entirely coincidental.

ATRIA BOOKS and colophon are trademarks of Simon & Schuster, Inc.

Manufactured in the United States of America

ISBN-13: 978-1-4165-4883-6

Copyright Notices

This book is dedicated to "Aunt Barbara," for showing up at all my local events, worrying about me getting enough sleep, and for being such a wonderful and supportive friend to my mother and the entire family. Thanks for being so open-minded and nonjudgmental. Those who choose to judge should first judge themselves; thanks for recognizing that. You are much loved and appreciated.

Contents

Introduction

Succulent: *Chocolate Flava II* has been a labor of love. I would like to thank the contributors for their patience and for allowing me to share their talent with the world. Erotica has truly exploded over the past several years, particularly in the African-American market. I am pleased that the surge has occurred and will continue to try to give exposure to those who deserve to be read in this genre. The pleasure that I derive from being able to give others the opportunity to shine is indescribable. It is an honor to do so and I appreciate all of those who may have submitted something but did not get selected. There will be many more anthologies to come.

The success of the first *Chocolate Flava* surprised even me. It surpassed all sales expectations, as did *Caramel Flava*. It is my hope that you will enjoy this volume as well, because a growth has occurred. Many of my readers have expressed that *Chocolate Flava* was one of their favorite books. This will surely also become a favorite; it is definitely one of mine.

In my determination to shed the world of sexual oppression

and repression, I am delighted to announce that *Zane's Sex Chronicles* will premiere on Cinemax in April 2008. It has been such a marvelous journey and I am looking forward to the next leg: television and film. *Addicted* will be in theaters in 2008 and I want to thank all of you in advance for your support of both efforts.

I do need everyone to do me a tremendous favor. No book, no movie, and no television show can truly succeed if people do not know it exists. Word of mouth is essential and I need all of you to ask everyone that you know to join my email list by sending a blank email to Eroticanoir-subscribe@topica.com. I want a million people on my email list; no, millions of people. For that, I need your help. Please spread the message to everyone you know. I would be deeply grateful for it.

With that said, I want each and every one of you to realize that you are truly loved and appreciated by me. I hope that you enjoy *Succulent,* which could have been called *Suck-U-Length* because a lot of that is going on in here. Also, please look for four select stories from *The Sex Chronicles: Shattering the Myth* on audio. They are hot! You can purchase them as an audio download online.

Remember to love hard but fuck even harder!

Blessings,
Zane

Succulent

The Quiet Room

Michelle J. Robinson

Patrice wasn't sure which throbbing she wanted to quiet more—the throbbing between her legs or the throbbing in her head. For two consecutive weeks now she had awakened with a vicious headache, which today had progressed in severity. Yet, despite the pounding in her head, she still got jittery between the legs watching that tall, dark, delicious man pass her desk. His name was Trevor and his ass looked like it was built from stone. Every time she saw his bald head she thought of how much she'd like to shine it with her own "special" lotion. Just as she was daydreaming about rubbing her thick, swollen pussy lips all over his face and head, she realized he was speaking.

"Good morning, Patrice."

"Good . . . good morning, Trevor," she stuttered.

"Hot enough for you?"

Patrice wanted to say, "Hot as a goddamned furnace— wanna blow it for me?"

Instead she said, "A little too hot," and left it at that.

"Well, try to stay cool and let me know if you need a fan or something. I believe we have some extras in the storage room."

Trevor was the firm's facilities manager and it was his job to make sure that their office ran like a well-oiled machine and that the partners, attorneys, and staff were comfortable.

Her mind running on overtime, Patrice thought some more about *his* "well-oiled machine" and how much she'd like to grease it; that is, before reminding herself she was married.

Trevor hesitated a moment, as if he wanted to continue the conversation, but instead wished her a pleasant day and continued walking.

Trevor couldn't help but notice feminine, felinelike Patrice. Her slanted eyes and agile body reminded him of a jungle cat that, when tamed, purred like a kitty cat. Years ago they had a phrase for women built like Patrice—*a brick shithouse*—and that she was; standing approximately 5'5", Patrice wasn't a big woman, but those 38Ds, those shapely legs, that tiny waist and round ass, meant she seldom went unnoticed; especially not by Trevor. He often visualized the stunning contrast of his dark chocolate complexion against her light chocolate form.

The stress at home was clearly beginning to get to Patrice, and this morning's headache made it impossible for her to function at the most basic of levels. Since leaving work and going home was definitely not an option, she decided she would use her lunch hour to get it together.

She had heard that there was a room in the office called the Quiet Room where you could go to nurse an illness or maybe even catch up on a little sleep if need be. As long as the room wasn't occupied, it was on a first-come, first-serve basis. The key was kept at the receptionist's desk, so Patrice went to retrieve it, hoping that no one else had.

"Hi, Gladys," Patrice offered with a smile.

The receptionist at Perkins & Brightmon was a haggard old crone with a disposition to match. Patrice thought her face would crack, trying to play nice with the old bitch, but she hadn't maintained her station in the corporate sector without her fair share of sacrifices.

"Is there a key to the Quiet Room here?" Patrice asked.

"Of course it's here. Where else would it be?" Gladys answered snidely. "Sign the book and take the key that's in the pocket. If the key is there, then it means the room is free."

Patrice signed the book that Gladys motioned to and took the gold key from the binder pocket. There was a spot for IN and OUT. She signed her name and jotted 1:00 p.m. in the IN box. As she walked away, she realized she had no idea where the Quiet Room even was.

"Oh," she uttered, not really wanting to ask the old woman anything further. "Where is the room?"

"Go through the double doors; it's the second door on the right."

Patrice found the room with little difficulty, stuck the key in the lock, and opened it. She walked in and surveyed her surroundings: beige walls, a brown leather chaise with a blanket and pillow, a small cherrywood side table, on which there was a silver lamp with a white shade. Next to the lamp was also a first aid kit. She opened it, seeking anything that might get rid of her horrible headache. Nothing.

It occurred to Patrice that the only thing she probably needed was a short rest. Things had gotten so unbearable at home, and dealing every night with someone you despised could definitely be a contributing factor to consistent headaches. As much as she hated screwing her pot-smoking, non-working, lazy-ass husband, Patrice was as horny as a fucking rabbit. She had taken to masturbating at every opportunity. Although she was horny—headache and all—she knew that this was neither the time nor the place for satisfying her basic desires. However, there were often things even your own mind couldn't control.

Surprisingly she drifted off to sleep almost immediately after lounging on the chaise and pulling the heavy gray wool blanket up to her chin. It didn't take long for her dreams to take hold.

"Drink it!"

"Drink every last bit of it!"

"Mine tastes just like vanilla milkshake, baby."

"Here it fucking comes. Open your mouth wide . . . wider!"

"Ahhhh."

She sat outside at an ordinary sidewalk café in Paris, except, instead of being clothed in her usual fashionable best, she was completely naked, without even a pair of panties. And as she sat sipping a thick white liquid from a long-stemmed champagne flute, at least a dozen men of various colors and sizes stood circling her, their dicks in their hands, jerking feverishly. One, a tall, bald, chocolate, strapping brother with granite pecks and a cock that could bench-press a barbell, had maintained quite a rhythm, sliding his right hand up and down his burgeoning erection, allowing his pre-cum to lubricate his efforts. He aimed directly for Patrice's mouth, hoping to make the money shot.

"Open wide, sugar. You've never tasted joy juice like this before," he uttered breathlessly.

Patrice obeyed every word and kept her mouth as wide-open as was physically possible—anxiously awaiting her reward.

All sorts of men were in the circle, some were white, some Hispanic, some tall, others short. Some looked like they spent hours in the gym while others were of average physical condition. But none of that mattered one bit to Patrice. Her focus was on their dicks and the circle-jerk that they were all engaged in.

One short man with long, black, wavy hair, who appeared to be Mexican, gripped his café-au-lait cock so tightly she was sure the strangled look on his face wasn't passion, but pain.

"Fffuckkkk!" he groaned as he blasted Patrice's swollen, ample globes with his sweet, sticky offering.

She ran her index finger over her breasts and retrieved a dollop of cum. The paltry appetizer only left her more famished than before, and she lifted her left breast and began devouring what was left with her own mouth, enthusiastically lapping at her now rigid nipple with her tongue, nibbling and biting until her nipple was raw and her pussy sopping wet.

While others aimed for the long-stemmed flute she was holding, still others seemed intent on splattering her pert, erect nipples with their cum, as she waited for each of them to explode one by one. Her dark chocolate man of steel appeared to be close to detonation, so Patrice removed her lips from her breast and opened up as wide as her mouth would stretch.

"Here it comes, sugar!" he bellowed.

His aim had a perfect landing directly inside Patrice's eagerly awaiting mouth.

"Drink it all!" he bellowed. "Don't waste a fucking drop. You never tasted nectar like that, baby. Never!"

As Patrice reached out in an attempt to milk Man of Steel's

cock of any remaining cum, it was as though an invisible barrier kept them from touching. This game had rules. She could watch them hand-fuck themselves and they could spew their lava at Patrice, but she couldn't touch them, nor them her.

However, Patrice enjoyed acting as "orchestra leader." She pretended she was the leader, conducting the orchestra and the multitude of dicks stretched out before her, the instruments. As she barked instructions, she reveled in the overwhelming feeling of control.

"Faster, faster," she called out to a tall white man with a long dick that curved ever so slightly to the right. Patrice wondered what that curved cock would feel like bouncing off the walls of her cunt. As quickly as she noticed this arched appendage and began fantasizing about what wonderful things it could do for her G-spot, she was distracted by a dick of modest length with more than impressive width. This display brought new meaning to the words *beating his meat*. The sight of his large, masculine hands wrapped around what could easily have been a tasty slab of beef made Patrice hungry beyond words. When his sudden forceful jet began gushing toward her, Patrice graduated from plain old hungry to ravenous. The crescendo of cum sputtering and spurting forth was her rewarding melody, but she needed more.

Suddenly her pussy began to feel painfully neglected, and Patrice threw her left leg over the arm of the silver chair she was sitting in. She played with her protruding button of bliss. The hard metal against her pliable flesh only made her hotter. Her pussy was starving for one of these dicks to fill her up to the hilt; maybe even two or three. After all, she did have three holes to accommodate.

To her right, a 6'9" Schwarzenegger look-alike, with the

most beautiful chiseled jawline, cleft chin, and olive-colored skin, intermittently slid his hand slowly up and down his adequately sized cock, taking turns jerking himself off and slapping his cock against the flat of his left hand. It seemed as though each time he slapped his cock against his hand, he swelled to cum-inspiring proportions, causing Patrice to finger-fuck herself with mounting enthusiasm. He slapped, and she plunged first one, then two, then three of her fingers deep inside her pussy, flicking at her clit with her thumb and causing a rush of juices to flood the hard, cold metal chair she was now glued to. The suctioning noises of several hands wrapped around several cocks and the assortment of masculine grunts and groans that formerly filled the area of the café were now drowned out by Patrice's moans and the slapping of one rapidly swelling dick against one open hand. However, the slapping sound suddenly changed to more of a knocking sound. Patrice assumed the heavy weight of his ever-expanding cock had caused the shift in timbre, yet the sound increased in such severity it was almost deafening. That's when she awoke.

Outside the locked door of the Quiet Room, someone was urgently knocking.

"Are you okay?" came the call.

"Oh, shit!" Patrice muttered to herself.

As she removed her slippery hands from her panties, she realized where she was and what she had been doing. The room reeked of pussy, and she had probably done the same thing she did when she was at home. Although she made every effort to avoid any possibilities of fucking her deadbeat husband, including making the guest bedroom her own room, she would often have an especially nasty dream and he would hear her moaning. She would find him standing over her in the middle of the night, hard as a baseball bat and wanting to fuck her with a fierceness. She would inevitably be pissed with herself for moaning in her sleep, and she now realized that is probably what had happened there in the Quiet Room.

She rose from the chaise, adjusted her clothing, and sprayed a little of her Chanel No. 5 into the air, hoping to camouflage the lingering scent of sex. Then, she opened the door, pretending to be half asleep.

It was Trevor.

"Are you okay? I thought I heard someone crying," he lied.

Trevor, more than anyone else, knew the telltale sounds of passion—and the scent of it. The smell in the room confirmed his suspicions. He had long been attracted to Patrice, but had heard that she was married. He was never one to interfere with a marriage, but the murmurs he had heard from outside the office had made his dick so hard he wanted to throw her down on that chair in the middle of the day and fuck her until she spoke in tongues. However, if he did that, it would probably be the last thing he ever did at Perkins & Brightmon; not that he hadn't had his fair share of quickies in the infamous Quiet Room. Those were reserved for off-hours, when he was relatively sure no one would be in the office. It did occur to him that he had one damn good perk working as Perkins & Brightmon's facilities manager. Ensconced in his office was something only a relatively few people at the firm were aware of. One of his responsibilities as facilities manager was to observe what was going on in the firm—who was stealing, staff comings and goings. To facilitate that responsibility, cameras were strategically placed in various sectors of the office. One of those sectors was the Quiet Room.

No one ever asked to see the tapes, unless something was

stolen or someone was hurt (which never happened), so Trevor often satisfied his lustful urges by watching tapes of the infamous Quiet Room. If his boss only knew what went on in there, that room would probably have been shut down a long time ago. The carnal delights that were satisfied after hours between attorneys and secretaries, janitors and partners, would have made media history if he ever published those tapes. But for now, none of those couplings interested him. All he wanted to see was that beautiful little kitty Patrice in action. He always thought she moved liked a feline, but outside that door, listening to her purr reinforced his perceptions. He would wait until everyone left for the day, shut his door, and watch Patrice pleasuring herself while he privately did the same.

By 8:30 p.m. everyone in the firm had left for the evening. Patrice was terribly embarrassed and sure that Trevor knew what she had been doing earlier that afternoon. She wanted to talk to him, but didn't want to do it during the day while everyone was there. Besides which, she had been so busy working all day that she couldn't have gotten a free moment if she wanted. She decided she would wait it out and find her way to his office when she was sure everyone had left—everyone except Trevor. Around 8:45, Patrice took a walk around the floor and saw the light on in Trevor's office. She was sure she hadn't seen him leave, so she decided to knock on the door. This time she was the one who heard the telltale evidence of passion. Before she lost her nerve, she opened the door to his office only to find Trevor, dick in hand, looking at one of his many monitors.

"Why don't you let me do that for you?" she asked huskily.

Trevor, shocked and surprised, fumbled, suddenly realizing he hadn't locked the door and what a stupid chance he had taken. However, he quickly recovered when he realized what she had said.

"Oh, kitty, please do," he responded.

Patrice crossed the office to his side of the desk and was surprised to find, instead of the downloaded porn she thought he was watching, that he was indeed watching her. It was mesmerizing, watching herself fuck her pussy the way she was doing—in her sleep. No wonder her husband would stand over her in the middle of the night, desperate to slide his pole inside. He had probably watched her many a night without her knowing the show she was putting on for him.

"Kitty, is your pussy still as wet as it was earlier today? Can I taste it?"

Trevor knocked everything off his desk, except for the two monitors, and grabbed Patrice up in his arms, setting her down on the desk. He pulled down her already saturated panties, spread open her legs, and began lapping away at her pussy with such zeal that Patrice was squirming and squealing within minutes. With the flat of his tongue Trevor assaulted her pussy with such a lashing that her legs turned to jelly. He then probed ever so deeply inside her dripping wet pussy with his pointed tongue, tongue-fucking her cunt until her eyes rolled up into her head. He found her throbbing, erect clit and tortured her sweetly with licks and nibbles that sent electric charges throughout her entire body. Kneeling down on the floor, feasting on this syrupy pussy, Trevor's dick dripped pre-cum in anticipation of Patrice's walls capturing his cock and holding tight, while he thrust himself deeper and deeper inside her. He raised himself from the floor, eager to share Patrice's tasty delights with her.

"Oh, fuck! You make me feel so good! Make me feel good,

Trevor. Please make me feel good! I want your cock buried deep inside of me. Oh, please, please!" she pleaded.

He smothered her pleas with his mouth. He took Patrice's face into his hands, gazed into her eyes, and kissed her so urgently, Patrice could think of nothing else but how good he made her feel. He explored her mouth with his tongue, not wanting her to miss an inch of her exquisite taste. She tasted like heaven on earth.

Trevor lay on top of her on the desk, his head in her breasts, licking them, tasting remnants of mother's milk lacing them. Suddenly he was reminded that less than a year ago the office had thrown Patrice a baby shower. His dick, hard between her legs, wouldn't permit him a conscience. All he could think of was the heat radiating from her pussy. He held fast to the desk above both their heads and plunged his stiff, throbbing, anxiously awaiting dick inside her, afraid to move; the sensation was so euphoric he was sure if he moved even an inch, it would be over long before it started. He rested himself there; that is, until Patrice began to gyrate rhythmically against him with her pelvis, grinding him ever deeper inside her pussy. Even from her spot on the desk, she couldn't control the urge to feel his dick up to the hilt of her pussy. She gazed into his dark, sexy eyes and increased the speed at which she circled his dick with her pussy. Then, something happened that had never, ever happened to Trevor in his entire life. He had had his fair share of pussy, but nothing could prepare him for the earth-shattering orgasm unchartered territory provides. As Trevor continued fucking Patrice relentlessly, she began scooting farther and farther back on the desk so that her back was bent over the desk and her head was hanging down. Her back bent so far back Trevor was afraid he might hurt her, yet the two lovers couldn't stop, even if they wanted to. It was now out of their control.

Patrice began a sexual chant that engorged Trevor's cock even more, then suddenly the combination of unveiled passion and nature caused Patrice to discharge mother's milk from her breasts so quickly and with such force and intensity it was as though her breasts were cumming, only turning Trevor on all the more. He gripped her with all his might, raising her along with him from the desk and backing her up against the nearest wall, devouring her breasts, biting at her crimson nipples, feeling them grow inside his mouth, poking insistently with his tongue, as he tried in earnest to extract even more of her sweet nectar, burying his head in the feminine curve of her neck to muffle his moans before they escaped from his throat. He repeated over and over, "Purr for me, sweet kitty. Purr for me, just the way you did for yourself."

Playas of a Greater Game

Anthony Beal

He made it so easy most days that in fleeting spaces between the passage of seconds Rosalind could almost pity her lover, Lord Eryq of the shaven head, the brow perpetually scowling on the best of days beneath the weight of the unenlightened world, God bless his warrior's heart. Let heaven help any woman so foolhardy as to risk seeking to love him on any day other than the best, for Shakespeare never penned tragedy like that which would ensue and had on more occasions than he'd ever admit. Your typical angry young African-American male, Lord Eryq was not, however, and few implications stood capable of drawing forth resentment as magma-hot or as voluminous as did that one. "Typical," indeed! He was not scornful, he was merely a thinker thinking, because that's what thinkers do, thank you kindly. Perhaps he did devote an inordinate amount of time to pondering life's many injustices and humankind's myriad shortcomings, but that was a problem of which he stood fully aware, and it was all his, not yours. Not unless you wanted to make something out of it.

And he hoped you wanted to make something out of it.

Before their relationship had aged a fortnight, Rosalind had successfully learned not only the rules of engagement, but also the best conditions under which to abide by or flout them, co-ordinating her actions with these right down to the temperature or time of day or part of the city in which they found themselves. Here, a wink of her impossibly blue eye at a restaurant wine steward as he refills her flute without being asked. There, a kiss of greeting applied haphazardly close to the lips of a long-missed male friend who's known her since the two of them were young enough to share a bathtub at her parents' home without impropriety. Here again, a smile allowed to linger on her face for a second too long at a coffeehouse barista's innocent flirtation; textbook flirtation bestowed upon all female customers alike in hopes of encouraging nothing so much as generous tips. Rare was the day that Rosalind's manipulation of these ostensibly innocuous seedlings of social grace failed to germinate. More often than not, they bore poisonous and irresistible fruit of the sort that would quickly become Rosalind's addiction; the sort that invariably placed her Eryq at physical odds with the various objects of attentions she contrived for precisely that purpose. His temper, the archetypal gift that keeps on giving, always paid her handsomely for her efforts.

Nights like tonight tended to place Rosalind's sympathies with the unsuspecting lambs to whom the slightest extension of her favor deemed superfluous in Eryq's eyes embodied criminality damning and dangerous. Rosalind might never know whether it was by blind luck or by Eryq's stubbornness that the altar of his ire always came to collect the sheep, but never their shepherdess. A thing of which she did feel certain, though, was that she would go on leading the unassuming to ultimate sacrifice upon that altar for as long as that scythe that her lover carried in his mouth remained sharp.

"Fool, I'm talking to you! I said, 'Do you have a problem?' " Eryq demanded, proving for all time that the grandeur of her art and artifice lay in consistently steering them, her and Eryq, to public locales populated by men as ready and able as oiled honing stones against which to grind him. The light-skinned brother dining alone at an adjacent table on the outdoor terrace of Eryq's favorite chophouse, the brother with the cleft chin and eyes as green as limes, appeared to be such a stone.

Those eyes as green as limes retrieved the gauntlet, the one that Eryq's glare had cast down between them, without flinching. He appeared to have no idea what new and unspoiled worlds of spilled blood and shattered dinnerware had been promised to him the instant he'd returned the surreptitious smile that Rosalind had made such an unsubtle point of delivering to him over Eryq's shoulder.

"Did I say anything to you that suggested that I had a problem?" Rosalind's lime-eyed sacrifice asked Eryq, looking by turns amused and disinterested in a way that Rosalind knew would only fuel Eryq's anger.

Eryq shoved his chair back, away from their table. Then things began rapidly happening as the lime-eyed brother's chair lost a leg to Eryq's temper. As table linen got dragged to the floor, toppling plates, saucers, and filled glassware over the table's edge and into oblivion against hardwood floors. As the tip of Eryq's boot introduced itself to the fragile ribs of a stranger. As fists accustomed to this drill kissed that stranger upon both his cheeks. As the establishment's manager phoned police. Then Eryq was hauling Rosalind up out of her seat, tossing enough cash onto their table to cover the cost of the meal that they'd not experience the luxury of finishing, and bounding purpose-fully out of the establishment with long, emphatic strides that left Rosalind the options of skipping to keep up with him or being dragged along the ground.

Seconds later, the rust-colored Pontiac that he'd probably never stop customizing tore out of the parking lot behind the chophouse with Rosalind at its wheel because Eryq was an angry driver on the best of days, and because Rosalind knew every conceivable shortcut back to his apartment.

Territorial, the lovemaking that spilled out of the car and into Eryq's third-floor walk-up. Shedding clothes like serpent skins, their knot of grappling limbs and smacking lips found Eryq's bedroom. In darkness, her teeth and fingertips stalked onto his body like armies storming an unclaimed continent. Rosalind's eyes crossed in the dark as his kiss drew the air from her lungs. Feral, his clutch beneath which smoldered libidinous fires that threatened to sear its every sampling of Rosalind's flesh.

Nothing Lord Eryq did ever left Rosalind feeling as deliri-ously wanton and powerful as she did immediately following a dustup between him and some unnamed flavor of the day with whom she'd chosen to innocently flirt. In that invariable instant that always found Eryq confronting the unfortunate, Rosalind was both girl and woman. She was goddesshood unbridled, un-disputed, immortal omnipotence through whom flowed and to whose whims bent all the energies of the universe. She was an ebullient child at play, guiding two posturing puppets in cir-cles about one another, choreographing their ritual dance to first blood, a ceremony that fed her evolution like nothing else.

Rosalind's hands stole impressions of Eryq's physique like

lusting thieves. Her fingernails bit into his beefy shoulders. Sending his fingertips to swim amidst the curly sable sea of her hair, Eryq filled the windy, berry-painted O of her mouth with his tongue and discovered electricity in her kiss.

Lord Eryq's gladiatorial spirit ran as rampant across her ivory nakedness as it had across the jaw of the lime-eyed brother at the chophouse. Rosalind lapped the aphrodisiac of his sweat from his every sinew as he stalked her most sensitive regions. Spreading spastic hues of coral and rose in anticipation of his mouth, she could do little but dance along with his tongue where it raved inside her, coaxing forth honey-sweet viscosity to glaze her inner thighs. Every shiver that he inspired was a village burned, every frenetic gasp a terrain surmounted. He slashed. She burned. And in truth, this was the way she liked it.

The truth, too, was that instances like this were the only times that Rosalind felt equipped to suffer his company, or to allow herself the briefest respite from loathing him.

But a deal was a deal.

"You and your white bitch need to learn some motherfuckin' consideration for the rest of the people living in this building," Eryq heard upon opening his apartment door to squint into the light of dawn. He no longer wondered on mornings like this how early his neighbor and onetime bedmate Celestine must have gotten out of bed in order to greet him at this hour, or how long she'd spent crouched beside her apartment door listening for the sound of him opening his door to retrieve his daily newspaper. It disgusted him sufficiently just to know that she had.

It served him right, and Eryq knew it did, that his every morning-after should begin with the crowing of the harpy next door. With him alone rested all fault for his having broken the first rule of the one-night stand: you never hook up with someone who lives close enough to you to track your every move. He would not seek to blame it on the general air of New Yorkers' emotional and sexual neediness that had marked that first New Year's Eve following 9/11, nor upon the fifth of Cutty Sark that he'd helped his partner Tulane demolish at the New Year's party they'd all attended in those days before Rosalind, before the club to which he now belonged.

Because he'd heard her voice before realizing he'd heard it, Eryq's reaction to the head stuck out of the next apartment door down the hall from his was not immediate. His brain had registered only the vaguest impressions of scowling espresso-dark features, of a black gauze headwrap, of words that seemed to lean, indicative of the speaker's Caribbean lineage. Failing to get an initial rise out of him, she squawked a second time.

"I know you can hear me, simple-actin' motherfucker. We sure as hell heard the two of y'all going at each other like motherfuckin' savages. I got motherfuckin' children over here. Little ones don't need to be woke up in the middle of the damned night hearing that motherfuckin' shit."

"Those little ones whose delicate little ears you're so concerned about," Eryq replied, "you talk to them with the same mouth you're using right now to talk to me?"

Blindsided by the question's implication, then affronted by it, Celestine raged, "Nigga, fuck you. You and that nasty-ass club you belong to." A rarity was the conversation between Eryq and Celestine that did not end on such a note.

"Go inside, Celestine," Eryq sniffed. "If words like *nigga* and *motherfucker* represent the extent of your arsenal, then you'll never defeat me in a war of words."

He closed his apartment door and immediately forgot about Celestine.

Eryq could be an arrogant prick, and he knew it. Eryq could fuck like a god, and the devil was in him knowing this as well, and knowing that Rosalind knew it. Turning that arrogance on the general public and then racing home with him to reap the bedroom benefits of the resultant altercations was the best vehicle Rosalind had yet discovered for reconciling the two. It was also the most effective form of precoital masturbation she'd ever known. Nothing brought the heat like watching her lover fight for her as if she were a prize to be won, as if her orgasms were spoils of war to be earned upon battlefields of her covert choosing. Knowing this to be a fool's fantasy, one more befitting a prepubescent, did nothing to diminish Rosalind's arousal at the mere thought. Their time spent together was as much her indulgence as it was his victory lap, one to be savored in any and every manner she and her victorious warrior saw fit to choose. That was the game's first, final, and only rule.

"So what do you tell people when they ask you about meeting men the way you met me?" Eryq asked her the following evening after lovemaking.

"Those who have to ask wouldn't understand it," she assured him. "Those evolved enough to grasp the concept aren't blind. They know what this is. They know what we are."

"All right, then. By your estimation, what are we?"

Rosalind grinned at him. "Sugar, any way you spin it, we're playas. Of a greater game."

"Eryq might be an asshole, but I cum hard every time," she

would later tell her husband by cell phone. "Behave and tonight I'll let you hear us fuck."

She kept her word. Eryq came without suspecting anything.

Every so often, his guilt overwhelmed him.

"Hello?" The cracked, listless female voice sounded smaller than Eryq had known it to be in the past.

"Hey, baby," he said, hoping the term of affection sounded less strange to her ear than it felt leaving his tongue. The five months since their last face-to-face encounter might as well have been five decades for the awkwardness he felt now.

"Hey. What do you want?"

It was the one question to which Eryq had failed to rehearse a satisfactory answer. "I don't know. I guess I just miss you a little."

"We agreed not to speak."

"I just . . . wanted to hear your voice for a minute," he admitted, cursing his weakness.

"Well, time's up. Good-bye, Eryq."

"Ananya, wait, please? I have some things to say." He'd anticipated that this conversation would not go easily. That hadn't kept him from hoping it might.

"So do I. You knew what toll this arrangement would take on what we had. You knew what it would mean, but at the same time, you wanted what you wanted, and that's always been the bottom line, hasn't it? Do whatever it takes to satisfy your wants and needs and damn the consequences."

"Listen, I didn't call you looking for a fight," he began.

A peal of her laughter belched forth without any lilt of humor. "Sorry. It's just that, if you think it over, that's kind of funny. Given the circumstances. Anyway, you want to tell me important things, then show up next month at the place and do what you have to do. You remember where the place is."

"Yeah, I remember where it is."

"Great. Right now I've got to go freshen my lipstick and climb back between Alphonse's legs. That man likes him his brown sugar, don't you know. Unlike some men I know, black women are still good enough for him."

Eryq cursed the unbidden visual that accompanied Ananya's closing remark, one involving her caramel-colored perfection mashed beneath a hairy Mediterranean club member named Alphonse. It seemed that for everything that had changed between Eryq and Ananya, one thing remained constant: his wife was still peerless and unrivaled when it came to twisting the fucking knife.

"You don't care who suffers, so long as it's dark meat you're riding, do you?" Eryq asked, storming naked into their bedroom one month later. They were to visit the club that evening, where Eryq would participate in one of the quarterly tournaments responsible for bringing him and Rosalind together.

"Where is all this coming from?" she asked, noting the strangeness of his facial expression. It was that of a man who didn't know where he was or how he'd come to be there. Damn Ananya for always knowing how best to push his buttons.

"I'm talking," he said, tossing the comforter and sheets from the unmade bed, "about you and your husband joining the club, coming there looking specifically for a big, dumb Negro." Eryq climbed onto her with a deadness behind his eyes usually reserved for men to whom he was about to hand a thrashing.

"Your husband never had to fight for you," he told her,

shredding the nightshirt she wore, "and when he finally did, he lost. He lost you to a big, bald-headed nigger with a big, black dick for you to spin on. Isn't that how you planned it? So how does the rest of the fantasy play out? When do we get to the rough stuff?"

"I don't know what you're talking about," Rosalind insisted, pulling away from Eryq's advance.

"Is this what it's all about? Is it this right here?" he asked, grasping his cock at its base and dragging her toward him. "Is it all about this? Come on, sister! Admit it! Admit it!" He punctuated each demand by slamming his naked body down to spear her sex and drive the air from Rosalind's lungs. Pelvic lunges of mounting savagery ground her protests into odes to his cock delivered through chattering teeth.

"You're a fine one to question anyone's motives," Rosalind told Eryq a short time later, bouncing wildly astride his hardness. "You think anyone believes you don't attend every event hoping to spy a new piece of Caucasian or Latin or Asian ass waltz in on the arm of some man who you can't wait to take apart? Don't crucify me just because you lust as much as I did for experiences neither of us had ever had, and I'm the only one of us honest enough to admit it to myself."

"Fuck you," Eryq grunted.

"Yes, you are, and you've loved every minute of the past six months, haven't you, shithead? We were only supposed to have three, but you've so relished playing schoolyard bully under the guise of defending your white queen's 'honor.' Don't lie that you haven't. I've loved it, too. Having a strong, able lover fight for me and win. I've exploited the hell out of it." They rolled. Rosalind found herself on her stomach.

Lord Eryq's helmet kissed Rosalind's lubed anal pore. His

unceremonious entry, the curl of his spittle-flecked lips, the mounting depth of his lunges, testified to his growing disdain for this woman who was not Ananya. Not to be outdone, Rosalind punched her fingernails through Eryq's mattress and flung herself backward against his crotch, affirming the mutuality of the sentiment.

"Nothing's ever made your 'big, black dick' as hard as that, has it?" she shrieked, feeling Eryq collapse fully onto her, rutting riotously. "Handing down beatings to any unenlightened soul who you thought didn't understand us as a couple!"

They came together in ecstatic agony, each one's orgasm fueling the other as they lay clinging to one another like first-time lovers fearful of being swept apart by the tempests ravaging their flesh.

"What are we, by my estimation?" Rosalind gasped, echoing his question from weeks ago as they lay panting. "Sugar, we're a good old-fashioned grudge fuck waiting to happen."

The "club" had changed locations three times since its inception two years ago. Tonight found it underground, in the basement of an abandoned warehouse on the east side of town near the river.

Membership was by invitation only. The first rule of the club was that there was no club. The club was a myth fashioned by church shills to smear the swinger's lifestyle. The club was an urban legend invented by sex-hungry teenage boys. The club was anything that kept news of its existence from leaking to the wrong person and bringing it under suspicion of the unenlightened.

Eryq and Rosalind descended into the club's arena, a gymnasium-size room with poor lighting. Posted signs directed ladies to one side of this room, where folding chairs awaited, and men to the other. To the ladies, an open bar offered assorted libations. Eryq fingered the plastic disk in his back pocket, the one bearing Rosalind's name.

Their host, a middle-aged African-American gentleman wearing a graying beard and a simple turtleneck and blazer, took the stage to open the evening. By this time, nearly a hundred married couples stood present. A lot of these, Eryq noticed, were new meat. When the host spoke, he was brief, because tiresome rule recitations took time away from the main attraction.

"Welcome, guys and dolls," he sang, "to this evening's main event: 'Come Out Swinging,' where we don't sweat the petty things and don't pet the sweaty things, at least not on-premises. If you're here, then you know the drill. Fellas, the object is simple: fight to the last man and leave with his tag in your hand. Make sure that your most recent swapmate's full name is legible on the plastic disk hidden on your person. Remember, three months is a long time to go with some other dude balling your baby, so either defend these with your life or surrender your sexy wife. And as always, the rule stating that no weapons of any kind are to be used or misused will be strictly enforced. Gentlemen, you may begin."

A maelstrom of fists and feet. With their wives watching, every husband present threw himself into a bare-knuckle brawl in which he engaged every three months; one that would determine, by his successful capture of an opponent's plastic disk, whose wife he would spend the next three months making love to.

Their host spoke again as blood and sweat flew. "Don't forget that our next social will be Turnabout Night. That's right, sisters, it'll be your chance to fight for your right to hard lays as only your neighbors' husbands can deliver them, so come out swinging."

Eryq located Alphonse and dove at him, prepared to bring Ananya home to stay.

Emma's Triangle

Tigress Healy

My friends think I'm nuts but that's not it. I just have different morals than folks. I believe in the old-fashioned way of doing things. Holding men accountable for their actions. To me that don't mean treating their fuckups with anger and violence. It means figuring out how to exploit them.

See, I'm fifty-three years old, which more than qualifies me to be grown. I got a few gray hairs to testify to my wisdom, two grandbabies, and a long, black dildo named Harry—see what I mean? And I ain't never been a dumb woman. How the kids say? "No, never that!" So when that young girl came knocking on my door talking 'bout she twenty-two years old and pregnant by my husband, I had to let the bitch in, if nothing other than to see if she was smoking crack!

Had to be.

But I understood. To a young, struggling girl, ain't nothing like an older man—specially if he gray. I remember those feelings. Feeling like older men were more handsome and mature 'cause they wore business suits and nice cologne (which by the way don't apply to James). Thought they had lots of money 'cause they were established (again, not James). Felt like they were intriguing 'cause their world was different than mine.

Chile, boo! If that girl really knew James Leonard, she woulda known that first of all, he's gassy, and two, he got gout on his big toe. Flares up every six months in time for us to have sex. Even fucking with his socks on, that shit is nasty. Heard it come from being lazy. Well, that sound about right. And far as having money, I can't say it enough—*James Leonard ain't got none.* The other day, Social Security called here talking 'bout how *he* owe *them* a check! But the girlfriends don't know these things. Got they head too far in the clouds.

Jordan Eller, what she call herself, the girl who knocked on my door. Pretty girl, too. Long, bronze hair, light skin, got them hazel eyes, good eyes. Big-chested and big ass. Thick legs. Earring in her tongue. Knew right away she been fucking longer than me, which I thought was interesting, so I let her in. Hospitable as I am, I offered her a glass of homemade lemon-ade, but she declined. I suppose she thought I was trying to poison her, but that certainly wasn't the case. Far as I was con-cerned, if I could get her to stick around, she could take over my wifely duties. Then me and Harry could run off into the Caribbean sunset.

So, sitting on my couch, we get to talking and she tells me how she used to be a teen runaway but now that she's legal she works for an escort service that don't pay much (in other words, she a ho). That's where she met James. Sucked his dick for fifteen dollars, and I was mad as hell. After all those years of marriage and commitment, I been sucking his dick for free? I coulda saved up for a vacation for Harry and me if hada been charging James properly.

Anyhow, one day James bought her a gift of flowers and she fucked him on the spot wit' no condom. Ended up getting pregnant. Said she didn't believe in abortion 'cause she got morals plus she didn't wanna expose her fetus to the dicks of different men. Problem was, if she got out "the business" as she called it, she wouldn't have money to take care of it—"it" being the little bastard child she was carrying. Said she was scared and confused and needing James's advice. Said she got the address from his credit-card billing information.

"Well, he ain't here, baby. Probably getting his dick sucked again. Where's your family?" I asked, being as compassionate as I could.

"Miss Ma'am, I don't have no family. Like I said, I ran away when I was young."

"Call me Emma, chile, and I understand. I've fucked other women's husbands in my time. Never got pregnant by them but I guess I was just lucky."

Jordan's face turned rosy like she was embarrassed of what I said, but with my husband's baby growing in her stomach, it was too late for that. Shoulda been embarrassed before she opened them legs.

"Where you live now?" I asked.

"In a women's shelter. It's filthy and it has bedbugs but that's all I can afford, and I can only stay there two more days."

"Been to the doctor yet?"

"Only the emergency room to confirm the pregnancy, but not for prenatal care 'cause I can't afford it. Homeless women ain't eligible for Medicaid. Well, they don't come out and say you ain't eligible, but they make it too hard for you to qualify. You ain't mad at me, Miss Emma, is you? 'Cause you ain't acting like you mad."

"Nah, girl. How can I be mad at a professional ho? If I was, it would only be jealousy. Every woman wants to be a ho at some point in her life. I'm sure of it."

"Oh."

"Well, look here, chile. Since you went and got yourself knocked up, why don't you come live with us? That way me and James can make sure your needs is met."

"What do you think he'll say?"

"Why you care if I don't? I'm fine wit' it just as long as you be a good wife to him so I can snuggle up to Harry."

"Who's that?"

"My boyfriend! We in a *very* serious relationship. But don't concern yourself wit' dat. Just know that you and your baby will be fine. You need a ride back to the shelter to get your stuff?"

"No, ma'am. I ain't really got no stuff."

"Well then, go on and use my phone to cancel that ho job you got 'cause you don't need it no more. It's time for you to be a real woman, not a ho. There's a guest room down the hall and to the right. You can stay in there tonight and the nights you ain't wit' James. On the nights you are wit' him, I'll stay in there. And just so you know, I want dinner ready every night by seven. Be sure to make my steak medium-rare."

That's how it started. I believed I was doing the right thing—helping the less fortunate in the community, giving a baby a future, and making time for me and Harry.

The first night I heard them fucking, I couldn't believe James could make a woman feel so good. I had told them they didn't have to hide their sex 'cause sex made labor and delivery easier, plus, I wasn't gonna hide what I was doing wit' Harry. Even though I knew I had said that, hearing them bump 'n' grind took me by surprise. The bed was shaking, Jordan was moaning, and James was grunting so loud and gutturally that I actually got horny. I left the guest room and shuffled to the bedroom to see for myself. I only had to push the door open a tad to see in. The scent of steamy sex got to me immediately. In an instant, my pussy was wet. I stood frozen in my spot and watched.

James's black ass was kneeling on the bed holding Jordan's yella legs open like a V. His long, thick dick plunged in and out of her oozing pussy. The expression on his face said he knew he was dicking her good. She moaned and purred as she rubbed her clit and pulled her nipples. Her titties shook and shimmied like *Saturday Night Fever* as he pumped into her. He bent over, sucked her nipples, and smacked her ass without ever losing rhythm.

"Oh, Jamie, baby, fuck me hard, baby," Jordan moaned.

"You like that, huh? You like Daddy's big dick in you?"

"Yeah, Daddy. I love your huge cock in my wet pussy."

"Aw, shit!" he said, slamming his pelvis into hers.

"Fuck me! Fuck me!" she yelled, massaging his nipples. She pushed him back to assume the doggie-style position. Opened her pussy lips wide and said, "Here, Daddy, fuck this juicy pussy."

"Shit," James moaned, as his balls smacked against her ass. His grimace revealed that he felt good to the core. He reached under and rubbed her clit.

"Fuck me, Daddy," she cried, backing her twat into his meat.

"Yes! Call me Daddy," he said, taking long, deliberate strokes. "I love fucking this sloppy pussy!"

The bastard was showing off, fucking her with no hands. Had 'em laced behind his head like he was riding a bike.

"Daddy, I wanna taste you. Put it in my mouth," Jordan said, pulling away from him. She brought herself to a sitting position and teased his dick with her tongue ring. She showed him a mass of white saliva on the tip her tongue.

"Here," he said, stuffing his cock in her mouth. She bobbed her head up and down as she sucked his cock and licked the length like it was a chocolate Popsicle.

Get the fifteen dollars, I silently cheered. But Jordan wasn't thinking about that. She was thinking about the hard dick in her mouth and the slime that trickled down her chin. Grabbing his cock like a prize, she eagerly licked the head in circular motions as she jerked it. Her snakelike tongue flitted about, teasing the base of his dick.

"That's right, suck my big cock, baby. Suck me good," James muttered.

"Damn right, I'm gonna suck it," she said with her mouth full of cock.

"Oh, shit, I'm gonna cum, baby. My balls are filling up!"

"Not yet, Daddy. I haven't licked them yet. Lay on your back," she said, dropping his dick from her mouth.

She licked and sucked each nut before putting the whole sac in her mouth. She juggled his balls with her tongue, but before he could cum, she sat on his face. Told him to stroke his dick, which I knew he was accustomed to, and he stroked it while eating her young pussy better than he ever did mine.

"Yes, Daddy! You're a good Daddy. Eat me, Daddy!"

That was my cue. In a few short moments, Jordan would be screaming for mercy and so would James, and I wanted to be with Harry when it happened. I went back to the guest room and fucked myself frantically with the tip of Harry's dick. Little did they know, we came in unison that night.

After the second month of intense fucking, I permanently gave up my spot in the bedroom to stay in the guest room with Harry. It wasn't a big deal. The way I saw it, this was a special time in Jordan's and James's lives and I was too much of a woman to stand in the middle of that. As a grown-ass woman who had already paid off her house, I certainly wasn't going to *leave,* but I didn't have to sleep in the master bedroom.

Toward the end of Jordan's seventh month, the fucking stopped cold—like a witch's titty. It really wasn't none of my business except I was nosy and horny. In truth, as long as Jordan got to her doctor's appointments and ate every day, my job was done. And as long as she cooked, cleaned, ironed, and fucked James, *her* job was done, and I didn't feel guilty in the least. I had earned the right to sit around and collect my retirement check and gossip on the phone about her. But the energy in the house was different when they weren't fucking. I had grown accustomed to fucking Harry while they went at it. Their drought was affecting my sex life.

Secretly watching and hearing my husband make love all those months made me attracted to him all over again. Sure, I was a little jealous that he was more passionate with her than he ever was with me, but in honesty, I knew I didn't have young pussy. That didn't mean I wanted them to stop, so I called Jordan into my room one day to try to find a solution.

"I don't know what happened, Miss Emma. I think he's afraid of hurting the baby."

"That's bullshit. Any doctor will tell you that sex eases the delivery."

"Well, maybe he doesn't know that. You sure you ain't mad? I mean, you talk about him like he's not your husband."

"He's *our* husband, dear. Remember that," I said.

"Okay." She thought for a moment. "Maybe he ain't attracted to me because of the extra weight."

"If so, he got a nerve! He ain't no Billy Blanks!"

"Maybe not, but I still care about how he sees me."

"Chile, you fine! Have confidence in yourself! Other than that, how ya feeling?"

"Okay, except . . . well, you said I could confide in you about anything, so here goes. Miss Emma, these days, I been feeling real horny. I don't know if it's the pregnancy or what, but I try to masturbate sometimes and can't finish 'cause I get embarrassed that James is laying right there. I don't know what to do."

"Your milk come in yet?"

"Just the clear stuff."

"Lay back," I instructed. "Since we women have to stick together, I'm gonna help you out this time, but don't you tell nobody about this."

"Yes, ma'am."

I shook my head at myself, thinking I should be ashamed of what I was about to do. I had been watching Jordan's sexy ass for eight long months and knew she was a good fuck. I wanted to try her out for myself. Why should James have all the fun?

"Close your eyes," I said, sliding my hand up her nightgown. I tickled her clitoris till her pussy secreted, then I pushed three fingers inside. Being conscious of the baby, I didn't go too deep, just deep enough to make her moan. I kissed her neck while her eyes were still closed. Stuck my tongue in her mouth. Our tongues swirled like chocolate and vanilla pudding. I groped her swollen titties but she was shy about touching mine. Finally, I got to tongue-fucking her pussy.

"Shit, Miss Emma, that feels good!"

I licked her cunt faster.

"Shit, Miss Emma! Oh, shit!"

I made slurping noises as I lapped her cunt, which added to both of our excitement.

"I wanna watch you eat my pussy, Miss Emma," Jordan said, opening her eyes. When she saw my tits, she snatched them into her mouth and sucked them like a starving child while she played with my kitty.

"You don't have to do that. I want *you* to cum," I said.

"But you've been so good to me, Miss Emma. I gotta lick your pussy in return."

I gasped as her tongue ring met my flesh and traced the inside of my pussy lips.

"Eat me," I moaned, holding her face between my legs. I writhed as she sucked my bulging clit. Watched as she finger-fucked herself and licked the juices off her fingers. Next, she grabbed Harry from the nightstand, sucked him, and put him at the entrance to my pussy.

"Do you like sucking and fucking my husband?" I asked, maneuvering my cunt onto Harry.

"Yes, I love his giant cock and how he fucks all my holes."

"Fuck me like he fucks you," I said, gyrating on Harry.

"Do you think you can handle it?" she asked, twisting Harry deeper into my hole. She fucked me in long, hard strokes, then in short, soft ones while licking my clit.

"Yeah, fuck me, eat me!" I shouted before succumbing to orgasm.

"My turn," I said, snatching Harry out her hand. He was still wet with my juices but I shoved him in her pussy anyhow. When she had enough of him, she mounted me. We rubbed our pussies together while her humongous titties flapped over my mouth. I reached for her nipples with my lips, like a seal, not caring that milk squirted out.

"Tasty," I said, squeezing her ass like I owned it. I stuck my thumb in her asshole while she squealed in delight. Finally, we got in sixty-nine position on our sides and lapped each other's cunt.

"Oh, shit, Miss Emma! I'm cumming!" she exclaimed.

"Now tell me if this shit ain't better than fucking lame James!"

Having sex with Jordan didn't solve the problem though. A pregnant woman still needed affection from her man to make the energy in the household right.

The plan was to wait until he got ready to call an escort, which we both knew he was doing, and present him with a cheaper option.

"Uh, James," I said, in that tone that made him scared.

"What's happening?" he asked, reminding me of that seventies sitcom.

"What's happening is you're about to have a baby soon and his mother needs attention."

"I do give her attention. I say 'Good morning' and 'Good night.' "

"I ain't gonna let you be a deadbeat, James. You got her pregnant, now she needs sex, and lots of it. Hell, I recently realized that I need sex, too."

"Well, what you want me to do?" he asked, looking from Jordan to me.

"Go in the room and get naked, James. Be waiting on the bed."

When he left, I removed Jordan's shirt, stroked her round belly, and kissed it as we sank into the couch. We tongue-kissed as I fondled her clit. I drank from her breasts as I unfastened my clothes.

"We're gonna make him want you," I said, grabbing her by the hand. "Let's go in the room and face our man."

James's dick sprung like a plant when he saw our naked bodies—the one of the old lover he had fallen for so many years ago, and the one of the young lover that was carrying his child. We got in bed on either side of him. He reached for her first but I didn't mind. While he hungrily sucked her tits, I greedily placed my mouth over his erect penis. His semen was so sweet I wanted to scoop some up to bake with.

He moaned as I deep-throated him, and she moaned as he squeezed her ass. Unable to wait, I mounted my husband and rode him while Jordan took up licking my ass and his balls.

"Fuck, Emma! Your pussy is so good," James moaned.

"Yes, James! Shit, Jordan!" I returned. Her warm mouth felt delightful on my ass as I pounced on my husband's sturdy cock.

We switched positions. I ate Jordan's pussy from behind, rubbing her belly as it hung low, while James slid his manhood in and out of me doggie-style. I almost came right then. But being the woman I am, I had to remind James that this session was about him making Jordan feel good, not me, so he laid her on her side and put lubricant on her anus. He slid his cock in her ass, placed his hands around her belly, and grunted as he butt-fucked her.

"Oh, yeah, baby," she cried. He placed his thumb on her clit but I pushed it aside so I could do it. I lay on my side facing her. As he moved in and out of her ass, Jordan and I kissed deeply and explored each other's body.

"I need my dick sucked," James said, kneeling between us. We took turns jerking and sucking his cock until it glistened with saliva.

"Fuck me, James," I moaned as he slid his cock in my ass. Not even Harry could work me like that.

James took turns fucking us doggie-style, rubbing Jordan's belly all the while. Eventually, we went back to sucking his cock, and he came hard, rubbing the jism on our tits and lips. I took pleasure in being the one who swallowed the bulk of his cum.

While Jordan and I continued to make love, James got it up again. He plugged his dick in my pussy, making me cum as Jordan sat on my face, letting me lick her twat.

Seconds later, her orgasm sent her into labor. After her six weeks of celibacy, we were at it again. We don't see nothing wrong with an intimate triangle. And as for Harry, I hate to say it, but he don't live here no more.

Beauty

Wanda D. Hudson

His appearance is massive, but he has a subtle mood about him that pacifies me. Every time he emerges I get weak, so weak my limbs can't stabilize me. He shows himself in times of passion—times when I summon him to act—times when I need him to take me in and soothe me.

No one knows of the affection I have for him. The first time I saw him I knew he had to become mine. He's my aphrodisiac. Every hour he fills my mind and I can't concentrate, can't react. My thoughts stop. Beauty—the only name that does him justice. He is my on-and-off switch that decides when I should operate and then shut down. I don't care that he owns me. I gave myself to him willingly, from the inside out.

The first time Beauty and I were introduced I was caught off guard. We were chatting, as we had always done for the last few months. For some reason my chat buddy decided that I was ready. If I had been asked first, I would have said that I wasn't prepared. The sight of him was too overwhelming. I was speechless and in awe. Since our first encounter I have craved his presence. I beg for him to come near. Perfection kissed my face when we met.

Was he a hallucination? There was nothing in my world to compare Beauty to. Up until him my existence had been composed of tattered shambles and noise. Too much noise for me to comprehend anything feasible. And suddenly he surfaced. Big. Bold. Aggressive. The frame that surrounded him had to fight to keep him from bursting out. My eyes bucked slowly, my mouth hung long. Everything that circled me stopped. Silence. He made me take notice. To him I'll pay my dues.

A sweet shock hugged me. I was a bit embarrassed but I couldn't turn away from the view. I had to have him. I reached to caress him and felt him through the screen. Ahh . . . a love affair was born. My fingers exuded energy as I clicked my keyboard. I was no typist but I felt that the faster I plucked, the closer he would come to me. The delusion I had of once stroking one hundred words a minute surpassed me. My heart pulsed as I asked why that wonderful specimen was kept closed in.

wlv: Whoa!!!! Where did that come from???

jrb: lol

wlv: No, seriously . . . where do you keep all of that?

jrb: lol u r hilarious. I keep it in my pants

wlv: How do you walk? Does it stick out?

jrb: lol I wear tight underwear when I go out and when I stay home I wear boxers

wlv: How long is it? Do condoms fit?

jrb: 12 inches

wlv: Get outta here! That's a lotta meat!!!

jrb: stop it! lol

wlv: I can't help it! That thang is PURTY! LOL

jrb: well, u know u can have it anytime

My entire body coursed with sexual stimulation. Pedicured toes tapped the floor, twitching rapidly. Then legs tensed. Looking down, I realized those out-of-sync body parts belonged to me. I panicked, floated, then came back down to earth. Thankfully we were on the computer and he couldn't see how shook he had me. Pacing was the only thing I could do to regain my composure. Long strides took me around the room in circles. Racewalking was never one of my favorite sports, but I kept striding as if someone were on my tail. Noticing my lit-up message box caused me to huff a bit more. Deep breaths did nothing to send my jitters away. I took slow, guarded steps back to the computer.

jrb: u there?

wlv: Yeah. I had to get something to drink.

jrb: so r u gonna answer me?

wlv: Answer what?

jrb: I said u can have it anytime. u want it?

wlv: BRB

All of that could belong to me? My chat buddy was born with a gift of a god. Control slid from my body. Sensations raced through my veins. I was near fainting and ran to splash water on my face. Appropriate behavior would have no place in my life if Beauty tantalized me. Once I passed the thoughts of temptations and indulged in the actual act, he could never be with another.

wlv: Hey, I gotta run. Will you be on later?

jrb: for u sure

Would this work? I was undeniably interested. He had me in the palm of his soul. A quick, simple flash of a photo made my every essence become soft, claylike putty. My heart was his. It was too early to let on that I had come apart upon the sight of such exquisite splendor. Somehow, some way, I had to make him want me. Beauty had to come inside and not leave. He needed to know that I was the key to his new home.

For the next two days I purposely didn't log on to Instant Messenger. I did, however, wake up in the wee hours of the morning to check to see if he'd sent me any off-line messages. My insides shuffled and then sank when I saw that they didn't miss me like I feened for them.

In all of my misleading previous relationships I had fallen prey to what I thought was an ever-conquering love. Sex had always been a demon in disguise to me. Sex used my body to deceive my mind into believing I was in love. When my body wasn't satisfied, the demon backed away. At this moment my head was clouded with confusion in relation to Beauty. I fulfilled my sexual fantasies simply by looking at him. The intense stimulation of twelve hard inches of man delving deep into my canal had never before been done. My body would be loose and uninhibited to all of the things he requested of me.

Every night I envision him in my sleep. He walks toward me in a lavish manner, with Beauty leading the way. Beauty carries himself like a stallion. He is a pedigree that comes in second place to none. The ribbons I want to wrap around his winning form are gold and red and midnight blue. Best in show will be his only moniker. Oscars, Golden Globes, or SAG Awards aren't allowed in his presence. Those statues are awarded for pretending to be something you imagine. His performances are real and satisfying. A script is never printed for him to follow. He takes the lead and directs you in the role of your lifetime. And this happens only in my dreams.

My "playing hard to get" game ended before I even had a

grasp on the rules. It was 3:47 in the morning and I waved the white flag. I had woken myself up, yet again, with a drenched dream about Beauty. They had come to my place and used lace scarves to secure my arms and legs to my bedposts. He stood over me as Beauty steered him to a warm, wet place that he could rest in after he drained all that held it confined. My own screams of pleasure awoke me in a lusty sweat, and I ran to the computer to find my savior.

I began typing a heated email, which gave them directions to my home and my telephone number. Before clicking the send button I logged on to see if he'd left me a message. They were online.

wlv: Hey U . . .

jrb: sup sexy

wlv: What have you been up to?

jrb: I've been thinking about u. I feel bad for turning u off like that.

wlv: What are you talking about?

jrb: u know, showin u my stuff like that.

wlv: Are you serious?

jrb: yeah. I mean, u never answered me. I thought I made you uncomfortable

wlv: No, I wasn't uncomfortable. I like your stuff very much!

jrb: lol

wlv: By the way . . . uh, how is he doing?

jrb: lol he's fine. missing u

Here was my chance to work the magic pass that I was dealt. I wanted them to be a constant source of gratification in my life. Beauty's partner was fine. His body was chiseled. My lips needed to roam his six-pack and savor each drop he allowed me to taste. He told me he stood six feet even, which would only heighten the experience for my five-feet-eight-inch frame. This was the man I wanted. Single, sexy, and trying his best to get some of me.

wlv: Oh is he now? Hmm . . . well, we are going to have to do something about that.

jrb: u tell me what u want and we'll make it happen

They couldn't hear the moans they called from me. The sounds were deep and resonated throughout the entire room.

wlv: What are you doing this Saturday?

jrb: whatever u want

A man at my beck and call is what I want. A fine man like you is what I need.

wlv: Well, I get off work at six. Can you come over at nine?

jrb: how about this . . .

wlv: Don't leave me in suspense!

jrb: how about I pick u up from work . . .

wlv: Go on . . .

jrb: bring u to my place . . .

wlv: Uh-huh . . .

jrb: and treat u better than u have ever been treated?

wlv: I'd love that. But I have to wash and change clothes first

jrb: no excuses. I can wash u here and u don't need clothes

wlv: Oh my!!! In that case, it's a date!

jrb: lol I can't wait to see u sexy

I couldn't respond as my body smiled.

jrb: sexy u there?

wlv: Yes. I just had a moment

jrb: u r going to have many more

wlv: Really?

jrb: girl, I got my eye on u. u know I want u

I became antsy in my seat. We wanted each other.

wlv: What do you like about me?

jrb: where should I begin?

wlv: I'm being serious!

jrb: me too. okay, those lips . . . mmmm

jrb: those eyes . . . mmmm

jrb: that pic u sent of those loooooooooooooong legs . . . mmmm

jrb: and me pullin that hair . . .

wlv: Ooooh . . . I'm ready!

jrb: so are we

wlv: can you show him again?

My nipples perked when Beauty looked at me. I inspected him a bit further. Long and solid, he stood at attention. He had a slight curve toward his tip, which would enable him to reach all the right spots. I closed my eyes and simulated hip movements in the chair. I thrust and swirled each time I felt him hit the bottom. I panted and grabbed the sides of the desk when I felt an orgasm approaching. Beauty inside of me would be magnificent.

jrb: what u doin over there?

wlv: Having another moment

jrb: can I come over now?

As bad as I craved Beauty, I wanted our first time to be an experience. They offered to pick me up. To me, it would be like riding in a chariot. Never in my menial existence had a man made me feel special. This man had accomplished that over a couple of months with a keyboard.

wlv: Don't jump the gun. I want the whole shebang!

jrb: okay, okay. send me an email with the directions and I'll see u at 6

They logged off before I could send another message. I quickly sent an email with the particulars to my workplace. Then, I ran to my closet and assaulted all of my clothing. I snatched things from every direction in the pursuit of love. When he saw me, Beauty had to sense that I was the thing that they had been missing. He would rise up to greet me and tell me how wonderful he thought I was.

After rummaging through every drawer, closet, and storage bin I had, I decided on a nice knee-length, sheer, lilac slip dress that had a split up the back. A comfort support was sewn in for my breasts, so all I had to wear under it was a thong. They already had unlimited access to my heart, and my body would be no different.

Forty-eight hours stood in between Beauty and me. The majority of the time was spent staring at the computer screen waiting for him. A few times I had the ugly thought of being stood up, but Beauty was a gentleman. Real men never make promises and in reality plan to break your heart. A real man would never present himself to you by putting on a facade. He would never show the type of man he hoped to be, or the man that didn't have a lineage in his family tree. When you're on the computer, people do that. I became a bit withdrawn thinking that Beauty belonged on someone else's body.

The last man I had met over the World Wide Web was a fake in every sense, syllable, and consonant of the word. He told me things that made my values flutter. I changed the outlook I had for my life because of a few emails and messages he sent. He told me he loved me, and that everything that was wrong with my life he would fix. I walked into our relationship with grimy shutters over my eyes. As I cleaned them off bit by bit to see what he really offered, I became disgusted. I had nothing to give to anyone at that point because he had broken me down as low as he was and seemed satisfied that I ran with the same misery he did. The sad thing is he had no Beauty, and a man with Beauty would know how to treat a woman who wanted someone to love.

That Saturday my hours at the publishing company dragged by. For the past two months I had to go in six days a week just to keep up with all the submissions we were receiving. The chief editor had the bright idea of extending the deadline on a new-manuscript contest, and we, the editing paupers, had gotten stuck reading some half-decent work.

I began cleaning and closing up things at 4:30. My cohorts had left at 4:00 so I was alone wandering in my sexual thoughts. At 5:25, I went into the bathroom to refresh and primp. I sprayed my body with an exotic mist. Inhaling it was an aromatic seduction, and tension that had been built trickled away. Hurriedly I left the bathroom, closed and locked up the office, and went and stood outside to await my nightcap.

During one of our conversations he'd told me that they drove a silver Navigator. I saw one coming up the street, and it slowed as it grew closer to me. I watched the vehicle come to a halt and saw the object of my desire get out. This moment happened in slow motion. He grabbed something off the passenger seat, then came around to greet me.

As he extended a bouquet of flowers, his luscious mouth spoke. "Sup, sexy?" Then it broke into a wide grin.

All I could do was breathe.

"You don't have to speak. I got this."

He took my hand and led me to the truck. Once I was comfortably seated, he laid the flowers on my lap and closed the door. I was in some sort of mystic trance and didn't come out of it until I heard the locks click.

"You just sit back and relax. Tonight, the world is yours." Beauty and his chauffeur pulled off and led me to my fortune.

After riding for twenty minutes in dramatic silence we arrived at their home.

"Well, sexy, we're here. Are you ready for us?"

"You know I am. Everything within me is at your disposal . . . have your way."

I fought not to look at Beauty. The first time we saw each other had to be in plain sight.

He opened the door and I was met with candles and incense that unbolted my senses. The scent was endearing and drew me in. It held me prisoner for life with no pardon. I belonged with them.

I followed them up the stairs to a sumptuous bedroom. The ceilings were high but I didn't concentrate much on my surroundings. More glow from candles illuminated the room. The aroma pulled me in deeper. Their spirit floated in this room.

He stopped in front of me and turned around. "Let me put those up for you." He left the room with my bouquet, but in less than a few seconds they returned.

"We have to undress you." They stepped toward me. All I could do was breathe. Beauty touched me as he reached around to unzip my dress. It fell to the floor and I sighed. I stood before them in my thong and my shoes.

"Step out of those, please" was their next command. I obeyed without a care. Then it was their turn. He unbuttoned his shirt and took it off. His chest was outstanding. He unbuckled his belt and his pants disappeared before my eyes. Beauty was free in an instant. Today he wore no underwear to pin him down. I don't remember him removing his footwear; Beauty had seized my functions. I performed on his schedule now.

They stepped back in front of me and Beauty searched his surroundings. I spread my legs to give him enough room. He was delicate yet firm, very firm.

"We'd like to give you your bath now." Still, I could only breathe. They placed me in front of them and hugged me from behind. Ahhh, Beauty roamed my backside. Satisfied he found a resting place. They ran my bathwater, removed my thong, and picked me up gracefully to place me into the tub.

"Is the water warm enough, sexy?"

"Uh-huh."

As he cleansed me, I watched Beauty. Well-behaved, he waited patiently for his turn. He massaged my back, my feet, my thighs, and my entire body. Then, he lifted me out of the tub and carried me to the bed. He laid me in the center of it. The sheets wrapped around me as if they were asking what took so long. For the first time I realized music had been play-ing. The song caused juice to summon for them. Prince's "The Beautiful Ones" let me know we were meant to be.

He began kissing my body. He started at my forehead and lay a trailed melody of love down to my stomach. I wanted Beauty now. I put my hands on the side of his face and pulled him back up tenderly. Our eyes met. I said nothing. All I could do was breathe.

He said, "Do you want him . . . or do you want me . . . 'cause I want you."

Ahhhhhh . . . Beauty began his slow slide of ecstasy into my domain. Ahhhhhh . . . nectar flowed from the tap he burst. He continued to go deeper, and deeper, and deeper.

Ahhhhhh . . . my breathing quickened to short, heightened, fast blows. He spread my legs and held them open wide. I grabbed the headboard rails and braced myself. He continued to go deeper. I released just because.

"Oh, sexy, you feel so good."

Still, Beauty delved. I tensed and released, sucking in what I could of him. I wanted him all, all of the time. He dove down into a terrain that had never been explored, as only he knew how.

I felt myself expanding. The intensity of the moment escalated as he continued his journey. When it was pelvis to groin, he thrust lightly. I moaned. He thrust again. I sighed. He thrust again and I begged him to let Beauty do the work. He did. I went into a Mediterranean Sea of emotions. I bounced and buoyed as Beauty pushed me to the edge of losing consciousness and brought me back. He kissed and fondled my breasts as they worked together to show me I was the one they longed for. Beauty sped up his discovery of me, and I could no longer muffle my cries.

"That's it, sexy. Let it out."

And in harmony we bonded. I freed more of a potion that was designed for him, and he allowed me to have his in return. We lay panting side by side, as I looked at them.

"Were we what you expected, sexy?"

"You were better than I ever imagined."

"Will you stay the night?"

"Yes."

Then they kissed me. Each time Beauty touched me that night, I gave him more and more of who I was, and this day he is mine. At last, Beauty is in the eye, the body, and the soul of the beholder.

The Best Psychic in Town

It was a sunny day, cloud-free, that I could notice from the nearby window. The sound of laughter brought me back to my present moment. My feet were hurting because I had been standing on them all day. I was staring out the window looking for Genie, a woman I'd just met. I checked my watch: it was 4:25 in the afternoon. I sucked in my breath and went back to my booth. *This is her first visit here and she might be late trying to find the place,* I thought.

My name is Aine. I am a natural hairstylist for Natural Beauty Hair Salon on Henry Street. I do braids, twists, dreadlocks, and regular press and curls for the little girls. I just turned twenty-five. I am very good at my job and horny as hell.

I turned away from the window and watched my coworker Keisha. She was finishing up a client's dreadlocks, and as usual, it was a fine-looking brother. Keisha was laughing and spraying his freshly twisted locks with sheen.

She turned to me and said, "I'll be ready for my reading in a minute, Aine."

The man's ears perked up. "Reading?" He turned to Keisha and asked in a rich baritone, "She does readings?"

Before she responded, I grabbed my purse and walked toward the bathroom near the rear of the salon. After entering, I slammed the door. Admittedly I was a bit irritable, but my period was due any day and I was PMSing like a motherfucker.

The "readings" that Keisha was referring to are something else that I am good at. I do tarot readings at the salon to bring in some extra cash. The clients love it because I am usually accurate. I have met people who have done tarot or "flipped the cards" since childhood and such. That isn't the case with me. I developed a genuine interest in divination a few years ago, and it burgeoned into a reputable talent. I really get a lot of information from my readings through clairaudience and clairvoyance, which is something I really enjoy because I am nosy as hell. Not to mention the best psychic in town.

I pulled down my pants and underwear to check for any spots of blood. None were there. I bent down and unfolded the folds of my pussy and slowly stuck a finger inside. I shuddered as I imagined how good it would feel to have a strong, thick dick inside. It had been a few months now since I had had such an experience, and quite frankly, the horniness that my PMS was bringing didn't help any. I pulled out my finger, and though it was covered with my juices, there was no blood.

I was feeling really aggravated then. I checked my watch: it was a quarter to five and Genie still was not there. She was supposed to get her braids done, and that would have been two hundred extra bones in my wallet. With much resignation, I realized that she may have been canceling her appointment. *Just as well,* I thought, while washing my hands in the sink. *Leaving work early for today may be a good idea, especially with a canceled appointment.* Those two hundred dollars from Genie would have helped out a lot. I laughed to myself as I thought about a saying from a popular movie that summed up my current situation: *Two tears in a bucket, motherfuck it!*

I still did not get a word from Genie. I knew the girl had my phone number and it was getting late. I walked from the bathroom and headed toward the front where my booth was located. The salon was abuzz with customers, lighted with vivid gossip, while the smell of aerosol sprays, foamy shampoos, and incense hung in the air like a fog. I got to my booth and began gathering my things. *I am outta here,* I thought.

Someone tapped me on the shoulder from behind. I turned and it was Keisha; she had a pained expression on her face.

"Look, girl, I have to leave early. My son got into a fight at the rec center and they're calling me to get him."

She pantomimed choking someone around the neck. Her animated pose made me laugh. She had had problems with Hakimm since he'd started high school the year before. That was why he was enrolled at the rec center on weekends—to keep from fighting.

"I'm gonna have to cancel the reading today. Maybe another time?" Keisha glanced past me to the clock on the wall. "Your client still coming?"

I scowled at the clock. It was five after five and still no Genie. "Nah, I am about to go, girl."

"Well, hold up." She turned and beckoned someone to come forth. "He's a walk-in. I told him about you and he wants a reading."

I turned around and this fine-ass man whom I had never before seen sauntered up to where we stood. I immediately liked him because he walked with confidence—as if he didn't let anyone stop him from what he wanted. A bit self-centered, I guessed, but I quickly blocked that from my mind.

Keisha grinned as we shook hands. I realized that he was staring at me but I diverted my eyes away from his burning gaze. *He thinks really high of himself,* I thought. *He doesn't care what people think of him. He is not bound by social restrictions of any kind.*

"My name is Denver." His voice was like syrup and I felt as if I were being drenched in it while he spoke. "Keisha told me that you do readings. How accurate are you?" He looked at me with excited anticipation.

"Very." I beamed proudly. "I'm one of the best." I checked my watch. "I suppose that I can stay to give you a quick reading."

"Good!" His countenance relaxed as he grinned. He was a good-looking man. His skin reminded me of coffee-colored velvet, no cream. His eyes glinted with softness, yet spiced with determination. His nose was positioned perfectly above a sensuously full mouth that was framed by a beautifully mani-cured goatee. I smiled as I imagined what his sexy lips would look like glistened by the balm of my sleek pussy juices.

Keisha said good-night and left while Denver and I retreated into the employee lounge in the back near the bathroom. I closed the door for privacy. I had my favorite deck of tarot cards in my hands. As we sat at a card table, I smiled because I would have permission to look into his personal business. Es-pecially the business of whether he was single.

What I gleaned from his card spreads was that he had good fortune all the way around. I reassured him that he was going to be fine and that he had recently come into a windfall of money. I warned him not to get upset with the result of the legal issues that he was about to go through (of which he preferred not to talk and which I had surprising difficulty intuitively picking up the specifics of). He nodded enthusiastically to my spiritual advice and beamed. I was a little concerned about his mysterious legal matters, but that was swiftly overshadowed by my strong curiosity and magnetism toward this gorgeous man. *He is attracted to me. He loves to fuck. He is guarding a secret.*

To say that we got along would be a serious understatement. There definitely was sexual chemistry between us. It was little things such as his staring at me a long time. He would grab my hands and caress them. He even rubbed my arms with his fingertips. Lord have mercy!

The reading lasted for forty-five minutes and my watch read 5:50 p.m.

Another coworker, Tekeyia, poked her head in the lounge. "We're all going for dinner." She nodded hello to Denver. "You want anything, Aine?"

I rose from my seat. "Nope, in fact we're wrapping up this session."

"Okay," Tekeyia replied. "You'll be the only one here. We'll be back in thirty minutes." Then she closed the door.

A minute or so later, I heard the other stylists talking while they left out the front door. Soon, it was quiet throughout the salon.

Denver came up from behind and placed his hands on my shoulders. "Thank you for the reading. You're very good. I bet that you're good at many things."

I turned to face him. A delicious, musky scent wafted from

his neck into my nostrils. I breathed his essence into my nasal cavities. My pussy began to throb from desire. He stepped closer.

"I'm good at at least one other thing," I murmured.

He cocked an eyebrow, and before he could say another word, I gave him a deep kiss on those luscious lips. He wrapped his arms around my waist and pulled me closer. He parted his lips and introduced his tongue to my eager mouth.

We moaned in unison as our kissing became more passionate. We explored each other's mouth and body. He kneaded the flesh on my thick ass like a pastry chef. I felt his dick get harder through his pants as I grinded against his muscular body. I imagined that he might be big enough to fill up every inch of my deep, cavernous vagina. He rubbed my firm nipples through my sweater and they hardened with his touch.

I am getting ready to fuck a man that I don't know from Adam or Eve, I thought as he took off my sweater and bra. He grinned like a kid in a toy store when he saw my tits. They are large and generously fill a DD cup. He grabbed both and jiggled them. I didn't mind because his hands were warm.

"Let me taste your tits," he commanded as he bent his head down. His tongue's light tease was the precursor to his mouth. It sent chills up my spine, the way he was sucking my tits. I grabbed his head and watched him ravish my breasts. He grunted and made slurping sounds. I felt warm drool trickle down the underside of my breasts and roll downward toward my stomach. *He likes to eat pussy. He wants his dick sucked. He is not forthright about his legal situation.*

Suddenly a rush of alarm came upon me. *My period! I might already have started.* I felt wetness but it could have been from my being aroused. I didn't know for sure and I grew nervous as Denver moved from sucking on my tits to unzipping my pants. *Shit!*

"No wait!" I said. "I have something I need to tell you." He looked at me puzzled, but he did stop. "I might be on my period. I don't know for sure."

To my surprise, he smiled and continued to take off my pants. "Let me check it out," he replied softly. "If you're on, then we'll stop. Now, if you are not on . . ." He grew quiet when he got to my panties. He pulled them down and grinned. "Look, you're dry."

I glanced down. My panties were rumpled at my feet, and sure enough, there was no blood; just the wetness of being aroused. I sighed in relief as Denver stood up and suggested that I sit on the nearby sofa.

I sat on a plush sofa that was next to the card table. My heart raced as Denver stood above me and gently parted my bare legs. He then kneeled down between my legs and started to kiss my stomach. He gave me soft kisses over my abdomen and circled my belly button with his tongue. He watched me intently as I moaned and threw my head back. He then headed down to my special honey pot and gingerly pulled back the moist folds until he found the clit. With a groan, he began licking my clit and rubbing my already hard nipples. He bobbed his head as he gave my pussy a good washing. I gyrated my hips in time with his rhythmic cunnilingus so that he could eat me at just the right spot.

The sounds that he made turned me on even more. "Aw, shit. This pussy tastes good," he whispered in between licks.

He licked, chewed, and gnawed me into ecstasy. I reached my climax within a few minutes of his mastery. He didn't even stop until he sopped up all of my pussy juices with his tongue.

My body trembled with rapture as my mind was being bombarded with intuitive information: *He loves the thrill of the chase. He is a skillful lover. He is afraid of telling the truth.*

He stood above me and unzipped his pants. His dick was long and thick and engorged with want. It pulsated and quivered in front of me and I was transfixed. The language it communicated in was ancient and appealed to my erotic side. I knew what to do. Denver eyed me sexily and licked his lips while I licked the tip of his dick. I washed his stiff shaft with my tongue and didn't stop until he moaned, "Suck this shit. Yeah, you like sucking big dick."

His breathing was staccato as he took short breaths. The way he gripped the back of my head was a signal for me to give him more pleasure.

I entered his dick into my mouth and didn't stop until his head reached far deep in my throat. He grunted as he moved his hips. Ah, his dick was strong and sweet. It turned me on to feel his manhood in my mouth, baptizing him with the moisture of my hunger.

I must have done my job with excellence, because soon his smooth pelvic movements became jerkier. I felt his rod vibrate inside my mouth. I watched him from below as he squeezed his hands behind my head. "I'm coming!" he yelled, guiding me back on the couch. My back had landed on the back cushions just in time for me to see milky white jism project from his dick and land square on my nipples. He moaned as he rubbed the fluids onto my luscious breasts. I was sprawled out on the sofa, naked, dazed, and physically spent. I smirked as I thought about Genie and her canceled appointment. It turned out to be a good thing because I got to act out a really freaky love scene with a superfine brother.

He soon sat next to me and began putting on his clothes. He kissed me on the cheek. "Thank you for this, I really needed it."

I blushed from his remark. "I don't do this often, you know. It has been a few months since my last relationship. I guess I didn't know how horny I was."

"You don't have to explain," he said, touching my arm. "Life is too short and we have to go with the flow sometimes."

He made a wave gesture with his hands to add emphasis. What an interesting day this had been for me.

He finished dressing and stood above me. I had already put back on my sweater and was now pulling up my pants. He watched me and smiled.

"I would like to see you again, if at all possible," he suggested, helping me zip up the fly to my pants. I detected some genuine warmth from him and it made me smile. *He thinks before he acts. He cares about people. His judgment is not sound.*

I mentally shooed the annoying random thoughts as if they were flies. Something felt amiss about his situation, but we had already fucked so what was the use of crying over spilt milk? Besides, the brother was fine and a good lover. . . . It may have been the start of something special. I am the best psychic in town; if he was up to no good, then I would have found out by then. Believe that.

Suddenly, the sound of the front salon door swinging open and my coworkers' laughter ushered out the previous settling quiet. Denver and I looked at each other and laughed. It was all so funny to me. There I was earlier that day, bitching and complaining about some random chick who'd canceled her appointment. Now, I found myself finishing up a freaky scene worthy of a trashy romance novel with my tits covered with cum.

• • •

It's so good to be home! I exclaimed after turning off my shower faucet. I dried myself, lotioned up, and put on my robe. I walked to my living room and sat on the couch next to my phone. I live alone in an apartment, which is fine because I get to walk around with my robe open. I wished that I had roommates though, so I could have regaled them with the thrilling fairy tale of Denver and me. I kept thinking about him. He was so nice that he gave me a ride home after our "frolic" in the employee lounge. We exchanged numbers. He paid for my reading, and you know what else? He even paid for what I would have earned if Genie had kept her appointment. That's right . . . two hundred big ones. And we were going out the following week. He *was* single, free, and interested in me! Could things have gotten any better? Whoever said that sleeping with a man too soon would never amount to a lasting relationship could go and kiss my black ass.

I was about to call because I was thinking about him when the phone rang. It was Genie, the chick who'd left me hanging earlier today.

"Aine, I'm so sorry that I canceled today." A distinctive strain was in her voice. It even sounded as if she had possibly cried before she called. "I'd like to make another appointment at a different time, but I also called you because you told me when we first met that you do readings. I need some help with a situation."

I smiled. Yep, the damn best psychic in town. That's me. "What's your situation?"

"Girl, I'm going to kill that motherfucker!" she shrieked. "My stupid-ass husband. He said that he wanted a divorce but we still live in the same house. I thought after five years, we could make it work but I guess not."

I felt a slight pull in my stomach as she spoke, her voice choking up. "Not only have I found out that he wanted to end our marriage, I discovered that he stole a couple of hundred dollars from my purse this morning. That was the money that I was gonna use to pay for you to do my hair."

I felt bad for her telling me her story, but my stomach was still aching and it bothered me. I felt a curiously sinking feeling as she spoke on the phone. *No, that can't be right . . . something is not right,* I thought.

"And, girl," she continued, "he took the car while I was asleep this morning and his monkey ass used it all day! Then he had the nerve to come home and take a shower. Probably fucked some bitch! I confronted him about the money and he denied it. We're the only ones who live in this damn house! I bet he spent it on some dirty heifer!

"That's what I get for marrying a no-good, broke-ass boy! I pay for everything! He was a street hustler when I met him. Thank God for the prenup!"

I pulled the receiver away from my ear because she was yelling so loud. My stomach was still aching. . . .

She finally calmed down. "Basically, that's my situation, Aine. I didn't call you because I was so upset by everything today. I know that we don't know each other that well, but I feel comfortable talking to you about this because you're psychic. So what I wanna know is, is my husband dating or has he fucked someone new already?"

I felt queasy. *I am the best psychic in town. Nothing should get past me.* A lump formed in my throat as I asked her, "What's your husband's name?"

"His punk ass is named Denver, girl," Genie snarled.

Pain shot through my body as I dropped the receiver. I held my stomach and bent down from the pain just in time to see a tiny stream of crimson fluid trickle down my leg.

My period had started.

Fondling My Muse

Randy Walker

The week ended with my head in a daze, stories circling my brain. I could still feel a slight cramp in my hand from all of the homework assignments I'd struggled to complete over the week. I had known that the Black Writers' Workshop would be exhausting when I applied several months ago. Like many others in attendance, I had felt the need to do something affirmative to prove to myself that I was in fact taking myself seriously as a writer. This was my chance to be around people and call myself a writer without being ridiculed. I wasn't a computer programmer anymore. I was just someone who was working on his short stories, aiming at getting a book completed by the end of the year. So when I packed up my things for a week in New York, I had no idea that I would meet her, the muse who would get me through the week.

I first saw her during the opening-dinner meet and greet. She didn't really stand out much either. She had a funky Afro, kind of like N'Bushe Wright's do in *Dead Presidents.* Her Stevie Wonder T-shirt hung lazily from her body, and if it had not been for her shorts riding up those long, sculpted legs, it might've taken me a little longer to really notice her. She had a casual beauty like that of Sanaa Lathan, the kind of beauty that was subtle in drawing attention. I had always found that type of woman irresistible.

After introducing myself and learning that her name was Meredith, I began to keep an eye out for her during our workshop breaks and during the meals we ate at the university cafeteria. On the second day, while having lunch, I spotted her at a table with several of her classmates.

"Excuse me," I said as I approached. "Do you mind if I sit here?"

She looked up at me and smiled. "No. It's cool."

I sat down diagonally from her, introducing myself to the two other women seated nearby. Since I was the only man at the table, the women quickly directed their attention toward me.

"So where are you from?" the woman named Rachelle asked.

"Mississippi," I responded.

"Ooh, you probably had to escape slavery to get here," said the one named Diamond.

"And I ain't never goin' back. Nah, sur. I's likes my freedom!"

They laughed, but I hardly noticed anyone except Meredith. She had a sexiness that danced just beneath the surface, and at that moment, all I wanted to do was undress her, lay her down on her stomach, and plant kisses all along her chocolate, moon-shaped ass.

"You here for poetry or fiction?" Meredith asked.

"Fiction."

"Really? Me, too. Whose your workshop teacher?"

"Jonathan Cadet."

"Man, I was trying to get him for my class. I'm taking Cynthia Wordley. She's great though."

"Well, I'd love to read some of your stuff sometime," I said.

"I don't know," she said. "Like Erykah Badu says, 'I'm an artist, and I sensitive about my shit!' "

Her smile made me smile, and from then on I found myself mysteriously sliding into this groove, writing the same kinds of stories all week long for my workshop. The first story was about a man and a woman who met at a sex anonymous meeting and fell off the wagon soon afterward. The second story was about a guy having repeated wet dreams about the same woman every night. The third story was about a woman who caught a man jacking off at a stoplight late one night and offered to finish the job for him. It had gotten to the point that when I came to class, Mr. Cadet would have an assuming smirk on his face. One day he flat out asked if I was trying to accomplish something thematic with my collection of randy stories.

"I don't know. I think I'm just following where my muse leads."

He nodded. "Well, it's good to have a muse. Stirs the creative juices."

Creative juices? I wanted to swim in those.

But I was a little too nervous to really step up and put it out there with Meredith, so I lay low and chatted with her during the brief moments when we'd connect during the day. Nothing special. Just enough to keep my imagination sparked. Before I knew it, the last day of the workshop had arrived, and the realization that I would probably never see her again began to sink in. I had written all of these stories about being with her, all of these *fantasies,* and it was about to be over. Just like that.

Another realization dawned on me, too: I had spent the entire week writing out my sexual frustrations with stories that I would probably never be able to use professionally, not unless Zane found one of them worthy of publishing in an anthology. If I didn't put it out there with Meredith, then I would have wasted a week.

That night I didn't see her at the banquet, and when a group of my classmates decided to go out for drinks, I kept an eye out for her, hoping our paths would cross going in and out of pubs. When I didn't see her out and about or hanging out in front of the dorm with other students, I began to question whether she had already left, headed home. When the thought that I had completely blown it set in, I promised myself that if I should see her before the program officially ended the following morning, then I would put it all on the line.

I knew that she was staying in a room at the end of the hall on the floor above mine, so in a final attempt to contact her, I went up to her dorm room a few minutes before eleven that night and knocked on the door. I could hear shuffling as the door opened slowly.

"Yeah," she whispered, squinting her eyes against the light of the hallway. It was pitch-black in her room.

"Just wanted to see you before you dipped out tomorrow."

"Oh, okay," she said, barely coherent. "How are you doing?"

"I'm good. And you?"

"Just tired. I gotta catch a flight at eight in the morning, so I have to get up at the ass crack of dawn."

"Oh," I said, chuckling at her joke.

She would be at the airport in a few hours, and I wanted to

kick myself for not coming by her room earlier or even trying to get at her before the last day. I could just have wished her well with her writing, but I knew that if I didn't tell her how I felt, I would never get the opportunity to. The words came out in a blur.

"Meredith, I know that this is really bad timing, but I just had to let you know that I've been feeling you all week. I can't stop thinking about you. Hell, all of the stories I wrote this week were about you."

She looked at me for a moment as if I had told her that Malcolm X was really a Baptist preacher.

I continued, "I hate that it took me this long to tell you, but I couldn't let you leave without knowing that I am really attracted to you, your voice, your smile, your personality. On that first day when I saw you, something in me wanted to connect with you."

The more I listened to myself, the cornier the stuff I was saying sounded. I was messing up big-time, but at least I was getting the basic idea out there. She had an expression on her face like "This nigga is crazy," and I couldn't blame her.

"Well. That's all. I was hoping to talk with you a little bit before you left, but I didn't want to cut into your sleep. I guess I should lay it down myself."

She nodded her head.

As I started to walk away, she said, "You wrote stories about me?"

"Yes," I said, turning around.

"Well, were they any good?"

"I don't know if they were, but it felt good writing them."

She smiled as she closed the door.

• • •

A half hour later, I was lying on top of the covers on my bed listening to Raheem DeVaughn on the portable boom box I had sitting on the desk in my room. Although the lights were out, I could still catch a mild glow of light through the blinds, reminding me that the city was right outside my window. I had been staring at the ceiling so long, lost in my thoughts, that I had assumed I was asleep.

The knock was soft, but somehow I still heard it. Dressed in only my boxers and a T-shirt, I got up and walked to the door. Looking through the peephole, I could see Meredith standing there in an oversize Clark Atlanta sweatshirt, her flannel pajama bottoms hanging down over her New Balance running shoes. I opened the door, and my stomach immediately started to churn with butterflies.

"Come in," I offered. I cleared off a spot on my bed for her to sit down.

It took everything I had in me to suppress my smile. She had actually come to my room! It didn't matter what for either. She was there, and that was really all that mattered.

"Hey, Marlon, I just wanted to take a look at some of your stories. I don't think any guy has ever written a story about me before. I just had to see what you had to say."

"No problem," I said, pulling out the stack of stories I had printed out during the week. I had arranged them in the sequence in which they were written, so the sex-aholic-meeting one was on the top. I handed them to her before I realized that I should be embarrassed by how blatant my stories were. Meredith had really brought out the freak in me.

As I sat in the chair by my desk, facing my bed, I watched

her read the first story. She nodded occasionally, as if to say, "Interesting." When she finished the first story, she placed it back on the stack resting next to her on the bed.

"So *I* inspired you to write a story about two sex addicts?"

"Well, sort of. More like motivation."

"Motivation? Are all of the stories like this?"

Now I was really embarrassed. "More or less."

She lowered her head for a moment as if to reflect over what she had just read. Lifting her head, she slid out of my bed and stood up in front of me. "I am Meredith Jones, and I"—she sighed, in a voice of mock frustration—"am addicted to sex."

I looked at her with my eyebrow raised, and just then I saw her smile, that same smile from the first day I had had lunch with her. I stood up from my seat.

"I am Marlon Shepherd, and I, *too,* am addicted to sex."

The words were nearly identical to the words in the story, save our names. I could feel my erection starting to push the fabric of my boxers.

"So, Marlon, what do we do now?" she said, looking down at my erection.

Her mouth sealed around mine before I could catch my thoughts, and her tongue danced against mine, causing me to ease my hands slowly down her back, around her waist, and onto her ass. She moaned as we fell back onto the bed.

I lifted her sweatshirt and smiled when I realized that she wasn't wearing a bra. I held one of her breasts in my hand and flicked my tongue across her nipple, quickly enveloping it with the warmth of my mouth. My hand eased down into her flannel pajama bottoms, and at that moment I realized that she had only been wearing the sweatshirt, pajama bottoms, and sneakers—nothing beneath!

Slowly I went over the length of her body, massaging her muscles with my fingertips and replacing the sensation with my mouth. I made a soft, wet trail from her neck, down below her navel, and as my lips reached the inner part of her hip, I lifted her legs to drape over my shoulders. She eased toward me, allowing her clit to rub against the tip of my nose before sliding down onto my tongue. She rocked into me as I licked and sucked, her hands holding my head as she moved her body back and forth. I cupped my hands beneath her ass, lifting her into me, and her legs shot out, erect, as she screamed out in ecstasy, shivering.

I stood back from the bed, admiring her sexy body reclined in the light of the room, her wetness dripping down onto my sheets. She slowly sat up on the edge of my bed and slid one hand up my T-shirt onto my chest, as she pulled my throbbing erection from my boxers with her other hand and ran her tongue along the entire length of my shaft. I moved my hips forward involuntarily as she took the head into her mouth. As she worked me back and forth with her hands, I did everything I could to keep from cumming. I wanted to feel her sliding up and down me before I came.

Wetting up my shaft with her saliva, she guided me between her legs and eased me into her hot wetness. The warmth worked its way down my shaft as I wrapped myself completely around her. Her hands rubbed my back, and I stroked her as if it were the last thing I would ever do in life. Lifting her legs into a V formation, I eased myself into her until she gasped. As I rotated my hips, I looked down at her beautiful, sexy chocolate complexion; her full, firm breasts; and her athletic body. I massaged her calves with my fingertips as I held her legs spread.

"Ooh, I like it!" she cooed. "It feels so good!"

I smiled, but I couldn't respond because she felt so incredible that I could cum if she so much as wiggled a toe. I wanted to hold off and enjoy her all night. I didn't want her to get on that plane the next morning and leave without knowing that she was all that.

We rolled over, and she climbed on top of me, sliding her hips into mine. I could feel her wetness dripping down my balls as she pushed into me and wiggled her body. And when she was ready, she did a Kegel pull that made me scream out.

"Oh, shit! I'm gonna cum!"

She pulled me into her as I felt myself exploding in what felt like a psychedelic Technicolor orgasm, my erection throbbing in repetition as her walls tightened around me. We held on to each other for what seemed like one interminable moment before realizing how late it was.

As she dressed, I watched her cover up her perfection with each piece of clothing I had taken off earlier.

"I want a copy of the stories," she said.

"Take them. I have the files on my laptop."

I walked her to the door and kissed her. "Sleep well," she whispered, caressing my face.

I offered to walk her back to her room, but she refused, saying that she was fine. She only asked me to do one thing for her just before she left: she asked me to write this story.

Shiny, Nappy People

Been

I'd started braiding hair in my apartment on the weekends for a little extra cash. My job in cubicle hell didn't pay for shit, and besides, there were these funky red leather boots on Zappos that I just had to have. (Hey, a girl needs her footcandy.) Anyway, I didn't mind doing it. I actually kinda liked braiding hair. There was something relaxing about it, comforting even, especially since my mama had up and bought herself a pine condo four years ago.

Braiding hair had become a refuge; one of the few times, other than fighting or fucking, that I had a legitimate excuse to lay my hands on other black folks. And I needed an excuse because somewhere along the line, between childhood and adulthood, it had ceased to be okay to touch the brown, black, and high-yellow people who were related to me by blood. And a girl can really miss that, ya know?

So running my fingers through the soft, nappy, kinky spirals of brown-skinned strangers was my answer to paying some clueless shrink $120 an hour to listen to me bitch and moan about how much I missed my dearly departed mommy. Braiding was, well, braiding was therapy, black-girl style.

So, maybe you can understand why when my celly rang one Sunday afternoon, and Amani asked if he could make an appointment for some cornrows, I was real quick to say, "Cool. Why don't you just swing on through now, baby."

Amani was the kid brother of this chick from work who sat three squares down from me on the cubicle farm. Fatima was mad cool, and I figured if she was okay, her brother had to be awwright, too. That, and the fact that I wasn't doin' shit except painting my toenails a tasty new shade of Urban Decay's Asphyxia, made me more inclined to overlook a tiny, little, inconsequential detail like I was inviting a complete and total stranger into my crib.

Twenty minutes after the first call, my celly rang again (which reminds me, I really gotta change that annoying Beyoncé "Ring the Alarm" ringtone, but I digress). Anyhoo, Amani told me he was pulling up outside my building. I went to the window and spotted a honey-brown-complexioned brother parking a shiny, white Jetta with gold rims. *Cute,* I thought.

I told Shorty to "Look up. . . . No, higher, baby. . . . No, to the right of that big red sign over the sushi restaurant. . . . Yeah, that's me, Kiki, waving at you. I'm in 3A. I'll buzz you in, okay?"

Moments later, I heard a knock on my door. I opened up and stepped aside to let this tall, fine, caramel piece of ass come in. Amani was wearing all white from head to toe, a sexy Good Humor ice cream man, and he commenced to doing a nice little broh-man swagger right into my tastefully-gawdy-yet-minimalist-with-a-Moroccanish-Indian-sort-of-vibe studio apartment and looked around.

"Nice place, Kiki," he said, picking up the gleaming golden

statue of a Hindu goddess that sat on the mantelpiece over my bed. "So, who's this supposed to be, Shiva or somebody?" He raised a curious eyebrow in my direction.

"No, playa, that's not Shiva." I tried my best not to sound like a know-it-all. "Shiva is a dude. This little beauty here is Sarasvati. And, since you asked," I said, flipping open my handy-dandy book on Hindu deities I just happened to have, "she is the goddess of knowledge, speech, poetry, and music."

Amani cut his eyes at me in a way that said, "Shut the fuck up," and continued scoping out the apartment, admiring my Eastern-flavored decor every now and then. I was admiring something, too. Mmm-hmm, like the way those white linen pants were skimming his deliciously shapely derriere. *Goddamn, he must* live *at the gym,* I thought. Now usually, my rule was to avoid those ego monsters known as gym rats who loved a mirror more than I did, but Amani was looking so damned tasty that I figured sometimes you just gotta forgive a person's shortcomings . . . know what I mean?

Amani and his fine, fine behind made their way over to my bookshelves, which covered two walls of my bedroom. His eyes darted curiously across the endless titles.

"Damn, you got a lotta reading material in here and shit, girl. What are you, some kinda librarian or bookworm or somethin'?"

I preferred to think of myself as a book whore, but tomayto, tomahto. "Yeah," I said. "Something like that. Actually, I was an English lit major in college and I guess I just can't ever kick the book habit."

"Let's see. What do you got here?" Amani asked rhetorically. "Hmmm, a section of Caribbean cookbooks, a whole 'nother section on Buddhism, some shit in French, oh, and what do we have on this top shelf here? Oooh, Kiki got herself a little porn section."

"It's called erotica, thank you very much," I huffed indignantly, snatching my steamy copy of *The Sexual Life of Catherine M.* out of his hands and putting it back on my, errrrrr, ummm, "erotica" shelf.

"Well, if it looks like porn and quacks like porn," Amani teased, winking. "What else you got? *Kamikaze Lust, Lovers' Yoga,* the *Kama Sutra, Going Down: Great Writing on Oral Sex, Tantric Orgasms?* Ms. Lady, I do believe you is a straight-up freak perpetrating as some kind of ghetto-fabulous hippie intellectual."

I rolled my eyes. "Didn't you come here to get your hair 'did' or something, if I remember correctly?"

"Yeah, that's right. The cornrows." Amani took a seat in the kitchen chair I had moved into the living-room-cum-bedroom for braiding purposes. "I really do need to get my wig smoked in a hurry because I'm going to the Wizards-Heat game later tonight and I want my stuff looking right."

"No problem. I got you, boo. You're dome is gonna be looking sharper than Allen Iverson's when I'm done with it, my Nubian prince."

He smiled at me, revealing a set of teeth so white and pretty, they would put Taye Diggs out of business, and lips so soft and juicy even Angelina would have to hate on him.

Putting my mind back on work for distraction from the tingling feeling I was beginning to get in the recesses of my cunt, I started combing through his long, billowy 'Fro. Gently, I worked some coconut oil through his tresses, massaging it occasionally deep into his scalp. Amani's strong, textured hair was thirsty for this moisture and started to gleam almost immediately. I noticed how the beautiful honey-brown skin at the side of his neck shone also, and overall he gave the impression of a shiny copper penny in human form. I started to think about how I'd like to spend that penny when . . . my goddamn Beyoncé ringtone rang again (damn, I *really* gotta change that).

"Whatchu doin'?" my friend LaTonya asked.

"Co-chillin' with a client," I said, as nonchalantly as I could.

"Co-whoin' wid a what?"

"Girl, I'm braiding hair, okay?"

"Oh, excuse me, Ms. Lady, for not bein' up on all the ling-O. We still on for seven o'clock tonight or what? I am fiending for a mojito."

"Nah, girl. I don't think I'll be done by then," I lied, knowing good and well the style Amani wanted should only take me an hour and a half, max.

"Okay then, sweetie, I'll catch you at yoga class tomorrow night?"

"Oh, fo' sho, gurrrllllll. I'll be there."

Amani must have closed his eyes and gone into full-on chill mode while I was on the phone with LaTonya. I half wondered if he was actually asleep, which would be okay by me because I wanted a chance to drink in that sexy man without having to pretend anymore I wasn't staring at him. And I wanted more time to feel on him. I started braiding real, real slow, redoing sections that didn't need to be redone, shifting from one foot to the other. Oh, my feet didn't hurt or nothin', don't get it twisted. I just had to shift because the very smell of him (the coconut oil mixing with some kind of warm patchouli scent he was wearing) was making my crotch twitch like a muthafucka. Amani noticed my restless movements and looked up at me seductively. So, he wasn't sleeping after all.

"Kiki, you getting tired?" Aww. He sounded genuinely concerned.

"Naw, I'm okay, boo. My back is just a little achy from spinning class earlier today," I lied.

"Aw, that ain't no good. Want me to sit on the floor so you can get more comfortable?"

"You don't mind?" I cooed. "Yeah, that would be cool."

I sat on the edge of my bed and positioned Amani on a plush, velvet Moroccan poof on the floor in front of me. Wrapping my legs around the sides of his finely sculpted torso, I began braiding down the last remaining section of his unruly 'Fro. I could feel Amani's body heat radiating through the fabric of his tight white T. My legs burned with anticipation of I didn't know quite what . . . yet. When he breathed or stretched, Amani's shirt tugged upon the exaggerated outline of his magnificently worked-out chest. Was it my imagination, or was his body getting hotter by the second, too? My question was answered moments later, when I felt a man's hands drifting up and down the back of my calves. Warm, coarse palms wandered over the flesh of my thick, curvy legs for what seemed like an eternity. Then slowly, almost imperceptibly, Amani turned himself around so that he was kneeling between my open thighs. With one hand he slowly eased my body down toward the mattress, while the other spread apart my willing limbs even farther, as far as they could possibly go (without morphing into Dominique Dawes, that is). I could feel Amani's warm breath against the fabric of my panties, then the insanely delicious brush of his lips grazing their white lace edges. Exquisite torture as he slowly nibbled at the lace, working his mouth ever so lightly across my snatch, like a butterfly fluttering over the petals of a flower. Tenderly, his fingers pushed aside the satin crotch of the panties and spread open the lips of my anxious pussy. My healthy brown legs quivered uncontrollably as soft, pillow-light lips brushed my vajayjay just once before I felt his warm, sensual mouth begin to explore the wet folds of my coochie. He groaned softly, that unmistakable *mmmmm,* you know, the *mmmmm* we reserve for sexual pleasure and eating Krispy Kreme dough-nuts? When his tongue shot inside the walls of my cunt, I reached for the closest pillow I could find and screamed into it like a white girl at a Dave Matthews concert. Not a good look. It was one of my Eastern "decorative" pillows from Pier 1, and though it did an okay job of muffling my cries of pleasure, I ended up with a mouthful of silver sequins. Before I had a chance to reach for another, more practical pillow to shriek into, Amani had grabbed me by both legs and yanked me even farther over the bed's edge so that my dripping cunt was prac-tically sitting on his long, hard spear of a tongue; a melting chocolate Häagen-Dazs bar skewered on top of her own per-sonal Popsicle stick.

Amani threw my legs up over his shoulders and continued to eat me so, so, so, soooo good, as I admired my glossy new Asphyxia pedicure behind his head. Damn, but that boy could eat a coochie. And he didn't seem like he wanted to stop . . . *ever.* Typically, I can almost sense that "I've done my duty, now it's your turn to do me" vibe coming over a brother, but not Amani. Oh, hell, nawww. This sweet thug was acting like he had found himself the juiciest peach in the farmers' market, and he wasn't 'bout to let it go until he had sucked every last drop of nectar and sweet flesh from its pit, which was fine wid me. I had to pray those sequins I was swallowing weren't too terribly toxic, 'cause this man was fixin' to keep me squealing into my "purely decorative" pillows all night long. I couldn't take it. I threw my head backward in wild abandon as he suck-led at my screaming honey trap, and there, looking down on us with a vaguely approving, serene little smirk, was Sarasvati, the golden goddess. I swear, it was almost like she was talking to me as Amani lapped at my pussy. Like she was saying, "Mmmm-hmmm, girl. That's right. That is where a man *belongs* . . . on his knees, prostrate, between our legs, worshipping the *pu-nah-ny*. Don't fight it. Let him bow down. Let him lick, let him suck, let him nibble, let him bite, let him rub, let him fondle, let him taste. Let him give the almighty pussy its due, sister."

Hours and countless screams into my poor, poor mangled pillow later, I gazed down upon Amani's beautiful, brown face still nestled between my moist legs. Stroking my hands over his neat, pretty cornrows affectionately, I said, "I think you missed your basketball game, boo."

Amani smiled up at me mischievously, his face still gleam-ing with my juices. "Mmmm-hmmm. I know," he replied sar-castically. "Sisters is always trying to keep a brotha from enjoying his NBA game. That's okay though, Shorty, 'cause I was doing a little goaltending of my own down here."

"Goaltending what?" I asked, playing dumb and giggling.

"This juicy little cunt of yours," Amani responded, plunging first his fingers and then his tongue back into my waiting yoni.

I *thought* about reciprocating. I *thought* about getting on my knees and unzipping that man's pants with my teeth, taking his pretty brown cock in my mouth and sucking on it long and hard until his cum trickled down my lips like honey. I *thought* about blindfolding his sexy ass and taking him out to the back alley behind my apartment, letting him fuck the hell out of me on the steps of the fire escape, fuck me hard against the cold, redbrick walls of my building. Yeah, lying there on my back, this beautiful black man's face buried deep inside my grateful cunt, I *thought* about a whole lot of things. But, in the end I decided to just lie there like a queen and savor this rare moment of complete female selfishness. I decided to let him just do his thang. Besides, with the way Amani was moaning with the pleasure of giving me pleasure, I was quite sure there would be plenty of other times in the future when we could try out some other tricks. But, even if there weren't any "other times," even if I never heard from this sweet, chocolate prince again after tonight, it felt so good and so right to simply receive this one time; to accept the adoration that was being given to me. I realized at that moment that it wasn't merely the "touching" I had been missing so desperately, but the being touched. And this amazing young brother with his talented tongue had touched me to my very core.

Almost Identical

Linda "Sunshine" Herman

I don't know why I listened to Joy. Even though I was born ten minutes before her, she was the bossy one. Everything was always about what she wanted, and I always gave in. Over the years we had shared everything from toys to friends. Now she wanted to share something more personal. She wanted me to pretend to be her while she traveled to the Bahamas with her "sugar daddy." That meant I had to entertain her live-in boyfriend, Roderick, while she was away.

"Just tell him you're on your period."

That's the best she could do? I was supposed to tell him that I was on my period for seven whole days?! Joy and I were identical but we were as different as night and day. Roderick, who had only met me once, should have been smart enough to know the difference. He and Joy had been living together for a few months. He should have known when she got her period. We were twins but not everything was the same. If you had ever watched *Girlfriends*, it was easy to see that she was Lynn and I was Joan, even though we resembled Toni. I just wished I had more of Maya's attitude though.

"Joy, that man ain't no fool. He knows when you get your period. Besides, I don't know what the two of you do for fun. What does he like to eat? What's your pet name for him?" I was giving in.

"Faith, you know me. I call every man Pumpkin. As far as eating is concerned, you're on your period, remember?" she teased.

"Ha! Fucking ha! I meant, what foods does he enjoy, freak!"

"I'm not much for cooking, so, he normally brings home takeout."

I learned as much as I could about Roderick Ford. After all, I would be Joy for the next week. Luckily for her I could request vacation without jeopardizing my job, and her sugar daddy, Hiram Sanders, was paying for my plane ticket. Of course I was traveling light. If I was going to be Joy, that meant wearing her skimpy clothing as well.

Joy and I have traded places before. I was the one who took all of our important tests in school. The teachers couldn't tell us apart. So, on test days, we were sure to dress exactly alike. Thanks to my study habits, we both graduated with honors. Thanks to Joy, we also graduated with reputations for being easy because she pretended to be me with my boyfriends. Even though I wouldn't go all the way, she would.

Now we're both twenty-four-year-old adults. I live in Atlanta, Georgia, where I work as an editor. Joy lives in Miami, Florida, and her job is being pretty and having fun. Every now and again she may take on a job as a waitress or a hostess. For the most part she is taken care of by men like Hiram Sanders.

Hiram, from what Joy has told me, is damn near fifty years

old. He is widowed and has two sons, both of whom are older than Joy and me. Hiram is filthy rich and loves nothing more than the company of a young, beautiful woman on his arm. He's not looking for another wife, which is fine with Joy. She's not looking for a husband. She simply wants someone to pay her bills when they're due.

I don't know how she and Roderick met. He actually seems like a decent guy. He's a painter and works full-time teaching art to youths. Even though he's thirty-three, he has never been married and has no kids. He seems to think the world of Joy, but I'm sure she only moved in with him because she needed a place to live and was between men like Hiram.

I arrived in Miami just hours before Joy was to leave for her cruise. She met me at the airport. My beautiful sister was dressed in a white tube top and no bra. I thought her breasts were going to fall out at any moment. She wore the shortest and tightest pair of jean shorts I had ever seen. If I didn't know better, I'd think Roderick painted them on her. The heifer completed her look with a pair of three-inch heels.

"Joy! You know I don't have any piercings!" I reminded her when I was nearly blinded from the bling of her navel ring. It had to be an entire carat.

"It's just a clip-on!" she said as she removed the diamond. "I haven't decided if I actually want the real thing."

Her long, curly hair was braided back. She had failed to tell me that she had gotten braids. My hair hung loosely on my shoulders. There was no way we'd have time to get my hair braided. Joy had told me that Roderick was normally home by six in the evenings. It would take longer than that for someone to braid my thick hair.

"What about the braids?"

"Just tell him you took them out, Faith! Dang!"

Even though I was doing her a favor, Joy was getting irritated with me. I don't know why she didn't tell him she was coming to Atlanta for a week. I felt so uncomfortable; going to their home and pretending to be her. Roderick would see right through me.

"Don't forget the art exhibit on Friday," she reminded me. That was the reason I had to be her. Roderick's work was being displayed at an exhibit, and of course he wanted his significant other at his side.

Joy gave me a tour of their small apartment. There was one huge bedroom. In the center was a king-size bed. Paintings of nude women of all colors filled the walls. They were beautiful and detailed.

It was easy to learn the apartment. There was nothing there but a bedroom, bathroom, and a kitchen. There was no living room area, den, nor dining room. The tour lasted all of five minutes, and after briefing me on a few things, Joy was gone.

It was only four o'clock. I had two hours to kill before Roderick arrived home. I decided to spend that time cleaning the messy apartment. The chairs in the bedroom were covered with clothing. The bed had not been made. I could tell Joy lived here.

"It smells good in here. I know my girl ain't cooking."

Even though I wasn't supposed to, I couldn't resist cooking. Roderick came home to the smell of fresh garden peas, baked herb chicken, broccoli-and-rice casserole, and peach cobbler. After cleaning the small apartment, I'd gone down to the corner store. If I was going to be there seven days, I had to stock the refrigerator with more than an onion and bottled water.

Before I could speak, Roderick planted a soft kiss on my full lips. Even though he had paint splashed on his clothing, he looked good in a white T-shirt and blue jeans. He even smelled good. It felt good being so close to him. He was more handsome than I had remembered.

"I went to the store and picked up a few things," I said, trying not to blush.

He put his hand to my forehead and asked, "You okay? You sure you don't have a fever?"

I laughed, despite the butterflies in my stomach. Joy didn't cook. It wasn't because she couldn't, though. Ma Ollie, our maternal grandmother, had taught us how to cook. Joy had no choice but to learn. Unlike school, she couldn't get me to stand in for her. Ma Ollie knew us apart.

"I just felt like cooking. Sit down and I'll fix you a plate."

Roderick and I ate our meal in the small kitchen. I listened to him talk about his students and what kind of day he'd had. I couldn't help but notice how good-looking he was. I was mesmerized by his Terrence Howard eyes and his Allen Payne lips. I wasn't supposed to be attracted to my sister's man, but I was feeling him. My nipples were hard and there was no denying the heat and moisture between my thighs.

Roderick unexpectedly joined me in the shower. I couldn't tell him that I was on my period. The man was down on his knees with his head between my thighs before I could open my mouth and say anything. His tongue said "hello" to my clit as they introduced themselves. He squeezed my ass as he stroked my clit. I wanted to say stop but I was speechless. I didn't notice the hot water turn cold because of the fire burning within me. When Roderick came up, without hesitation I went down. I took the full length of his swollen penis into my mouth. I licked it and sucked it with hunger. I hadn't had a man in over six months.

"I've never known you to be so unselfish," he moaned before picking me up and carrying me to their bed.

As he stared into my eyes, he entered me. A whimper escaped my throat as he gently pushed his love deeper and deeper inside my walls. Up and down and then slow circles. Up and down and then faster circles. Faster and faster circles, and then we both screamed as we climaxed. I called out his name. He called out Joy's name. My pleasure was quickly replaced by guilt.

"How's it going?" Joy asked the next morning after Roderick had left for work.

"Fine. Are you enjoying the ocean?"

"It's beautiful! Did Roderick buy the period thing?"

Why couldn't she just leave it alone and talk about her? "Yep."

"Good! Well, call me if you need to know anything. The only thing I can think of right now is the exhibit. Make sure you're there to support him for me."

I agreed and was happy to end the call. I had lied to my sister. Even worse than that, I had betrayed her by sleeping with her man. Worst of all, I had enjoyed it and was looking forward to being in his arms again.

Roderick and I made love every night after dinner. He used his tongue to explore every inch of my body. With him I always experienced orgasms. I was able to let go in a way that I had never done before. I felt free. I felt loved. I was falling in love with him.

"There is something different about you, Joy," he said as he watched me dress for the exhibit.

He hadn't said anything about my not having the braids. "My hair?"

"I like it better this way, but that's not it. You seem like a totally different person. I mean, I come home to a clean house and dinner every evening. You listen to me talk about work. I'm not complaining, but even in bed, you're different."

I couldn't help but be curious. "Better?"

"You're more giving of yourself. Before I felt like you were holding back. You seemed to enjoy me pleasing you but you were reluctant to do the same for me."

I could believe that. Joy was that selfish. She cared about her feelings above all else. I could imagine Roderick working hard to satisfy her only to be disappointed when she didn't put any effort into satisfying him in return.

"Well, enjoy it while it lasts," I teased as I put the finishing touches on my makeup.

I felt proud to be at Roderick's side that night. I met some of his students and was impressed by the display of paintings. Every artist was African-American or Latino. On canvas they painted their history, the present, and a hopeful future. I couldn't wait to get Roderick home.

As soon as we closed the door, I pushed him back against the wall. I dropped to my knees and unbuckled his trousers. I took him into my mouth and gave him what Joy wouldn't. Within seconds softness became hard as steel. I pulled harder and harder until he exploded.

"Irreplaceable" sang from Joy's cell phone. I knew it was her calling.

"Hello?" I answered as I headed toward the bathroom. Roderick mouthed "Hurry up!" as he headed to the bedroom.

"How was the gallery?"

"Joy, it was beautiful! Roderick is really talented!" I beamed proudly.

"He's talented but those art shows bore me. I'm glad you enjoyed it."

"So, how is the trip?" I asked, wanting to change the subject.

"I could live here! Girl, it's beautiful and Hiram is spoiling me rotten! You may have to take home some of the stuff he bought me. I don't have any idea where to put it!"

I could see her smiling through the phone. I wished she could live in the Bahamas. I sure would have lived with Roderick forever. In five days, I had fallen in love with him. I didn't know how Joy could live with him for three months and run off with old-ass Hiram for a week.

"You'll be back on Sunday, right?"

"Yes, don't forget to get out of the house before he wakes up. I'll go home and tell him I was out shopping. He'll never know the difference."

She was so wrong. He would know the difference. He would know that the loving and selfless girl was gone. He would surely notice that the selfish girl was back. He just wouldn't know why.

"Don't forget to take the braids out!" I warned before we hung up.

Sunday came too soon. For six nights I had lain with Roderick. We had made love every single night. Now, it was time to go. I kissed him softly on his lips, trying not to wake him, before leaving the apartment. I cried all the way to the airport and all the way back to Atlanta.

The only thing waiting for me back home was my job. I had no man and no true friends. Ma Ollie had died a year ago, and our parents had been dead since we were five years old. My mother had killed her husband after finding out he was sleeping with her cousin. She'd then killed herself. Ma Ollie had raised Joy and me with Grandpa Bill's help. He'd died of cancer the year we had graduated high school.

Joy hadn't called or flown up to kick my ass, so I assumed she didn't know about Roderick and me. When she did call a few weeks later, I was completely caught off guard.

"Don't forget about next week. Roderick and I are coming up for Thanksgiving."

I had forgotten. Thanksgiving was always spent at my place. I'd go to Miami and spend Christmas with Joy. We would go to South Beach and enjoy the sunny weather and look for celebrities. We had been fortunate enough to see Miami Heat center Shaquille O'Neal.

"Of course I won't forget."

"I hope you cook something good because he has been pestering me about cooking since I got home. Why in the hell did you have to go and cook for him?" Before I could answer, she continued, "You know Hiram wants me to spend Christmas with him in Aspen."

"I thought we were spending Christmas together in South Beach again."

"I've got to figure something out. Maybe you and Roderick can go to South Beach. I really want to learn how to ski."

There she was again being selfish. Only she didn't know how much it would mean to me to be with Roderick again. I agreed to think about it. I then tried to prepare myself for their visit.

When our eyes met, it was obvious that he knew. Roderick realized that I was the one who had been unselfish; the one who had cooked his meals and had cleaned his apartment. He just didn't know why I had done such a thing.

"I'm going to take a nap," Joy announced as she dropped her handbag on my white sofa and disappeared into the guest room.

"It was you. I knew something was different," Roderick finally said. "Why?"

"Roderick, I . . ."

"Please, don't lie to me," he said, his voice full of sadness.

I couldn't lie to him. I sold my sister out. I told him about her trip to the Bahamas with Hiram. I even told him about her plans to spend Christmas with Hiram and have me spend Christmas with him.

"Are you okay?" I asked when he covered his handsome face with his large hands.

"I'm in love with you, Faith." Before I could respond, I was in his arms. "I've been in love with you since the first night we made love."

"What is going on?" Joy startled us both. Neither of us had been aware of her entrance.

"Let me explain," I offered right before she slapped me hard across the face.

Roderick stood between the two of us. "Joy, we didn't plan this. You basically pushed us together when you used Faith while you were busy cheating with my boss!"

His boss? I didn't know Hiram was his boss. I had doubted that the two even knew each other.

"You slept with my sister! And, Faith, how could you do this?" Joy didn't wait for my explanation. She grabbed her handbag and stormed out of the house.

I knew where to find her. There was only one place she could be. She would be at the cemetery with our deceased loved ones. I had to go to her. But first I had to let Roderick go. I cared for him but I couldn't lose my relationship with Joy. She was all I had in this world.

"Don't say it," he said when he read my expression.

"She's all I've got." On that note I left him behind as I searched for my sister.

It took some time but Joy and I worked things out. She spent Christmas in Aspen with Hiram and I stayed in Atlanta. Having nothing to do, I decided to visit an art show at a nearby museum.

"You like that painting?"

Without turning around, I knew the voice belonged to Roderick. He had painted the portrait of the beautiful women. They were twins. One had happy eyes and the other wore sadness in her brown eyes.

"I guess I'm the one with the sad eyes?" I asked with my back still to him.

"Actually, you're the one with the happy eyes."

I faced him with a question in my eyes. I had always thought that Joy was the happy one. She had never seemed to have a care in the world. I, on the other hand, had always been the one to worry about every single thing. I had always been so focused on doing the right thing while Joy did the right now thing.

"I don't understand."

He explained his observations. "Joy is lost. She lacks direction. She doesn't know how to love anyone above herself."

True, so far. I nodded in agreement.

"You seem to have yourself together. You love unselfishly. You simply need to allow yourself to be loved in return. I want the chance to love you the way you deserve to be loved."

I gave him the chance he asked for. I gave myself the chance that I deserved. Joy wasn't happy at first but eventually we worked things out. In the end, I remained close to my sister and in love with Roderick. Few people understand, but sometimes there simply is no explanation when the love jones comes down.

Curiosity Stirred My Cat

Tyanna

"Thank you, God!" I said to myself out loud. It was Friday afternoon and I couldn't wait to get off work. I loved being a schoolteacher, but those damn teenagers were pushing me to retire sooner than I had planned.

I walked out of West Hartington High School, searching my purse for my car keys. "One of these days I have to clean out my purse," I said, finding them as I approached my car. I got in the car and drove straight home, trying to beat the rush traffic.

When I pulled into my driveway, I was surprised to see my husband's truck sitting there. He was never home at that hour. The front door was unlocked; I shut it behind me after I walked in. I didn't see any signs of him downstairs.

"Kamar, baby," I said.

I went back in the great room, spotting Kamar running down the carpeted stairs. I hated when he ran up and down the stairs. We lived in a home, not a jungle.

"Hey, you know the rules. There's no running going on in this house," I stated in dismay.

Kamar flashed his sexy smile, the one that always dampened the inside of my cinnamon thighs. He walked toward me and wrapped his firm arms around me, caressing my back.

"Hi, gorgeous," he said before softly kissing my lips twice. "How was work, babe?"

"Ugh, work! I'm so happy that winter break is next week."

He chuckled. "Okay."

"Wait a minute! What are you doing home from work?"

"I left some files in the den. I need them for the streamline and pipeline contract." There was a silent pause between us before Kamar spoke again. "I do have to get back."

"Okay, baby." I readjusted his necktie and fixed his shirt collar precisely.

"Thank you, gorgeous."

"Anytime."

"I'm glad that I got to see you before I went back to work."

Kamar kissed me good-bye and then he was out the door. What was I going to do now? I could call up a few of my girlfriends and find out what they were doing that night. Naw, I didn't think so! I loved my girls, but sometimes they didn't know when to go home.

I managed to busy myself with a bit of housecleaning and washing Kamar's funky-ass gym clothes as several hours passed. I finally took a break and settled down in our master bedroom. After taking a hot shower, I crawled into our king-size bed and snuggled up with my laptop. I decided to go online and check my emails. I came across two from my husband and read them. Kamar always wrote me little love notes while he was at work. I only wish his lovemaking was as passionate as his love notes. After reading his emails and responding to them, I decided to do a bit of Web surfing and browse through a few chat rooms: BLK Is Better, Fine BLK Men 4 U, and 30s Ebony 2 Love.

Less than ten minutes later, I was bored to death. I couldn't believe I even bothered looking in those corny-ass chat rooms. I needed to grade some research papers, but I had the entire following week to accomplish that.

Kamar wouldn't be home for another five hours. Lately he had been working late and I couldn't stand it. My eyes looked back at the laptop screen and saw an IM Catcher pop up with an instant message from an unknown buddy. I was feeling lonely so I opened the IM and replied.

KWC624: May I ask your age?

MAXXINE: I'm thirty-two.

KWC624: The picture in your profile is stunning, very classy.

MAXXINE: Thank you.

KWC624: How tall are you?

MAXXINE: I'm 5'9".

KWC624: You seem very intelligent.

MAXXINE: Thanks, again.

MAXXINE: Tell me something about you.

KWC624: Well, I'm a little too old for you.

MAXXINE: Okay.

KWC624: I'm 6'4" 218 pounds—athletic body, light brown skin and mixed parents. My mother is white and my father is black.

MAXXINE: Do you have a picture?

KWC624:   Yes, I'm going to email it to you now.

MAXXINE: Thank you. So, exactly how old are you?

KWC624:   Smile.

MAXXINE: Okay.

KWC624:   I'm too old for you, dear. What do you do for a living?

MAXXINE: I'm a high school English teacher.

KWC624:   Do you have a man now?

MAXXINE: Yes, I'm married.

KWC624:   Damn, just my luck. I should have known a sista as fine as you wouldn't be available.

MAXXINE: I appreciate the compliment.

We continued to chat as I waited for his picture to arrive in my mailbox. We talked about my relationship with my husband and other miscellaneous topics.

KWC624:   Mail sent.

I clicked on the mailbox icon and opened his email. I waited a few seconds before the picture downloaded completely. When it did, I was speechless. He looked so beautiful. His physical appearance reminded me of my husband. His complexion was perfectly bronzed. He had a chiseled face and well-defined arms. They were rippled with muscles. The brotha was built, a black Adonis.

MAXXINE: You're a very handsome man—debonair.

KWC624:   Thank you, dear.

MAXXINE: You're very welcome.

KWC624:   How long have you been married?

MAXXINE: Almost eleven years.

KWC624:   Hmm, I see.

There was a pause before he replied again.

KWC624:   So tell me . . .

MAXXINE: Yes.

KWC624:   What does an English teacher like you do outside of school?

MAXXINE: I'm a tennis instructor, as well as being an indoor track and field coach for the girls' team.

KWC624:   Oh really. I bet you have good form, too.

MAXXINE: LOL. Yes, I do.

KWC624:   Smile, what else?

MAXXINE: One of my favorite pastimes after work is hanging out with my girl-friends, going for long drives at night and to this local jazz club with my husband. I love going there, but I haven't been there in a few months.

KWC624:   Why is that, dear? You're un-happy with him.

MAXXINE: No. I love my husband, but

his business is interfering with our personal life lately. We hardly spend any time together anymore.

KWC624:   That's unfortunate. Does he know that?

MAXXINE: Yes.

KWC624:   Is he still at work now?

MAXXINE: Yes.

KWC624:   I would love to be with you right now.

MAXXINE: I'm sure, LOL.

KWC624:   I'm serious. I'm not talking about just sex. You seem very nice—devoting.

MAXXINE: Thank you.

KWC624:   What is it about your husband that turns you on?

MAXXINE: Don't you think you're getting too personal too fast?

KWC624:   I was just curious, dear.

MAXXINE: If you must know, I'll tell you.

KWC624:   Okay.

MAXXINE: Well, it's the way he looks at me; his eyes burn right into my soul. His body is smooth and hard. He's hot. Everything about him turns me on. There's also a softer side to him. He writes me these little love notes from work, telling me how much I mean to him. He tells me how much he misses me when he's away from me and how he can't wait to get home to me. He lets me know that he's in love with me. It's the little things like that, that he says to me. They mean the most to me. They keep my home fires burning for him.

KWC624:   That's very sweet, but if he's not careful, another man can replace him.

MAXXINE: I doubt that. He's it for me.

KWC624:   If you say so. What else do you enjoy?

MAXXINE: For the moment I'm enjoying our talk.

KWC624:   So am I, dear. What else do you enjoy?

MAXXINE: Well, I enjoy a few things. I like going to art museums, reading, music, a day at the spa, my husband and everything else in between. I sound boring, don't I?

KWC624:   You're interesting—mature. I like that in a sista.

MAXXINE: What does the KWC624 stand for?

KWC624:   Kenneth Warren Cooley is my name. June 24 is my birthday.

MAXXINE: That's a very appealing name.

KWC624:   Thank you. I'm assuming your name is Maxxine.

MAXXINE: Yes.

KWC624:   Nice.

MAXXINE: And what is Kenneth Warren Cooley's age?

KWC624: I'm 57.

MAXXINE: You had me thinking that you were some old man.

KWC624: LOL, well you are young, dear. I didn't think you would be able to handle me.

MAXXINE: Well, there's really nothing to handle.

KWC624: Not yet, dear.

I let that one slide and pondered the thought of where my conversation with Kenneth Warren Cooley might be headed.

KWC624: Are you there?

MAXXINE: Yes.

KWC624: I thought maybe I had scared you away.

MAXXINE: You didn't. Where are you from?

KWC624: I'm originally from Chicago. I'm currently living in Arizona, and you?

MAXXINE: Connecticut.

KWC624: Oh, really! I have family out there. I also do some business out that way with a few clients and other places along the east coast.

MAXXINE: What type of business are you in?

> KWC624: Investment   Banking.   You know, I have to fly out to Connecticut next week on business. I would love to see you.

Was this man for real? There was no way I was going to meet some man off the internet, no matter how fine he was. I was not meeting any man, period. Hell no!

> MAXXINE: I'm going to have to pass.
>
> KWC624: That's   unfortunate.   Maybe you'll change your mind, dear.
>
> MAXXINE: I don't think so. How come you're single?
>
> KWC624: Because I'm picky. I love a sexy black woman who is educated, honest, classy, loving and caring. Plus, I'm waiting for you to divorce your husband.
>
> MAXXINE: LOL, you don't know when to quit.
>
> KWC624: Quitting is not in my vocabulary.
>
> MAXXINE: Even when it's a lost cause. I'm happy with my husband.
>
> KWC624: Then why are you talking to me on the Internet?

Damn, he had me there.

> KWC624: I'm not trying to offend you. If he was doing his job, I wouldn't enjoy chatting with his sexy wife.

MAXXINE: Thank you.

KWC624: You're welcome. Think about what I said about meeting. I know we'll be good for each other—something new.

MAXXINE: Maybe next lifetime.

KWC624: Why not this one?

MAXXINE: I'm married and too young, sugah. Remember.

KWC624: I think you can handle me. I'll treat you right. I can teach you a thing or two that your husband can't teach you.

MAXXINE: You know you're wasting your time.

KWC624: That's highly unlikely. I like talking to you, dear. We should be having this conversation in bed instead of like this—kissing, caressing and pleasing you. Showing and giving you love and the attention that you desire.

MAXXINE: That all sounds nice, but I have to go.

KWC624: Aw, don't do that, dear. You want to call me and say goodnight?

MAXXINE: I'm tired, Kenneth.

KWC624: Okay, maybe next time. I want to chat with you again. I want to get to know you. I'll treat you right.

MAXXINE: I see. I'm sure you will.

KWC624: Are you really married?

MAXXINE: Yes. Why would I lie about that?

KWC624:   Just asking, dear. I hope I cross your mind tomorrow. I will think of you.

MAXXINE: You're too kind.

KWC624:   I'm just being honest. Think about what I said.

MAXXINE: Okay. Goodnight, Kenneth.

KWC624:   Goodnight, Maxxine. Email me tomorrow, if you think of me.

MAXXINE: Okay.

KWC624:   One more thing, what part of Connecticut are you from?

MAXXINE: The West Hartington area.

KWC624:   Oh, really! I have family in that area as well. I hope you seriously consider my proposition. I'll let you go. Sweet dreams, dear.

MAXXINE: Thank you. Goodnight.

After signing off the internet, my mind wandered into the damn gutter about Kenneth sexing my body. I wanted him bad, especially between my thighs.

"Maxxine, quit it!" I told myself.

I was a happily married woman—sort of. Yes, I was. I had to forget about him. That was it, problem solved.

I woke up later that night, feeling Kamar's hand rubbing the small of my back.

"Hi, gorgeous," he whispered in my ear before kissing it. I turned around to face him.

"Hi, baby. What time is it?"

"A little past one."

"I tried to wait up for you."

"You're so sweet." He pulled me closer and kissed my forehead with his soft L.L. Cool J lips. "I love you, gorgeous."

Then Kamar kissed me with a lip-teasing, toe-tingling, body-cracking kiss that stole my breath away. With one swift movement, he was on top of me. I gasped as he entered me, maneuvering all eight thick, long inches inside. I bit into his shoulder to stifle the scream that was so close to shattering his eardrum. The pleasure that I was experiencing rocked my soul. It was so intense that, within minutes, I was trembling with the most amazing orgasm that I'd ever had. Then I realized that Kamar was the one making love to me. Kamar continued to pump into me like a runaway train. He couldn't hold back any longer. I could feel his hot juices pummeling the walls of my pussy.

Then he cried out my name. "Oh, Maxxine, Maxxine! I'm cumming, baby."

I pretended to cry out to him. My voice was saying, "Kamar, cum for me, baby," but in my mind, I was seeing the face of KWC624: Kenneth Warren Cooley. I yearned to know what he would feel like inside me. Could Kenneth make my toes curl and crack my back, or was he all talk?

After we made love for the next ten minutes, Kamar drifted off to sleep, leaving me wide-awake and yet again unsatisfied. As I watched him sleeping so peacefully, I caressed his stubbly cheek tenderly and thought to myself, *Where did all your passion go?* I whispered those sentiments to him, but he was sound asleep.

I didn't do anything the entire weekend: no girlfriends, shopping, or work. My husband had started working on the weekends, even though weekends were our sacred time together, too. Well, except for during football season. Thinking about Kamar's work schedule angered me so I switched my focus to Kenneth. Fucking him was all I wanted.

"Maxxine, stop tripping, girl!" I told myself continually.

I couldn't take it anymore. I went upstairs, booted up my laptop, and got in the bed. My heart was pounding rapidly, then I started laughing. It was ridiculous to get so excited and moist over some man from online, but he was a fine piece of chocolate.

"He probably forgot all about our chat," I vaguely said to myself. "Well, here goes."

I signed on. I checked my emails and noticed KWC624 had sent three. Just seconds after I read the last one, I received an instant message from Kenneth.

> KWC624:   Hello!
>
> MAXXINE: Hi, I was just reading your emails. Thank you.
>
> KWC624:   You're welcome. How are you?
>
> MAXXINE: I'm doing well.
>
> KWC624:   That's good to hear, dear. So how for real are you? Do you want a good man?
>
> MAXXINE: I believe any woman would want nothing less, but I already have one.
>
> KWC624:   Well, that's what you deserve, Maxxine.

I didn't respond to his message until he sent me another.

KWC624: Have you missed me? Did you think of me at all after we signed off?

MAXXINE: Yes, I went to sleep with you on my mind.

KWC624: Really! What were you thinking?

MAXXINE: I was thinking about what you said to me.

KWC624: I want to be with you, dear.

MAXXINE: You know this will never work.

KWC624: Are you saying what I think you're saying?

I hesitated about his question. My mind was rambling all over the place. I couldn't think of an answer fast enough to type back before Kenneth did.

KWC624: Maxxine, are you there?

MAXXINE: Yes.

KWC624: You haven't answered my question, dear.

MAXXINE: I know.

KWC624: It's okay. I assumed too quickly. I don't want you to feel pressured into this.

MAXXINE: You know this will never work.

KWC624: Smile.

MAXXINE: This is crazy, but my answer is yes.

KWC624:   Aw, I wish you could see the
smile on my face. I'm exhilarated!
MAXXINE: Kenneth, don't get your hopes
up. I'm not promising you anything.
KWC624:   I believe we both know what
we're in for.

We continued to chat for the next ten or fifteen minutes before exchanging our cell phone numbers. Kenneth called me immediately after we both signed off. For the next two hours, we engaged in phone sex. Kenneth's oral sexual foreplay made me climax nine times. It was official. We made arrangements for the upcoming week to meet each other.

I was a nervous freaking wreck, waiting for Kenneth at the baggage claim in McCarthy International Airport. It was overly crowded, my patience was running low, and my heart was pounding through my chest. He should have been there by then. I had made plans for us to go to the Bushnell Theatre; different events were going on during Black History Month. What the hell! I shouldn't have been there in the first place. Black women didn't do crazy shit like that.

"What the hell was I thinking?" I asked myself out loud.

A man walked up behind me, wrapping his strong arms around my waist—squeezing me. He sucked on my left earlobe before saying, "Maxxine, it's too late to have doubts now."

Kenneth swung me around to face him. Shit, he was too fine! Just like Kamar, only taller and bigger. His dark eyes held me in a spell and time seemed to stand still.

"Maxxine, don't get shy on me now; not after all the things you said to me on the phone."

As he stood there grinning, I snapped out of my trance and spoke to him in person for the very first time.

"Hi, Kenneth."

Kenneth's touch felt so familiar to me, causing me to blush within his arms. His facial features struck me in a wicked way, as if we had met before. That thought quickly faded as he slipped his tongue in my mouth and our tongues intertwined in a passionate kiss. He was seemingly attempting to suck the life out of me.

I broke free from our kiss long enough to say, "Are you ready to go to the Bushnell?"

He eagerly replied, "Oh, yes, Maxxine."

We didn't make it out of the airport parking garage before Kenneth was feeling all over my ass and waist. He insisted on taking the stairs instead of the elevator to the ninth level. We stopped in between levels seven and eight of the stairwell.

"Maxxine," he whispered in my ear as he leaned over, "I want you! I want you right now." He flicked his tongue in my ear and it made me melt, causing friction between my thighs. "Maxxine."

Kenneth pressed my body closer to his, leaving no space between us. I could feel his cool-minted breath brushing against my face. More important, I could feel his steel pipe pressing on my stomach.

He asked, "Are you okay?"

I replied, "Yes."

His lips were soft and tender as our tongues intertwined once more. He forced his thick, long tongue down my throat, searching for my inner soul. He put his hand on the back of my neck to fill my mouth with his tongue. I let out a slight moan of bliss as I caressed his smooth-as-a-baby's-skin face. He used his free hand to unbutton my salt-and-pepper peacoat and squeezed my breasts at the same time. Just then I realized that I was about to commit adultery. I broke our kiss and he tried to put his tongue back in my mouth. I rejected it.

"Maxxine, what's the problem?"

"I shouldn't be here."

"Then we'll go wherever you want to go." He put his cold hands underneath my black cashmere turtleneck and caressed the small of my back. The coldness of his hands sent chills down my spine. I gazed into his eyes, searching for the right.

"I won't hurt you, Maxxine."

Everything within me wanted to reject his advance, but the desire to be with him was surreal. I wanted him inside me.

"I promise," he said before slipping his tongue back inside my mouth. Kenneth pulled my coat off and let it hit the floor before taking my turtleneck, designer jeans, and heels off. He let out a sigh as he looked me up and down slowly. His eyes were tracing the curves of my voluptuous body.

I unbuttoned his shirt as we continued to kiss. I removed his shirt and coat all at once. I wanted to feel his naked chest against mine and caress it with my soft hands. He unbuckled his belt and unzipped his slacks, letting them fall around his ankles, leaving him standing in his cotton briefs. I could feel the stiffness of his clothed dick pressing up against my body. I couldn't wait to have him inside me.

Kenneth backed me up slowly against the wall. He licked, kissed, and nibbled his way down my neck to my breasts. He popped both breasts out from my floral satin bra. He sucked on my right breast and squeezed and pinched my other breast with his fingers. I loved the warmth of his tongue sucking on my hard nipples. I caressed the back of his head, filling his mouth with my breast. My pussy was throbbing and my panties were so moist. Kenneth put his free hand in my panties and rubbed my swollen clit. He rubbed it so hard and continued to suck my breast as a moan of ecstasy escaped my lips. He rubbed and squeezed my swollen clit for a little while longer before sliding two fingers inside my wet essence.

I gyrated my hips and worked my pussy on his fingers. My moans were beginning to grow more as Kenneth stroked his fingers deeper in my wetness. He released his mouth from my breast and kissed my lips and sucked on them, while he continued to finger me. We both looked into each other's eyes. We stared at one another, and the next thing I knew, my panties were being ripped. Kenneth tore my panties off and pulled his aroused dick out from his briefs. I gazed down at his big, thick dick and it gazed back up at me. I wondered if his dick would fit in my pussy. He reached down and picked me up. I wrapped my long, toned legs around his sculpted waist. He slid his tongue into my wanting mouth. I wrapped my arms around his body. Kenneth elevated me up higher to position my pussy over his dick. Then he lowered me slowly onto his manhood, easing its way past my moistened pussy lips. I felt his head entering me and inching its way farther inside me. I moaned after his dick was all the way inside me, stretching my pussy beyond its limits. It hurt like hell, but felt so good at the same time.

"Are you okay? Is everything alright, Maxxine?" he passionately asked me.

"Yes," I uttered with bliss.

He continued to kiss me and fuck me up against the wall. He fucked me slow, grinding and pumping his massive dick into my tight pussy. I locked my legs around him tighter and pulled his body closer to mine.

"Mmmm, fuck me. Fuck me, Kenneth!" I whispered with ecstasy in my voice. I could feel his dick tickling my navel as our moans and groans grew more intense with pleasure. He continued to tear my pussy up against the wall for twenty-five minutes, before carrying me over to the staircase with his steel pipe still marinating inside me. Kenneth pulled his dick out of me slowly and put me down gently. His dick was still at full attention and covered with my sweet juices.

"Turn around and bend over for me, dear," he demanded.

I obeyed, resting the palms of my hands parallel to each other on the steps. Kenneth rubbed and squeezed my ample ass as he knelt down behind me on the stairs. I couldn't remember the last time my pussy had been eaten so well. He rolled his tongue into a tube and wasted no time licking and darting his tongue in and out of me. I moaned louder each time he sucked and nibbled on my clit. His strong hands grabbed my hips to prevent me from swaying back and forth so much. He worked his hot tongue forcefully over my cunt. I came four times from that snakelike tongue of his. My juices drizzled down my inner thighs and onto his tongue. He licked me dry before standing back up. Kenneth began stroking his shaft with his right hand and rubbing and fingering my pussy with the other. I was so fucking horny and ready to have him invade my sugary walls again. I told him to take my sweet pussy and fuck me hard. He grabbed my hips and spanked his dick on my pussy before penetrating me. He thrust it in quickly, all in one stroke. He moaned and so did I. I loved the curve in his dick. Kenneth definitely knew how to hit all my G-spots with his curved pipe. He pumped his dick in my pussy slowly, squeezing my ass. He increased his pace and caught a rhythm. My ass was in for one hell of a ride then. Kenneth fucked my little pussy with no mercy, spanking my ass and grabbing my hips to pull me up and down on his shaft. I could feel his balls slamming up against my clit as he pounded and thrust himself deeper inside me. I could hear him whispering my name repeatedly as he fucked me faster and harder.

My knees began to buckle beneath me. They were shaking and getting ready to give way. Our extremely intense moans accelerated. Each stroke of his inside me was better than the previous one. I could feel the sweat trickling down from his body onto my back and being absorbed in my skin. Kenneth felt so damn good inside me, tearing my pussy to pieces, slapping my ass, rubbing my nipples, and kissing my back. The more he fucked me, the louder I got. With each thrust of his hips, I could feel his dick. It seemed as if he were trying to touch my heart. I could feel myself sinking slowly to the floor as we both came in unison. Kenneth gave me a few more thrusts and then collapsed on top of me. We were both breathing rapidly after our exploding climaxes. We lay there for a few minutes in silence. My mind and body were numb. Kenneth pulled his long pipe out of me slowly and asked if I was ready to leave; I quietly responded that I was.

I drove forty miles out of the way from my hometown. I couldn't risk being seen by anyone who knew me—worse yet, Kamar! Though it was too late for all of that; the stains on those steps in the parking garage told a different story. Since it was Black History Month, I brought Kenneth to the Bushnell The-atre. I was stunned that he still wanted to go after he laid the pipe down so well. I was spent, euphoric and confused, but Kenneth insisted. Every day in February at the theater, African-

American culture was celebrated through various themes and events that contributed to the past, present, and future of our society. When we went, they had black artists showcasing their work in a monthlong exhibition, and they were showcasing several miscellaneous performances about the underground slaves and the unknown African-American heroes who had fought for freedom. I figured he would appreciate the exhibits; he did. I would have enjoyed it more with Kamar. My mind kept switching back and forth between Kamar and Kenneth. My husband was my heart and soul. There was no doubt about that, but Kenneth gave me something that Kamar hadn't been giving me in a long time.

There was complete silence on the way to the Hilton Hotel. I assumed Kenneth was going to say good-night and get his luggage from the trunk of my car, but instead he flashed that sexy smile of his at me.

"Maxxine, thank you for taking me to the theater."

"You're welcome."

"Are you okay?" he asked for the twentieth time that day.

"Hell no!"

"Tell me what's wrong."

I took a deep breath before speaking.

"I'm married and I shouldn't have even chatted with you!"

"I'm glad you did."

I looked away from Kenneth as he leaned over and brushed the hair behind my ear.

"Saturday is my last day in town and I want to spend the rest of the week with you."

I stared at him in shock. He couldn't have been serious.

"Kenneth, I can't risk what we did again—never!"

"Nobody is going to find out."

"I know that but—"

"Maxxine, no buts. All I want is to see you every day while I'm here. You know, you're not the only one who had doubts."

I raised my brow. "You had doubts!"

"Yes, you seem surprised."

"That's because I am. You were so determined and anxious for us to meet."

"I was, but I thought that maybe you would back out because of your husband."

"He should have been enough for me to back out," I said guiltily.

"But he's wasn't?"

"Kenneth, my husband is the love of my life."

"Can he make love to you the way that you desire, Maxxine?" Kenneth boldly asked. I didn't respond to his question; instead he answered it for me. "No, I didn't think so. Forget about him for the rest of the week. When I'm not in my meetings, I want to be in you."

I couldn't believe he had hit me with that corny-ass line.

"Aren't you a little old to be so horny?" I laughed.

Kenneth couldn't help but shake that one off. "You're never too old for good lovemaking."

"But I'm too old to be playing games with you or anyone else."

Kenneth unfastened my seat belt and unbuttoned my pea-coat again. He let his fingers walk up and down and swirl around my clothed right breast. My nipple expanded from his touch.

"I'm not playing, Maxxine. I'm going to show you what real lovemaking is all about."

I arrived home four hours later. Against my better judgment, I had let him have his way with me again. It was partly because I didn't plan to see him again, but mostly because I wanted his dick. I sucked his dick and he ate my pussy again. After he fucked me from behind in the backseat of my car and in the reverse missionary position, my back, neck, mouth, and pussy were so sore. I could barely walk straight, let alone stand. I took all my clothes off after turning the water on in the shower. I wanted to wash all my sins away: the way Kenneth kissed me deeply, me sucking his dick, him sucking on my pussy, caressing my soft body, and fucking my tight pussy with his King Kong dick. At that very moment I knew what I had to do. I had to make Kenneth history.

After drying off and correcting some of my students' research papers, I heard the front door open and close.

"Maxxine."

"I'm in here."

Kamar walked in the great room as he loosened his necktie. He placed his briefcase on the floor and sat down beside me. I was afraid to look at him. I didn't want to show any signs of guilt on my face.

"How was work, baby?"

"It was busy. Did you get my emails, gorgeous?"

Damn it, I had forgotten to email him back! I always emailed Kamar back—always. Instead I had let some man sex me down more than once. Even though it was the best sex I had ever had, there was no excuse for it.

"No, I didn't. I haven't checked it yet."

"Okay."

There was a brief pause between us before he asked, "What did you do today?"

Shit! Why did he have to ask that question? He hadn't asked me what I was doing yesterday.

He smirked. "Does the cat have your tongue, gorgeous?"

That's when I looked into Kamar's eyes and lied to him for the first time. "I'm sorry about that, baby."

"I left you several messages, between your BlackBerry and the house phone. I was worried about you. It's not like you to ignore my calls."

"I know, baby, and I'm sorry." I really was sorry. I hadn't been thinking clearly at all. How could I live with this sin for the rest of my life, when it hadn't even been a day and it was killing me?

"So, what were you doing?"

For a minute there, my mind registered Kamar saying, *So, who were you fucking?* I flipped the script on him and questioned him.

"Kamar, what's with all the questions?"

That's when he suspected something was up. "I see."

"You see? You see what?"

"I know what this is all about, Maxxine. You're still unhappy with me."

"What are you talking about?"

Clearly I didn't know where he was going with this one. *I'm still unhappy with him*—huh! I was happy with Kamar. I loved my baby with everything I had.

"I'm talking about my work hours." Kamar took my manicured hand into his and kissed each knuckle slowly one at a time.

"You know how I feel about that."

"Yes, I know. I haven't been committed to you like I'm supposed to be."

"What do you mean?"

"Over the past seventeen months all of my attention and focus have been on these projects at work."

"Kamar, I completely understand. You have a business to run. I get it."

"You're right about that, but I have a gorgeous wife that I've been neglecting emotionally and physically."

Kamar reached over and caressed my shoulder and neck. "I should have paid more attention to you and I will."

"We've had this talk before, more than once," I said sternly.

"I'm sorry, but you'll see. I have a surprise for you." Kamar smiled at me and got my full attention. I positioned my body to face him.

"Oh, really?"

"Yes."

I was curious. "What is it, baby?"

"All I can tell you is that I'll be home this Friday around four thirty."

"What happens at four thirty on Friday?"

"It's your surprise; a surprise that's well overdue."

Now I was suspicious. I wanted to know what the big secret was. I couldn't wait until Friday to find out. Several scenarios crossed my mind. One of them was having a baby. Kamar couldn't be asking me to have a baby. He didn't have time for even me, but then again, I could have been wrong. I put my work on the coffee table and began tickling Kamar, trying to force my surprise out of him.

"Tell me now, baby! I can't wait until Friday."

Kamar continued to laugh hysterically. I always loved the way he laughed. It made my whole heart smile. Kamar stopped

me from tickling him. He grabbed my wrists and forced himself on top of me in a playful manner. I looked into his beautiful
eyes and smiled at him.

"You know that I don't like to be tickled."

I kissed his soft lips before speaking. "Of course I do, but
how else am I going to get this secret out of you."

"You won't; not with this one. You'll get your surprise when
it's time, gorgeous." He flashed a smile at me.

Friday was only four days away, so I guess I could wait until
then.

"Okay," I reluctantly agreed.

"Good then. I'm going to grab a quick shower. Do you want
to join me?"

The next four days were incredible. I tried to cut Kenneth
out of my life, but his dick was so good to my pussy. On Tues-
day, I let Kenneth tie me up, drip hot candle wax down the
small of my back, and fuck me. On Wednesday, Kenneth fucked
me in the elevator and in a public restroom. On Thursday, Kenneth fucked me in the Jacuzzi adjacent to the wall-to-wall mirror in the bathroom. He said he wanted to see what we looked
like, fucking each other's brains out. On Friday I was going to
tell Kenneth that our sexcapade was over, but he fucked me
again without mercy in his hotel suite.

I was lying in bed with him in complete silence. I wanted
him to have me again, but I decided against it. Kenneth would
be tearing up my little pussy for another three hours if I let
him. He looked at me, kissed my shoulder, and asked if everything was alright.

I lied and told him, "Yes."

In such a short time I was becoming good at lying. I didn't

realize how easy it was until the lies started piling up on each other. I was so lost in thought that I didn't hear him tell me that he loved me.

"Maxxine, did you hear me?" he inquired, sucking on my neck.

Confusion must have been written all over my face. "Huh?"

Kenneth intertwined his fingers with mine and kissed them. He gazed into my eyes and told me again, "I love you, Maxxine."

Was this man serious?

"Kenneth, please, you don't love me."

"I do, dear."

"You love fucking me."

"I'm not going to deny that, but it's much more than that. I want to be with you."

I darted my eyes at him with disbelief. *How the fuck did I get myself into this mess?* I let go of Kenneth's hand and wrapped the sheet around my body as I got out of the moistened bed.

"Maxxine, where are you going?"

Kenneth got out of bed as well, with his curved dick bouncing around in the air, and walked over to me.

"What's the matter, dear?"

He caressed my cold shoulders as I revealed the problem.

"I can't see you anymore, Kenneth. It's over. I'm going to tell my husband about us. I have to go."

"Why would you do that? It won't do you any good."

"I don't keep secrets from my husband and I don't lie to him!" I yelled.

He stopped caressing my shoulders. "You're only going to hurt him."

"I already have, but he doesn't know it yet."

I walked over to the balcony sliding doors, looking at the vista for some answer to fix this. Kenneth followed behind me. I sensed that he was searching for some words to say, but he decided against it, and I spoke for him instead.

"I'm sorry, Kenneth. This is all my fault and I shouldn't have led you into thinking that we were going to have a committed future together."

"Maxxine, you have given me the best week of my life. I don't want that to end. You gave me a reason to live again. I want you in my life, dear," he said passionately.

That's when I turned around to face him and told him for the last fucking time it was over.

"Kenneth, you'll never see me again after today. I have to go."

"I have to meet someone in a little while. I want to see you later tonight."

What the hell was this? I know I wasn't talking to myself. Didn't he hear anything I had just said to him? What part of "it's over" didn't he understand? Kenneth knew what the deal was from the beginning.

"That's impossible. My husband has a surprise for me and I'm not going to let him down again."

"Please, just this last time. I promise. You won't have to see me anymore."

I looked Kenneth square in his beautiful dark eyes. "No, Kenneth. I'm going to take a quick shower, put my clothes back on, and then I'm leaving. I'm truly sorry, but it's over between us. My husband will be expecting me soon and I must go."

I could see the agony in Kenneth's eyes. I didn't want to hurt him, but I couldn't keep our affair going. He had known the deal from the beginning. It would only cause more damage later on.

After leaving Kenneth's hotel suite, I didn't go straight home. I never left the Hilton Hotel. I got on the elevator and ended up in the ladies' room on the lobby level sobbing like a baby. While sitting on the floor in the handicapped stall, I thought about how my life had become so screwed up in a matter of days. I had never anticipated that my winter break would be filled with blissful, unadulterated sex. If I were only more open and demanding with Kamar when it came to paying more attention to my needs, I wouldn't have been in that predicament.

I heard my BlackBerry vibrating in my purse. I hoped it wasn't Kenneth calling me. I unzipped my purse and pulled it out. I looked at the caller ID; it was Kamar. I hadn't realized it was after four thirty. I had been wallowing for nearly three hours. I cleared my voice and answered his call. He asked where was I and when was I coming home.

"I'm on my way now."

"Okay, gorgeous, I can't wait for you to see this!" he said anxiously.

I tried my best to be complacent. "Me either. I love you, Kamar."

"I love you, too. Now hurry up and get your beautiful self home."

"Okay, I will."

After talking with my husband, I freshened my makeup to look as if I hadn't been crying and that everything was fine. If only that had been even half the truth.

I arrived home twenty minutes later, nervous as hell. I had to tell Kamar what I'd been doing on my vacation, more like whom I'd been doing. When I pulled up in my driveway, I noticed an SUV parked next to Kamar's truck. What the hell was going on? I'd never seen that SUV before. I parked my car and turned off the ignition. I got out and closed the door. I walked up the cobblestone sidewalk leading to one of the main entrances to our home. I unlocked the door and walked in. I saw Kamar coming toward me with this huge smile on his face. The security alarm motioned that I was in the house.

"Kamar, I'm sorry that I'm late."

He kissed my tender lips twice.

He seemed so eager. "You're here now and that's all that matters."

"Baby, we need to talk. There's something that I have to tell you."

"Okay, okay, but after I show you my surprise. It's in the great room."

"What is it?"

"Come on, you'll see."

Kamar and I walked into the great room. He wrapped his strong arms around me and kissed my cheek. A man was standing at the patio doors admiring the view of the lake outside. He must have been so intrigued by the view that he didn't hear us enter. I was wondering what this was all about and what kind of surprise was this?

Kamar said excitedly, "Dad, I would like for you to meet my wife, Maxxine."

His father? I was stunned, confused, and happy to finally meet him. From the stories Kamar had told me, he and his father had never gotten along and Kamar had hardly ever mentioned him. I hadn't even seen photographs of him, but I assumed that Kamar had gotten his good looks from him. I could sense in Kamar's voice that the bad blood shed between them was finally in the past. His father turned around and I nearly had a heart attack. I couldn't believe this. Kamar was still holding me tightly; I was glad he couldn't see my face. His father approached me, took my hand into his palm, and kissed it softly.

Kenneth grinned. "It's a pleasure to meet you, dear."

Katrina

Samantha J. Green

I shifted uncomfortably in my seat. I was worse than a little kid at church when the Reverend Maple went into what I referred to as "disciple mode." He could bring the congregation to its feet during a sermon, but he had the gift of gab so bad, he could talk the paint off the walls.

Here I was, a twenty-five-year-young woman, and I was fidgeting like a five-year-old. I paid close attention when Reverend mentioned New Orleans. It was a soft spot for me, like most people, because New Orleans was such an important city in Louisiana. Even though Shreveport is in northern Louisiana, we still felt the effect of the tragedy.

Reverend concluded, "So if anyone would be so kind as to be a host family, please meet with Mrs. Williams after the services." I was among other church members who volunteered their home. After giving us information about the people we could possibly be hosting and taking our names, Mrs. Williams said, "We will have a meeting tomorrow night at seven for those who are still interested in being a host family."

The next night I pulled into the church parking lot at six forty-five. Glancing around, I was pleased at my church family's response to helping the evacuees.

"Sister Winfield," Mrs. Williams said, giving me a hug. "How are you doing?"

"I'm fine."

"Are you planning to host an entire family or a single?"

"Well, I only have one spare bedroom, but . . ." My jaw dropped and my eyes focused on the male who was standing behind Mrs. Williams. He had a patent on the word *fine*.

She turned around. "Mr. Brown, I want you to meet Ms. Theresa Winfield. She will be your host family."

He stuck his hand out and I shook it. He didn't let go of my hand right away. "It's nice to meet you, Ms. Winfield," he said in the most delicious New Orleans accent.

"Oh, call me Theresa."

"Okay, Theresa, but only if you call me Tony."

"Deal." I glanced at the retreating Mrs. Williams, who mouthed, *You owe me,* at me.

I suggested that Tony and I go out to eat to get to know each other better. Tony agreed. We were sitting at IHOP and I asked, "How long have you lived in New Orleans?"

"All my life. I graduated from Dillard—"

"A Dillard man," I interrupted.

"And you know this."

"What about your family?"

"It was just my mama and me growing up. She passed when I was twenty."

"I'm sorry."

"No, her life was very fulfilling. She was one of those women who knew how precious each moment was and lived life to the fullest."

"And taught you to do the same," I said rather than asked.

"Yep. And I teach that to my students."

"What do you teach?"

"I teach sixth-grade English."

"The sixth grade?"

"Yep, as kids make that transition from child to young adult-hood. I love it."

"I bet you do."

"So what about you? What are you passionate about?"

"My job."

"And what is it that you do?"

"I'm a therapist, children mostly, but I counsel families going through divorce. I know how rough that can be."

"Are you a child of divorce?"

"No. My parents didn't divorce, just separated . . . a lot. I remember how confused I was, and I don't want other kids to feel like that. I know I can't help every child, but I do my best."

Tony clapped. "Bravo. I'm scared of you."

I laughed.

"I'm honored to be in your presence," he continued.

"Oh, stop, I'm no miracle worker."

"Please, yes, you are. Theresa Winfield: miracle worker."

I put my hands over my head and adjusted an imaginary halo.

"What are you doing?" Tony asked.

"Adjusting my halo." We laughed. Getting back to reality, I asked, "Have you looked for a job here?"

"Yes, I've been offered a job at Green Oaks; freshman English."

"You should take it! I know they aren't your sixth-graders, but they're still transitioning from childish antics to adult ways."

"I'm sold on the idea. I'll contact Principal Cleveland Robinson in the morning."

"Good."

"You like getting your way, don't you?"

"Shoot! Do you like boudin?" I said sarcastically, referring to the infamous southern-Louisiana dish.

We both laughed. I couldn't remember laughing as much as I did with Tony.

When we got home, I showed him around. "The bedrooms are down this way. My room is to the left, straight ahead, and your room is to the right. Your private bathroom is outside your door and to the right."

"Okay, thank you, Theresa. I really appreciate this."

"It is no problem. And feel free to come to my room if you need anything."

His eyebrow rose at my double meaning. Instead of correcting myself, I went to my bedroom.

Tony and I learned a lot more about each other over the next couple of weeks. I realized we were getting closer because, over dinner one night, he asked, "So why are you still single?"

"I don't know; haven't found the man for me. Why are you still single?"

"Pretty much the same."

"Please, no woman has tried to hook you? From speaking

with you, I can tell that you aren't too bad. I live with you, and I haven't seen a habit that I despise."

"There was one woman." He shook his head. "I fell for her hard, but she wasn't the one for me."

"What did she do to you?"

"She told me that she couldn't see herself with me for the rest of her life."

"Damn, did she tell you why?"

"Yes. She was in love with another guy."

"Ouch!"

"Yeah, and she told me this after four years and a marriage proposal."

"Damn, she did you wrong. No wonder you're still single."

He laughed. "There have been some after her, so I'm not scarred or anything like that."

"That's good to know."

"So, have you ever been engaged or close?"

"I had a situation similar to yours. I was involved with a guy. I loved him, thought it was returned."

"What happened?"

"We weren't engaged or anything, but it was still serious, ya know."

"Theresa, what happened?"

Tears fell from my eyes as I relived one of the most humiliating moments, if not the most, of my life. "I went to his apartment. I let myself in because I had a key. Why would he give me a key if we weren't serious? Anyway, I go in and they were right there on the living room floor. It was like they couldn't hold their passion for each other until they got to the bedroom."

"He was a dumb ass. Did you know the girl?"

"No, thankfully I didn't know her."

Rather than say anything else, Tony enveloped me in his strong arms. I needed to be held, and he obliged. Our relationship grew stronger that night.

Tony spoiled me. Each time I came home, delectable smells would be coming from the kitchen. I enjoyed spicy foods, but Tony showed me what spices were all about. We would sometimes prepare meals together. He showed me how to make the most delicious jambalaya and gumbo. Over dinner we would discuss work. He loved his job and always had a story about one or more of his students. We would talk for hours about our days and the plans we had for the next day. Most nights, after we would part ways to go to bed, Tony would remain on my mind.

One night, I found myself unable to sleep until I pleasured myself. I closed my eyes and touched myself, imagining it was Tony's tongue circling my breasts, then going lower until he reached the juncture of my thighs. He would use his tongue to bring me to a climax so great I would forget every other man I'd ever been with. Then would come the main course: his dick. He would enter my body with one thrust. Soon we would join a rhythm that was old as time. And just as I was about to cum . . .

"Theresa, are you alright?"

I struggled to regain normal breathing patterns before I replied, "Yeah, I'm okay, Tony."

"Can I come in?"

"Umm . . . hold on for a minute." I pulled myself together as best I could. "Yes, you can come in now." He opened my door and was wearing boxers and a wifebeater. I had only one thought: *Beat me, baby!*

He laughed and asked, "What was that?"

Shit! I'd said that aloud. "Nothing."

He smiled and I was glad I was sitting down because I became weak in the knees. He gazed at me with those sexy bedroom eyes. "Theresa."

The way my name rolled off his accented tongue made my legs spread by their own accord. "Yes?"

"Remember when you told me to come to your room if I needed anything?"

"Yes."

"I need something."

"What?"

He leaned over until his mouth was mere inches from mine. "You."

When our mouths joined, I thought I'd died and gone to heaven. It was just the beginning though. I wanted to feel the rhythm of his talented tongue on my other pair of lips. As if reading my mind, Tony pushed me back on the bed and began a slow descent from my mouth to my throat, then to my chest. He paused to show equal attention to both of my breasts and nipples. His hands were as busy as his tongue. One caressed my ass while he inserted three fingers of the other hand in me.

"Mmm . . . ," I moaned.

His mouth traveled down my stomach and finally to my flaming heat. He licked the fingers he took out of me one by one, then used his hands to lift my hips so he could have better access to the essence of me. He first licked each of my thighs, then kissed me between my legs before using his tongue to pleasure me in the most erotic way. "Ohh . . . Tony! Give it to me now!" He lifted his head long enough to push his boxers off and place his chocolate-colored dick at my pussy's entrance. My femininity practically sucked him in.

"You feel so good, baby!" Tony said as he pushed and pulled in and out of me. He mumbled something, but it was said so fast, I couldn't understand him. My vaginal muscles clenched him as a climax ripped me from my head to my toes. Before I could fully regain my composure, Tony had me on top, his mouth was fastened to my nipple, and his hands were around my waist, guiding me as I rode him up and down. "Shit! You feel amazing, Theresa! I'm about to cum, baby!"

"You call me baby like that again and I'll be cumming with you."

"Baby . . . baby . . . baby."

"Cum with me, Tony!" I started moving up and down faster. He flipped me over and began riding me doggie-style. I could tell this was one of Tony's favorite positions by how hard he rode me. He gripped my waist, licked my neck, bit my ear, and pulled my hair. I could feel the front of his powerful thighs smacking the back of my thighs. I also felt the familiar sensations of an orgasm.

"I'm there, Theresa! Cum with me, baby!"

I did. I felt Tony shoot his load all the way to my stomach. He practically collapsed on my back. He rolled over and pulled me on top of him. We covered ourselves with a sheet. A half hour later, Tony woke me up for another round. This time, I satisfied a craving I'd had since first meeting him. I licked him from base to tip and everywhere in between. I had his balls in my mouth as I masturbated him to give him double the pleasure. His dick was my chocolate ice cream cone, and I licked him like it was the Fourth of July.

The sexual trysts between Tony and me were amazing. I'd

become a FANatic of his. Our appetite for one another was insatiable. He only ventured into his room for work clothes. Tony and I went to several events together. We went to movies and out to eat a lot. Occasionally I would surprise him at work. On Sundays we would attend church together. I could see myself changing for the better. I was no longer a fidgety little girl in church. When I felt myself become antsy, it was as if Tony knew and he would grab my hand. Mrs. Williams would catch my eye during service and flash me a knowing smile. I realized that she was happy for me. Tony was like a breath of fresh air in my life. We complemented each other. As much as we enjoyed going out together, we would have lots of fun relaxing in the living room watching television or playing cards or dominoes. Sometimes I'd lie across Tony's chest and listen to the rhythm of his heartbeat. We would lounge on the couch and listen to ballads. Love ballads. I didn't know how he felt about me, but I loved him. What had started out as lust, which had got fulfilled time and time again, had turned to love. Two weeks later, I found out how Tony felt about me, when he dropped to one knee in front of my church family and asked me to be his wife.

Now, six months later, I am Mrs. Theresa Winfield-Brown. We are currently expecting our first child, a daughter, whom we'll name . . . Katrina.

The Hard-Boiled Dick

Chris Hayden

Sam was cheatin'!

No 'bout a doubt it! He was creeping home at funny hours, getting up to leave in the middle of the night, coppin' 'tudes about nothin', slinking around the house when he *was* home looking like a mangy old mutt who had been caught in the garbage, and generally slippin' so badly that he was even forgetting to scrub the smell of his outside bitches off him before he came to bed!

How could he? LaTisha had always been the good and faithful wife! She resolved to put it to him righteous—but she needed *proof*!

A coworker suggested that she retain the services of a private investigator.

Sharpetta Kensington, P.I., had a posh office in an upscale part of town, but when LaTisha saw her—playin' a "Hell up in Harlem" black fedora (broke down gangsta-style), a butchy black pin-striped pants suit, some come-fuck-me pumps with stiletto heels—sitting with her feet up on her desk reading a racing form and smoking a cigarillo like a young Samantha Spade, LaTisha started to kick her to the curb.

During the interview, Sharpetta tossed off an impressive list of credentials, cases solved, and clients served.

"Make no mistake about it, I'm an ace dick," she said.

"Excuse me?" LaTisha said.

"That's slang for 'expert detective,'" Sharpetta explained. "I'm worth every dime, I ga-ron-tee."

Still harboring some misgivings, LaTisha cut her a check for five thousand dollars, her initial retainer.

A couple of weeks later, early one afternoon, the "ace dick" summoned LaTisha to her office.

"Mrs. Jenkins, yo' man is a dirty bird," Sharpetta announced.

LaTisha shouted, "Wait till he gets home tonight! I'll—"

"Chill. You need to catch him in the act."

"When, where, and how?"

"In about forty-five minutes. I have the address of the pad where Sam is hosting a live sex party this very afternoon. We can roll right on over there and bust him."

"I hope there's no rough stuff."

Sharpetta showed her a 9mm pistol and a Taser, then chuckled wickedly. "He won't harm a hair on your head."

"I'm not worried about *my* head," LaTisha said.

"I heerd *dat*! We'll take my car."

A little later they pulled up in front of a one-story, white wooden house in a quiet part of town.

"Snug little fuck pad, ain't it?" Sharpetta said.

"When I'm through with him, he'll wish he was doing time in Guantánamo Bay!" LaTisha said. "I don't see his car."

"He's a slick dawg. Parks his car across town and takes a cab here. Ready?"

They went to the door. LaTisha stood out of sight while Sharpetta knocked.

"Who is it?" a man asked.

"We're the girls for the party," Sharpetta said.

When the door opened, they bum-rushed the show.

"I'm a private investigator and this is LaTisha Jenkins, Sam Jenkins's wife," Sharpetta said, her hand on the gat in her shoulder bag. "Don't start no static, won't be none."

They stepped into a living room thick with incense and chronic smoke. With gaudy purple wallpaper and crotch shots from *Black Tail* magazine on the walls, big, fat, green silk harem pillows on the floor, red bulbs in lamps turned down low, and Tupac's "How Do U Want It" bumpin' on the box—it looked like the waiting room of a Las Vegas whorehouse with furnishings by Snoop Dogg.

Two guys, as cut and buff as a couple of chocolate Chippendales, and clad only in cutoff jeans, were standing in the middle of the floor looking *très* busted.

LaTisha gazed at their rippling torsos, the bulges in the crotches of their tight jeans, and their buns of steel and wondered if maybe Sam was on the down-low. For a New York minute Sharpetta stared at them as if her eyes would buck out of her head. Then she was all business.

"Where the hell is Sam Jenkins!" she demanded.

"Never heard of him," one of the hot studs said.

"Goin' for bad, eh? I got something for your ass." Sharpetta showed them her Glock. "In the back!" she shouted. "I'm gonna get to the bottom of this!"

Mumbling protests, they did as they were told.

LaTisha flopped down on a pillow. She felt drained.

How long had Sam been involved in some shit like you saw on *Cheaters*? How could he? How——

Suddenly LaTisha heard fearsome noise coming from the back. Bloodcurdling screams, cussing, calling on Jesus and unholy bumpin' and jumpin'——it sounded like the Rock and Booker T wrasslin' a wildcat in a one-stall shithouse!

They got the drop on Sharpetta! LaTisha thought. *Call the police! No! Not enough time!* She rushed out of the living room, down a short hall, and to the door of the room from whence the hellacious racket came——

And stopped. They'd got the drop all right——on Sharpetta's *drawers!* All of them were buck nekkid on a bed (Sharpetta still sportin' her gangsta lid). She was whacking the dudes off, and when she got them good and hard, she started blowing them: first one, then the other, then both simultaneously!

The men's eyes rolled up so only the whites showed; they groaned and grimaced in ecstasy! Then, slick as an acrobat from the UniverSoul Circus, Sharpetta switched positions so one of the dudes could fuck her doggie-style while she sucked the other one's cock until they all came and collapsed in a sweaty, satiated heap!

LaTisha was a married woman and no prude, but she had never seen such mad, scandalous fucking! When she was satisfied that they were still breathing, she wobbled back to the front room.

A little later Sharpetta joined her. Her clothes were disheveled, her hat was cocked ace deuce, and her hair was sticking every which way from under it. She had to lean against the wall for support.

"That's all for now!" she croaked weakly to the dudes in the back. "Don't leave town!"

Loud snores were their only reply.

When they got back to the car, LaTisha jumped in Sharpetta's shit with both feet.

"Look, babe, in my racket you got to do what you have to to get the dope," Sharpetta snapped, trying to get her face together in the rearview mirror. "You ought to commend my willingness to sacrifice my virtue for the cause."

" 'Babe'? 'Racket'? You sound like that dykey female cop on *The Wire*!"

Sharpetta looked at LaTisha out of the corner of her eye a minute, then, grinning slyly, set a damp wad of cash on the dashboard.

"What is this?" LaTisha asked.

"Your cut."

"My cut of what?"

Sharpetta snickered. "What them sorry sacks of shit was supposed to give the hos."

"Good God, Mama! Call the police!" LaTisha groaned.

"Hey! Slow your roll, cutie-pie." Sharpetta started the car. "Your man was here, alright, but he left. Those two mopes gave up the address he cut out to. If we're quick, we can get right over there and bust him!"

Her name was Delilah. She was frail and trembling like a little girl, but she was ready for grown-up games in a see-through nightgown and a pair of crotchless, black lace panties.

She sat on her bed, dabbing at her eyes with a hankie. Sharpetta and LaTisha stood on either side of her. LaTisha wanted to take her in her arms and comfort her, and she wanted to kick her ass.

Sharpetta was only in ass-kicking mode.

"Straighten up, you home-wrecking bitch!" she snarled.

"He was only here a little while. He acted like something was bothering him. We didn't do anything. Honest, I didn't know he was married," the girl wailed. "He never told me. I never would have dated him if I'd known."

LaTisha said, "Maybe we should just go—"

"Fuck this gold-diggin' bitch!" Sharpetta shouted.

"I'm not comfortable with this," LaTisha said, looking away from the weeping girl.

"Okay. I'll take a statement from her funky ass and we can blow this pop stand," Sharpetta said. "Say! I left my tape recorder in the car. Would you get it?"

"Sure," LaTisha said, happy to have an excuse to leave.

She was halfway to the car before she realized that Sharpetta had not given her the keys. When she got back to Delilah's apartment, the door was locked. She knocked. No one answered. She knocked again. Then she heard moans, cussing, calling on Jesus, and the hot and wet sounds of Divine Sixty-nine—mutual cunnilingus . . .

Sharpetta came out about half an hour later, grinning and freshening her lipstick. LaTisha was fit to be tied.

"Getting to the bottom of things again?" LaTisha asked.

Sharpetta shrugged and they walked to her car.

They could see the girl's apartment window from there. She was standing in the window naked. She mouthed the words *Bye, Mommy,* winked, and wiggled her ass.

Sharpetta blew her a kiss, then flicked her long, lascivious pink tongue at her. The girl giggled and started stroking herself between the legs.

"Silly ho," Sharpetta said to LaTisha as they pulled off. "Thinks she can get over on Sharpetta Kensington. I led her down a slippery slope."

"I *bet* it was slippery," LaTisha said. "How much is my cut this time?"

"Absolutely nothing happened in there that did not occur strictly in the course of business—and if it *did*, I didn't enjoy it!" Sharpetta huffed.

"I don't know if you can solve a case as good as Shaft, but you *sho'* is some kinda sex machine."

Sharpetta sputtered, then both of them broke down laughing so hard she had to pull the car over.

Sharpetta Kensington was a pistol! A real hard-boiled dick! Tough! Brassy! Bo-fucking-dacious! She'd shag a snake in a sandstorm—but fucking was her way to solve the case. If not an excuse, it was a saving grace! Maybe, LaTisha thought, if she had been more like Sharpetta, her marriage wouldn't be on the rocks.

Maybe if she had taken care of business rather than only being about business—

But what woman can make a home, keep her front up, bring home the bacon, and fuck like a rabbit every night to boot? Shit!

"So, what did you find out?" LaTisha finally asked. "I know she told you everything."

"Not everything," Sharpetta said.

"I bet you know where she buys those panties."

"Frederick's," Sharpetta answered. "But I don't know what she pays for them."

Sharpetta recounted Delilah's story.

"He didn't say where he was heading when he left, but she gave me a list of probable locations."

"Lead on then, Holmes."

"Elementary, my dear Watson."

Why do black men cheat?

They asked the salesclerk at the Booty Sto' where Sam copped hot movies.

"It's genetic," he explained, adjusting his clunky black horn-rimmed glasses. "Mother Nature has hardwired the male brain to pursue more partners than seem necessary to ensure the propagation of species *Homo sapiens.*"

"I'll homo your sapiens," Sharpetta cracked.

"I beg your pardon?"

"Let's go," LaTisha said.

"Excuse me," said the clerk. "What are you going to do about this bill for late rentals Mr. Jenkins owes?"

"File a claim in divorce court, Poindexter," Sharpetta said. "Until then, don't leave town!"

They asked the owner of the Peter Meter, where Sam bought his fuck books.

"Here's a story they tell about President George Bush the First," he replied. "Him and Mrs. Bush visited a farm one day. The farmer pointed out a rooster and said that it sometimes fucked thirty times a day. 'Would you please tell that to Mr. Bush?' Mrs. Bush said. 'I say, Mr. Farmer,' President Bush said, 'does that rooster fuck the same hen every time?' 'Nope,' said the farmer, 'different hen, every time.' 'Would you please tell that to Mrs. Bush?' he said.' "

When the women didn't laugh, the guy repeated it. Rolling their eyes, they headed for the door.

"Hey, what about all these books Sam ordered?" the man asked.

"I'm sure *you* can make good use of them," Sharpetta stated with much sarcasm.

On the car radio they heard a male caller tell Brass Balls, the host of *Testosterone Talk,* that he blamed slavery for the brothers' cheatin' ways.

"Would you believe I had a case where a *white boy* tried to use that one?" Sharpetta cracked.

They asked Ma Barker at the Toi Store, where Sam bought his sex toys.

"They never grow up. Just can't concentrate on one thang too long, baby!" she said. Then she showed them an inflatable rubber doll she was holding for Sam, which looked just like LaTisha and had working orifices.

"Here's who's beating your time," said Sharpetta to LaTisha. "Hey, Ma! You got any more of these in back?"

Their last stop was the Black Hellfire Club, *the* place for African-American swingers. These freaks were discreet: it was located in an industrial park and there were no signs, no lights, no nothing to give the slightest clue to the scandalous goings-on inside.

"It's supposed to be members only, but they let in all skeezers. You shouldn't have any trouble," Sharpetta announced on their way to the entrance.

"Thanks a lot," LaTisha said. "I don't know if I'm up to this—"

"Hey! You want to catch him in the act, don't you?" Sharpetta said. "Without eyewitness evidence all you have is hearsay testimony."

"This whole thing is just *unreal* to me. My dad never cheated on my mom."

"Leastwise you don't *know* that he did," Sharpetta said. "I guess these days that's just as good."

"If we drop it now, do I get my money back?"

"Hell naw!"

"Let's get busy then."

They still had to slip the bouncer/doorman a Benjamin.

The Black Hellfire Club was *smoking,* a copious cornucopia of copulation and exotic sexuality. It was dark and funky and cavernous as Mrs. King Kong's cunt. There were erotic paintings and sculptures everywhere and erotic films of all kinds—straight sex, gay, lesbian, gang bang, B&D, fetishism, masturbation—played nonstop on a dozen giant video screens.

The patrons wore street clothes, sexy costumes, or nothing at all. LaTisha saw enough nipple, tongue, penis, and vulva rings to pierce the Osbourne family.

On a trapeze suspended from the ceiling, a big healthy mama in a leather-and-lace French maid's uniform (and nothing on underneath) swung back and forth, giving everyone below a gander of her ample ass and pudenda.

"Wall-to-wall *freaks!*" Sharpetta exclaimed, rubbing her hands together greedily. "Er—disgusting!"

"I thought this kinda action was a *white* thang," LaTisha said.

"Blame integration, love. Let's fade to the bar."

LaTisha stumbled to the bar and sat down on a stool. Sharpetta ordered drinks. LaTisha downed hers with one gulp.

"Lay dead, babe," Sharpetta said. "Stop looking like Sister Mary Superior at a circle jerk and try to blend in. I'm gonna case the joint and see if I can bust your old man doing the nasty."

She got up, cocked her fedora, and swaggered away.

LaTisha's head was spinning. An old tune by the Time, "Wild and Loose," pounded in her ears. She felt a warm flush spread from her burning crotch to her tingling belly to the tips of her hard nipples to her neck and face.

Then she noticed a man sitting next to her.

Dark and lovely—damned if he didn't look like Wesley Snipes. Better than Wesley. This guy was stateside and didn't owe the IRS $12 million either. When she was home alone, in the shower, hot water trickling over her body, tickling her clit—she sometimes fantasized Wesley was Blade and he was going down on her—

He leaned close, then said, "Hello. I'm Dave."

"Isn't it warm in here?" she asked him.

He moved even closer. He took her hand. He touched her knee. He nuzzled her neck.

She pushed him away. What did he think she was? Then she remembered Sam and his fuck pad and Delilah and the rubber doll. She remembered they hadn't fucked in ages—

Everything was like a blur after that. LaTisha grabbed Dave by his lapels, pulled him to her, and kissed him long and hard. She stuck her tongue in his mouth so deep that he almost gagged. They were pawing frantically at each other—

They were moving across the floor, holding each other tight. They went upstairs. There was a room with a huge waterbed. On it a mass of people in various stages of undress writhed and sucked and fucked. She hesitated—then she kicked off her shoes—

Then everything else. Dave was fumbling with his clothes. LaTisha pushed him down on the bed before he finished disrobing. His dick was out and as hard as Japanese arithmetic. She straddled him and guided it into her cunt and started riding it like Blade rides that motorcycle, sliding up and down, grinding in circles, faster and faster. Cussing and calling on Jesus, she fucked him until a series of orgasmic explosions rocked her world.

She rolled over on the bed. Other hands touched her— caressed her breasts, back, and neck. Other mouths kissed her mouth, belly, feet, sucked her toes; other hot, wet, probing tongues licked her all over.

She lay there and let it happen. A woman put her arms around her neck. Sharpetta!

"LaTisha, your man is a dirty bird," the female dick whispered, nuzzling her neck.

"At least you lost that damn hat," LaTisha said, giggling and pushing away from her. "Stay on the case, girl!"

"Just as well." Sharpetta laughed. "Every time I fuck a client, I don't get paid."

An eternity later LaTisha staggered back downstairs to the bar.

"That drink was spiked with an aphrodisiac!" she stated accusingly to the bartender.

"You think we want to get sued or wind up in jail? Wasn't nothin' but orange and papaya juice," he said, giving her a knowing "Needed some excuse to get laid, eh?" look.

"Don't leave town," LaTisha croaked, wobbling away. She didn't try to find Sharpetta, Sam, or Dave. She took a cab home.

She stumbled into her house, stripped, showered, and fell into bed exhausted.

She was so out of it that she didn't hear Sam come in. She didn't see him until he was standing over her.

He stood there a minute, then fell to his knees, crying like a baby!

"I have been unfaithful to you, Tish," he wailed, grabbing her hand.

Now, of all times, he wanted to confess!

"Sam—"

"I have been a faithless, low-down, cheating snake! I have sullied our marriage, broken my vows, stained the sanctity of our connubial commitments."

Should she tell him he wasn't a Lone Ranger now? Maybe tomorrow. "Sam—"

"Tish. You knew. I know you did. I could see it in your eyes. Yet you never protested. You didn't leave me. You soldiered on, loyally. That's what finally brought me to my senses, love. That's what made me—are you falling asleep?"

"No. Yes. I had a rough day today. At the office."

"Daddy has a little something that'll perk you up." Sam got up and dropped his pants. He had a monstrous, throbbing hard-on.

If pussies could talk, LaTisha's would have yawned and proclaimed, "Not tonight, junior!"

"We shall consecrate our love anew," Sam said. "With a glorious bout of strenuous lovemaking!"

I don't know if niggas have rhythm, but they sure have lousy timing, LaTisha thought.

"Sam, I'm not in the mood," LaTisha said.

Sam stood there looking as if he'd just seen somebody slap his mama, then said meekly, "Sure. Sure, baby cakes." He stripped silently and got into bed with her. Then he took her in his arms.

"You just want to be cuddled, don't you?" he cooed. "Held. This is what I love about you. Your childlike innocence. Your—"

Her loud snores cut him off at the pass.

Anais

Camille Blue

"This is the last time that I dress you to return to him, Anais," my love said.

I gazed into Hamilton's fathomless, dark eyes and nodded.

Hamilton always washed me from head to toe before I returned to my husband. He would rinse away all the spicy, moist scents and residues from our love. His strong hands moved with gentle possessiveness as he parted my legs and eased his soapy fingers over and inside my vagina. He cleansed me, while branding me with his touch from the inside out.

Hamilton would then dry me in thick, fluffy white towels and lay me across his lap as he massaged cocoa body butter all over my tingling skin. When he finished my massage, he held out my deep purple satin and lace bra. I slipped my arms into the bra and fastened it. Then Hamilton dipped his hands inside my bra and adjusted my breasts, before drawing my silk panties up my legs and over my hips and butt. His hands roamed over my barely clad body. He almost smiled then, as if against his will. He seemed to hate to reveal the pleasure he got from handling me, before I had to leave him for another.

His tender attention continued as he smoothed my silk stockings up my legs and hooked them to my garters. I stepped into my black sheath dress and he drew it up my body. Like a child, I lifted my arms high and through the armholes of my dress. Hamilton zipped up my dress and held me close from behind. After a kiss on the neck, he bent and put my stiletto pumps back on my feet. He rose slowly, watching me the entire time.

I smiled up at my magnificent love, Hamilton Kincaid. His smooth, deeply brown skin stretched gracefully over his six-foot-four muscular frame. His thick, curly black hair felt like raw silk whenever I sank my fingers into it. His angular, chiseled face with its high cheekbones called to mind African royalty from years long past. But those lips of his were the sexiest that I had kissed or would ever.

"I love you, Hamilton," I said. I wanted him to feel my love in his pores and throughout all the cells in his body.

"Enough to leave him?" Hamilton's gaze captured mine in a relentless hold.

"Yes." The warmth of my decision cloaked me for a few seconds, before the fear of actually leaving my husband descended.

Hamilton kissed me so hard and long that we both were heavily and audibly breathing when we parted.

I gathered my coat and purse. I touched his cheek and left.

Hamilton and I had met at a jazz supper club, five months prior. I had been waiting to have dinner with my husband. After an hour, Justin had called to say that not only was he not going to meet me, but that he would not be home that night. I was preparing to leave when Hamilton appeared next to me at the bar. He gave me a slow smile that was sinful in its appeal.

"Stay with me," he said, then held out his hand.

My small hand found my way into his. I sat back down with a smile of my own. We talked for hours about everything from the state of the world to how celebrity-obsessed our culture had become. Hamilton asked me what made me smile. I fell in love with him then.

We met several times at different clubs and restaurants over the next three weeks. I held out for a month, before I let myself make love with him. Our first night of love was the genesis of many more nights of the most intense passion, pleasure, and cherishment that my body had ever known.

I smiled in sweet remembrance and returned my mind to the present day. I belted my black trench coat tightly to ward off the whipping, freezing wind of an early Illinois spring. I hurried to get in my car. With regret, I left Hamilton in Oak Park as I returned to my husband's downtown Chicago condo.

I let myself inside the five-thousand-square-foot, ultramodern condo with its stark black-and-white furnishings and white-marble-tiled floors. After five years of living in this showplace, I still felt like a visitor who had long overstayed my welcome.

My husband, Justin Alexander Watson III, strolled in late the next evening.

"Hello," I said. "Dinner will be ready soon. May I get you a drink?"

"Martini. Vodka," he ordered, and brushed past me on his way to the bedroom.

Twenty minutes later, he joined me in the dining room. I set the plate of prime rib, scalloped potatoes, and green beans with sliced almonds in front of him. I sat down in front of my dinner of skinless, grilled chicken breast with mixed bitter greens salad. I looked across the table and observed my absentee husband.

Justin was a handsome man. With his golden eyes, golden skin, golden fit body, and diamond-bright smile, Justin had it all and he knew it. He used his good looks, cunning, and legal skills to win many high-profile criminal cases. He was an anaconda in an angel's body.

"I'm leaving," he said.

"Your parents—"

"I don't need to be reminded of my parents' visit," he said with a freezing look. "Marisa's birthday is tomorrow." He took a sip of his drink and smiled at me. "I'm flying her to New York to celebrate."

Justin had stopped lying about his other women three years ago. Unfortunately for me, I did not stop caring about his affairs until almost a year ago.

I gave him the practiced look of hurt and acceptance that I had mastered. He richly enjoyed hurting me. I allowed him to think that I still cared enough about him to be emotionally hurt by him. It was imperative that Justin believe my charade. I had to be certain that he in no way suspected that I was loving Hamilton hard and good every chance Justin would give me.

"I guess I'll see you Saturday," I said in a subdued voice.

A tender half-smile curved his lips. I could tell that his mind was already on his beautiful sculptress who awaited him. Minutes later, he was gone.

My first thought was to go to Hamilton. My body craved his, but I had commitments that would keep me on the home front for the next few days. I stoked the embers in the fireplace in my bedroom. Then I snuggled into the down comforter and fantasized about my own lover across town.

Days later, I called Hamilton. He answered after two rings.

"May I come to you?" I asked.

"Come," Hamilton said.

My heart raced with anticipation as I smoothed down my little black dress. I tied a black-and-white silk scarf around my neck, then I checked my appearance. My body was slender, with breasts that were a bit large for my frame. My waist was narrow. My hips and butt were firm and gently curved. I kept myself in peak condition with a Justin-restricted diet and daily vigorous exercise.

My makeup was light against my pale honey-brown skin. I added a little mascara to emphasize my chestnut brown eyes, with a hint of lip gloss and blush to complete my look. My straight black hair was parted down the middle and flowed over my shoulders and halfway down my back. Now I was ready to see my baby.

When Hamilton opened the door for me, my heart beat quadruple time. He looked gorgeous in black slacks and a charcoal gray cable-knit turtleneck. He smiled at me, and like magic I felt happy and free. We kissed with slow sensuousness, until Hamilton tugged me inside his home.

"I wanted to cook with you tonight," I said. "I stopped by the store. They had some beautiful prawns." I kept talking because I saw the question in his eyes, but I didn't want to hear him ask it.

"I thought we could make Szechwan shrimp with noodles." I walked into the kitchen and Hamilton followed. I unpacked the groceries and avoided looking in his direction. "I could even make a Caesar salad."

Silence.

"Baby?" I asked as I gripped the head of romaine lettuce tight.

Hamilton turned me around to face him. His hands moved stealthily up my neck and cupped my head in his hands.

"Have you left him?"

"No, I didn't."

Hamilton left me standing alone in the kitchen.

"Hamilton?" I called out.

Nothing.

I started to shake all over as I walked into the living room. "Please, baby. Let me explain."

I watched his retreating back until he left my line of vision. Then I heard the quiet close of a door.

I let out a shaky breath and plopped down on the toffee-colored leather sofa. Hamilton had left his black leather jacket nearby. I tugged it on and inhaled his cologne and the fragrance of his body. I felt so weary. I curled up into a ball and rocked myself on the sofa, until I fell asleep.

When I opened my eyes, I saw Hamilton standing over me. His shirt hung loose and unbuttoned. He held a bottle of imported beer by the neck, while his eyes raked over me.

"Come into the bedroom," he said, then walked away.

I lay stunned for a few minutes, unsure of what to do. Then I decided to follow him. Only the light from the roaring fire and a few pale green pillar candles lit the bedroom. In the shadows, Hamilton leaned against the massive carved headboard of his mahogany bed. He was naked and sporting the most superb erection.

"Take off your clothes," he ordered.

"Hamilton, please. Don't be like this with me tonight."

He closed his bulging arms over his sculpted chest. "Now, Anais."

His coldness chilled me, even as I stood in front of the fireplace. Hamilton had never been this dispassionate with me. I felt so insecure.

"Do as I say or leave my home."

Now I felt a hot anger beginning to burn inside me. I felt sick to death of men treating me like a mindless possession.

I glared at him as I yanked the scarf off my neck and took off my dress. I kicked off my heels.

Hamilton's eyes narrowed as they drifted over the angry bruises all over my body. This was the first time that I had allowed Hamilton to see what Justin did to me. I usually waited until the bruises faded before I came to him. But now I wanted him to know the tremendous risks I took to be with him.

The harshness in his eyes vanished. He moved toward me.

"Stay on the bed," I commanded. "You wanted a sex slave tonight. Let me perform for you."

He frowned and looked as if he would refuse me, then lay supine on the bed and watched me. I stepped up on the bed and stood straddling him.

"Shall I dance for you?" I swayed my hips to India.Arie's "Brown Skin," which played only inside my head. I dropped the straps of my bra down my shoulders, before I tossed it on his chest.

I tugged free the tiny bows on each of my hips. I watched Hamilton as I seesawed my panties between my thighs. I repeated that slow motion once, then twice, before dropping my panties over his face. He removed them slowly as he inhaled my humid scent. I stroked my hands down my flat stomach and covered my most intimate part from his avid gaze. I stood naked, physically and emotionally, before I knelt down over his body and inched my fingers up his chest.

"Shall I suck your dick, baby?" I asked with a vicious little smile toying along my full lips. "Or should I back this thing up and let you hit it from the back? Would you like that, Hamilton?"

He placed my hands over his heart. "You are more than a body to me. Don't you know that?"

"I thought I did," I whispered. Then my anger and composure deserted me. "Until tonight."

"I'm so sorry, baby." Hamilton touched and kissed my bruised and aching neck.

I sighed and closed my eyes in pleasure. He caressed my sides and hips that were so tender from Justin's kicks and punches.

"I have to kill him now," Hamilton said.

"Then you would be taken away from me." I let tears fall. "And I don't know what I would do without you."

My eyes drifted to half-mast, as his lips moved over my breasts with tiny kisses and passionate tugs on my tight nipples.

I wrapped my legs around his waist and leaned into him. He felt so warm and hard against me as his powerful arms held me close and tender. The sweetness of him felt almost unbearable. Still, I needed more. My hands cupped the muscles of his strong back. I grinded my hips against him and silently urged him to join us.

"I don't want to hurt you," Hamilton whispered.

Hamilton was a demanding lover. We weren't always gentle with each other, but I always felt the love in our lovemaking.

"Only you can heal me," I said.

He reversed our bodies. I sighed as the softness of the bedding shrouded my battered body. Hamilton lifted my right leg and kissed my toes, then my ankle. His kisses traveled up my leg and moved to the inside of my thighs. I closed my eyes and smiled as his lips placed moist, angel-soft kisses inside my upper thigh. He moved deeper between my legs as his tongue swirled and ebbed and flowed inside my heat. Hamilton treated my other leg to the same lavish treatment, but much slower. I ached with the need to feel his talented mouth at my thumping center.

He loomed over me and tilted my pelvis to receive him. Hamilton's penis still felt tight and so heavy inside me, even after all the times we had made love. But then he moved and my body stretched to accommodate his largeness. His strokes were slow and measured. I could tell that he was holding back, trying not to hurt me, so I squeezed him tightly and sank my teeth in his shoulder. The salty taste of his skin flooded my mouth and made me bite harder, until I almost drew his blood. He groaned as he deepened and quickened his thrusts. I held on as long as I could, but my stamina was fading. I was so emotionally spent. My body let go. I continued to shake long after my unbelievable climax had ended.

Hamilton soothed my body with his touch, while our bodies remained joined. My body was lax and motionless and his was still hard and waiting for my desire to return. Inch by hard inch, touch by silken touch, kiss by sultry kiss, Hamilton aroused me again.

His hands guided my hips and he had me galloping on his big body, like the thoroughbred that he was. He revved up my body, then slowed me down so that I could go the distance with him this time. My body tensed, and the deep tugging, sweet ache in me needed to be released.

"Let it all go, baby," he said.

I followed his command with blind obedience. My release fueled his. Hamilton groaned and rode me hard twice, then a third time, before he relinquished his iron self-control and let his body experience the pounding release and pleasure that he had always given me.

After making love again, I lay on top of him, with my front against his back. We had not spoken in more than half an hour, but our silence felt comfortable. I caressed the back of his head before kissing the sweated out curve that his neck and shoulder made. I trailed my fingers across his broad shoulders and down his arms as far as I could reach. He captured my hand and brought it to his lips. I smiled and fell asleep.

I woke up cocooned in Hamilton. His embrace in his sleep was almost as fierce as when he was awake. I had to be careful not to wake him as I maneuvered myself free. I dressed without washing this one time. I wanted to keep the scent of him, and us, with me for as long as I could. He looked so beautiful lying in profile with the still-shy rays of the early-morning sun peeking into the room.

"I love you," I whispered to his sleeping form. I kissed his shoulder and walked out of his life.

I had not seen or heard from Hamilton in nearly two months. I mourned his absence from my life like a death in my family. His love continued to haunt me in my dreams and ever more so when I was awake.

So when Hamilton opened the door to me, after all that time, I did not know how I would be received. He looked astonished to see me. I knew I looked a sight, in old jeans and a ripped T-shirt, sporting a black eye and a busted lip. I stood, holding my sleeping baby in her pink *Dora the Explorer* blanket.

"This is my daughter, Maya," I said. "She's two."

"She's beautiful." Hamilton smiled at Maya and lifted her into his arms.

He reached for me with his free hand and welcomed us inside. We walked into his guest room and he laid Maya down on the bed. I covered her with her blanket and sat beside her.

"Will she be alright in here?" Hamilton asked.

I kissed Maya's forehead and stroked her brown curls. "Yes. She sleeps through the night." I looked at him with a silent appeal. "She is such a good girl."

"I'm sure she is." Hamilton turned the bedside lamp on low and we walked arm in arm into the living room. After Hamilton laid me on the sofa and covered me with a deep green chenille throw, he held me.

"Hamilton, the reason why I didn't leave Justin before now——"

"Is lovely and sleeping in my guest room," Hamilton finished my statement. "I understand, Anais."

"I told Justin I was leaving him. He went bananas! He punched me wherever he could land a fist. Maya ran in the room and hit him and bit his hand. He twisted her arm and threw Maya against the coffee table. I bashed the back of his head with his girlfriend's sculpture and got us the hell out of there!" My body shivered as I relived the last beating that I would ever take.

Hamilton kissed my forehead and rubbed my arms. "You're okay now, baby. You and Maya are safe now."

"Can you be a father to Maya? She's never really had a daddy."

"Yes," Hamilton said. "I've always wanted a daughter."

I took a deep breath as I prepared to let go of my last secret. "I'm pregnant; a little over seven weeks."

I peered up at Hamilton. He looked as if he were bracing himself for a blow that he saw coming, but could still not move out of the way. I took his clenched fist and placed it on my stomach.

"This is our baby. I haven't been with Justin in months." His fingers relaxed and spread out over my stomach. The warmth from his hand radiated throughout my body. He held my face and kissed me.

I frowned as a painful memory crept into my mind. "Justin says he is going to take Maya away from me."

"You must know that I would never let that happen," Hamilton said.

"Justin is very powerful."

"He doesn't have the monopoly on power. I have it, too, in abundance. Don't look so worried." Hamilton smiled and stroked a finger beneath my bottom lip. "Nothing that I am will ever hurt you or Maya or the baby."

"That sounds like something Michael Corleone would say."

Hamilton chuckled softly. "I'm not a godfather. You can trust me."

"I do."

"I love you, Anais."

I leaned my forehead against his. "You've never said that to me before."

"You weren't mine."

"I've always been yours. I simply wasn't free, until now."

The Visit

Memphis Vaughn Jr.

The Christmas season was not a good time to be alone. I couldn't make the trip back home to the Gulf Coast from L.A. until the week after Christmas. My close friend Erick had suggested I drive up to Oakland with him for the holidays and not spend it alone, as I had planned. After my breakup with my girlfriend back in October, he didn't want me to be alone and feeling sorry for myself. He suggested that his stepmother's Southern cuisine and hospitality would help get my mind off the breakup.

We arrived two days before Christmas to a quiet neighborhood of well-kept homes. His stepmother greeted us with warm hugs and graciously welcomed me into their home. His family was originally from Texas, and his stepmother was all the family he had now. His dad had died a few years earlier, from a heart attack at fifty-five, and his mother had died when he was twelve. When his dad remarried, his stepmother had raised him along with her daughter, Damara, from another marriage. Damara was a twenty-three-year-old graduate student at Stanford and was home for the holiday break. Erick and Damara's younger brother, Kelvin, was stationed in Iraq and would not be home for the holidays.

"Jayson, make yourself at home," his stepmother said, her Southern accent still intact. "Stay as long as you wish."

"Thank you, Mrs. Dillard."

She smiled. "Please, call me Linda. Mrs. Dillard makes me sound like an old lady."

That evening Erick's family hosted a holiday party; the other guests were some of Damara's friends and several neighbors. All of Damara's friends were attractive, but Damara was the stunner. She had nice, long legs and a butt that swooped out in the precise amount of curvature. There's nothing comparable to the well-shaped butt of a black female.

Damara was charming and intelligent and she matched me wit for wit as we chatted and discussed a wide range of subjects. I enjoyed watching her sashay through the room, and I could tell she enjoyed putting on a show. My mind alternated between thoughts of holding and caressing her body and focusing on the conversation in the room. I tried to fight those thoughts and not be disrespectful to Erick and his family.

Damara helped her mother serve the assortment of holiday food and drinks. Whenever Damara came near me, she would touch my arm or shoulder, and each time, I felt something surge through my body. I couldn't decide if it was static electricity or my own lust playing tricks on me. Each time she reached down to retrieve my plate or glass, it would put her curvaceous breasts on display. The clingy top struggled to keep her pendulous breasts in place, and I wouldn't have complained if they had spilled out right into my hands.

I also found myself catching glimpses of her mother—a

slightly older version of Damara, but with more generous curves. Linda, with her Southern charm, warm personality, and good looks, was the perfect hostess. I could imagine that in her younger days, she probably had to fight off the men wanting to jump her bones. I estimated that Linda was in her late forties, and with me being thirty-three, I was probably too old for Damara and too young for Linda. Fortunately, Erick was not aware of the interaction between Damara and me since he was too engrossed with one of the other females, who I later found out was an ex-girlfriend.

As it neared midnight, I tried to stifle my yawns, which resulted from the long drive up and from consuming multiple glasses of the rum-laced eggnog. I made a valiant effort to stay alert, but Linda finally caught on and suggested that I go to bed. I protested but she prevailed and led me downstairs to the guest room in the converted basement.

"I hope you don't mind sleeping down here," Erick's mother said. "It's quiet and you'll have your privacy."

As I surveyed the well-appointed bedroom, I quickly responded that it was nicer than my own bedroom. Linda laughed and gave me a quick hug before she went back upstairs.

I sprawled across the bed intending to rest my eyes for a moment before I took a shower. Just as I began to drift off to sleep, Erick stuck his head in the room and asked if I wanted to join him.

"Jayson, don't tell me you're wimping out on me already. We just got here." He poked me in the side. "Roz and I are going down to a club on the waterfront. Get up."

"Naw, man, you two go ahead. I don't want to be a third wheel. It's been a long day; I'll catch you in the morning."

"Alright, man. But tomorrow, you're gonna hang while we're here in Oakland. So get your rest now."

"Cool. Catch you later."

A few minutes later, I finally got up to take a shower. I heard a light knock on the bedroom door, and much to my delight, it was Damara.

"Just checking to see if you needed anything?"

"Thanks. I'm good and I have everything I need." *Except you,* I thought. As she stood there, I noticed her beautiful languid eyes were a shade of hazel and complemented her other facial features.

"You sure? I want to make sure your stay is very pleasurable." She stood there eyeing me, and the word *pleasurable* seemed to resonate through my mind.

"My stay has been great," I responded as I flashed a smile. "Your family has been very welcoming to me."

It was getting difficult to restrain the arousal that was forming in my pants as I scanned her body. Damara's sexy smile was having an effect on me, and I was doing my best to respect my friend and his home.

"Good," she replied. Just before she started to leave, she popped another question. "You didn't want to go out with Erick?"

"Uh, no, I didn't want to intrude on him and his date, since I would've been without one myself."

"I would've gone out with you. I'd be good company."

"Maybe I can take you up on that tomorrow. I was about to take a shower and call it a night."

"Okay. If you need anything, I'm right upstairs." She then winked at me and repeated, "Anything."

Her wink and continued offering of assistance had gone beyond normal pleasantries. We stood there for a moment, the sexual tension growing stronger with each passing second.

"So, if I need someone to wash my back, should I call on you?" I fired my volley and awaited her response.

"Sure. I can help wash anything else you may be having difficulty with." She looked at my crotch, which was reacting as if she had called it by name.

I pulled her into my arms, and our lips and tongues battled feverishly with pent-up passions. Our hands began to caress and explore each other's body. Her soft backside felt good as I grabbed each cheek and pulled her tightly against my groin. Her hands roamed across the muscles of my back and down to my butt.

We broke our kiss and began to undress each other. I quickly removed her blouse and lacy black bra to reveal the breasts that had teased me all night. Her dark, thick buds were tasty as my tongue rolled across her taut nipples, setting off her sensual murmurs of approval. Damara didn't waste any time helping me shed my pants, and I soon stood there with my pants and shorts down around my ankles. Grabbing my hard dick, she stroked it up and down and kissed my nipples. I suckled her full breasts as I slowly slid her panties down her long, shapely legs.

After extracting ourselves from the awkward tangle of clothes, I led her into the bathroom and we stood there for a moment gazing at our reflections in the mirror.

Despite her height, she appeared much shorter next to my six-foot-three frame. My dark skin contrasted against her café-au-lait complexion; yet the darkness of her nipples matched my skin tone and provided an ideal blend of our colors.

In the shower, we let the water cascade over our bodies. With her back against me, I felt my penis wedged between the cheeks of her curvy ass. I reached my hand around to stroke the sensitive nub that was nestled in a dense forest of soft curls. My fingers found their way to her molten vagina, which was already emitting its satiny fluids. My other hand caressed her nipples, causing her to moan and purr, like a well-tuned Ferrari.

The danger of knowing that her mother was upstairs heightened the pleasure I was experiencing. Damara squirmed in my embrace as I stimulated her clitoris. I wanted to break her off right then, but she spun around and pushed me against the wall. I watched as the water streamed onto her chest and made tiny rivulets down her honey brown body. She licked at the droplets of water that hung on my broad chest as she moved from my nipples down to my navel and ended with her lips engulfing my throbbing penis.

"Damn, Jayson, it's so thick."

Her hot mouth devouring my dick caused my eyes to roll back in my head. She sucked it in and out of her mouth, letting it pop each time she withdrew her mouth from the head. She played with my penis as if it were her own personal joystick.

She worked her mouth down my elongated staff, taking more than half of it in.

"It's too big for my mouth," she announced after withdrawing from my saliva-coated shaft. "But, I have another hole that I know can handle it."

"That sounds like a challenge," I teased. "Show me your skills, baby." I turned her around and parted the cheeks of her backside. I playfully nudged my penis toward her rump, but her hand swatted it away.

"No, not that one," she said, giggling. "You know which one I'm talking about."

"Oh, this one." I pushed the head of my penis against her tight opening, which eventually allowed me to ease inside her awaiting body, the wetness allowing me to glide in. Damara's well-rounded butt was made for the doggie-style position as I watched my dick wedge its way between her jiggling butt cheeks.

"Oh, shit," I moaned as she worked her abundant backside against me. By now the water had gotten cold and I turned the shower off as we continued our lovemaking.

Her inner walls gripped my penis, and I struggled to maintain control. Grabbing her titties, I began my assault on her quivering body. Damara matched me stroke for stroke and her shrieks of pleasure threatened to awaken the entire neighborhood. I stuck my fingers in her mouth to muffle her moans, but my own moans of pleasure betrayed me as my bass voice loudly reverberated in the tiled shower stall.

"I'm cumming! I'm cumming!" she screamed as she bucked back against me. That was all it took for me to reach my climax. After a few final thrusts, I pulled out and shot a stream of cum across her back and onto the shower wall. My eruption was like none I had experienced before.

After a lukewarm shower, we ended our sexual foray with more passionate kissing on the bed as we lay there wrapped in towels. I wanted her to stay with me the entire night, but we both thought about the possible repercussions if we were found that way in the morning. After one more lingering kiss to her succulent lips, I watched her slip through the door and back upstairs.

My dreams that night were extremely vivid, and they continued to play out one sexual situation after another until I found myself awake and trying to determine where I was. I felt a presence in the room and thought that maybe Damara was returning for another bout. After my eyes adjusted to the dim light that seeped in from outside, to my surprise I saw Erick's stepmother.

"I hope I didn't wake you," Linda whispered, standing right inside the doorway.

"No, I was half asleep," I lied.

"I was checking to see if everything was okay." Her gaze scanned my body, and I then realized that I had fallen asleep wearing only the towel. The towel, now tangled beneath me, left my naked body fully exposed to Linda. Her stare was locked on my erect penis.

"I see that something else is fully awake," she said as she sat on the edge of the bed, her body right in my face. The intoxicating scent of her perfume hung languidly in the air. The thin, silky robe exposed her luscious thighs and the bra and panties she wore.

"Jayson, I'm here to help you with anything you need," she said, her voice soft and soothing. "Erick told me about the breakup with your girlfriend. I know that guys can get real depressed when these things happen, especially during this time of year."

I was embarrassed about her knowing about my personal life and wished Erick had not told all my business.

"I'm doing okay," I responded.

Her sexy voice and the feel of her fingers grazing my lower thigh caused my penis to respond, and I attempted to cover up my nakedness.

"Don't be ashamed if you were having a wet dream. It's natural to have those feelings," she said. Even in the dim light of the room, I could see the desire in her brown eyes. "I can help you with things, if you want me to."

As her hands slid farther up my thigh and hip, I knew exactly what she meant. After a fulfilling bout of sex with her daughter, I had to admit I was turned on by her, too.

"I know I might seem too old for you, but—"

"No, Mrs., I mean, Linda. You are very attractive and not too old for me. But I don't want to disrespect your hospitality by doing something improper."

"Don't be silly, Jayson. I want this more than you realize." She leaned over and kissed me on the nape of my neck, and my dick sprang up like a rake being stepped on.

"We shouldn't be doing this. What if Erick or Damara come down here?"

"Erick's still out and Damara is asleep," she said in between kisses. "It's only you and me."

Her kisses lingered on my nipples, making my penis leak pre-cum. My hands began to stroke her soft body. Age had been kind to her body, which was just as supple as her daughter's.

"Your body is beautiful," I said as I pulled the robe from her shoulders, then slid down the bra straps to unveil her abundant breasts. The caramel color of her large breasts was accentuated by the darker nipples and areolas. I hadn't noticed how big her breasts were until now as she leaned over and placed my dick between them. The pre-cum created the perfect lubrication as I slid my hardness between those soft mounds. Linda snaked her tongue out across the head of my penis as I pumped back and forth. Her tongue was longer than any other I had ever seen, and she put it to good use as it flicked across the sensitive nerves of my prick each time it poked through the cleavage of her breasts. The sensations from both her tongue and her breasts were intense. I didn't want to cum too fast, but her actions soon brought me off as I coated her nipples with my pearly essence.

"I'm sorry but the feelings were too incredible for me to hold back."

"Don't worry, baby." She rubbed the sperm into her breasts, making the nipples glisten in the predawn light. "I'll make it hard again."

She stood up, peeled off her panties, and straddled me in the sixty-nine position. Placing her fleshy mound in my face, the combination of her feminine scent and the effects of her tongue began to bring my penis back to life. I thrust my tongue into her soaking vagina, causing her to swallow my penis. I soon felt it slip all the way into her throat, and her tongue snaked out to tickle my balls.

I returned the favor as I worked my tongue up and down her engorged slit—occasionally darting it deep into her fiery vagina. Before I knew it, my dick was as hard as cast iron on a cold day.

"Umm, I love your hard dick," she exclaimed in between sucks. "I knew that you could get it up again."

I enjoyed her encouragement and offered my own brand of sex talk. "Yeah, keep on sucking it. Your mouth feels so good on my dick."

"You're going to make me cum by talking like that. Can you do that, baby? Make me cum?"

"If I do this, I'm sure you'll cum." I jabbed my tongue against her clit and she quivered.

"Oh, yeah. Keep doing that," she called out.

I sucked on her clit and she pressed her thick thighs against my head, almost smothering me. Her body began to thrash about and she moaned loudly, signaling her orgasm. She collapsed on top of me and her body continued to convulse for several more moments.

Now it was my turn to take control and I rolled her over and got on top of her. I kissed her thick nipples, causing them to harden and rise prominently. As our lips met in a torrid kiss, my tongue was no match for her long tongue. I felt it go down my throat, creating a new sensation for me.

I grabbed my penis and stroked it across the silky hair of her mound and found her opening ready for my entry. Linda's pussy was as hot as a boiling cauldron. I always savor the sensation of entering a hot and creamy pussy.

"Come on, don't be afraid to ram it in," she urged.

I took her encouragement to heart and began an urgent stroking that had the bed rocking. Pushing her legs up over her head, I pounded her insatiable punany. Her muscle control was amazing as it gripped my penis. She grabbed my ass and held on as I stoked the sexual fires.

"Work it, baby," she cried out. "Deeper, deeper."

"Can you handle it? You sure you want it?"

"Yessss," she hissed. "Let me feel that hard, black dick."

I stiffened my body and continued my assault on this forty-something woman who was sexing me better than women half her age. They say that women reach their sexual peak in their forties, and Linda was living proof. Since I had cum twice that night, I had much more stamina this time around. I began a steady, slow grind that caused Linda's body to undulate against mine.

I felt more sexually charged than ever, and it had to be because I had already made love to the daughter and now I was doing the same to the mother. I picked Linda up and stood with her bouncing up and down on my dick. Despite her thicker body, she was surprisingly lighter than I expected.

"That's it, baby. Take me in your strong arms. I knew you were a stallion when you hugged me coming through the door last night. Work that dick."

I heard the squishing of my dick pistoning into her vagina as she rocked her body up and down my ebony stalk. The sounds, the sights, the scents, and the sensations brought me to the brink of climax just as Linda reached hers. She convulsed repeatedly, then fell limp in my arms. I continued my thrusts until I surrendered to my own intense orgasm. I filled her with the remnants of my balls. She dropped to her knees to suck the remaining droplets from the tip of my penis.

I'd always remember my visit to Oakland. Both mother and daughter each visited me once more during my holiday visit. Luckily, neither ever realized what had transpired with the other. Nor did Erick. He had been right, the visit had cleared my mind of the breakup. I would welcome future visits home with Erick.

Riding the Friendly Skies

Lesley E. Hal

I stood before the mirror admiring myself. I loved the way my curves accentuated the Roberto Cavalli dress I wore. I teased my hair and the body curls fell just right. My makeup was flawless on my bronzed skin and I was glowing. I was always being mistaken for a younger Vanessa Williams, and tonight I would not disappoint.

I sat on my sofa, enjoying a glass of wine, waiting on the man I should've married years ago. Now here I was settling for a role I never thought I would play in a million years: his sideline ho, while another woman enjoyed the benefits of being Mrs. Tony Lambert.

I was too impatient, always shooting down his ideas. I told him countless times that his dreams of owning the first internet café wouldn't pan out. Boy, was I wrong! Not only did his dreams pan out, that little dream exploded into chains of internet cafés across the globe! My mother didn't raise me to take care of a man, so I was determined not to pour my youth into some man's pipe dream. What she should've taught me was how to look for the potential in a man and to stand by his side while he achieved his dreams. She always said a man was supposed to take care of a woman, otherwise do it for herself, and that's exactly what I did. Look where that got me!

I even told him not to waste money on buying stock in Google, but he went ahead with his gut and look at Google now! Had he listened to me, that gem would've slipped right through his hands. I've made one stupid mistake after another my entire life, and letting Tony Lambert, number seven on the *Forbes* list, go was my biggest.

I'd been wallowing in self-pity, agonizing over the decision I'd made. After his proposal, I had broken it off with him and had never looked back until now. I realized what a fool I'd been the day I heard he got married. I wasn't the type to bust into a wedding and shout for him to marry me instead. That was so cliché and beneath me. I'd finally worked up the courage to call him after five years of absence. To my surprise he was happy to hear from me. And that's all that mattered.

Just as I was about to take another sip of wine, the doorbell rang. I gave myself a once-over before sashaying to get the door.

"Bianca, you look . . . wow . . . gorgeous!" Tony was not only tongue-tied but also mesmerized. The electricity was still there between us after all this time. My thong instantly became moist.

I took in all of his sexiness. Six feet two inches of chocolate muscle stood before me. His deep dimples were begging me to poke a finger in one of them like I used to. I loved the way his hazel eyes undressed me from head to toe as he licked his luscious lips.

"Turn around," he requested.

I did, and slowly, so he could see what he'd been missing. We embraced each other and our lips connected. It was everything that I'd remembered.

He moaned and placed a blindfold on me. "Hmmm."

"You better hope this doesn't mess up my makeup and lashes," I threatened with no sincerity at all. Hell, for all I cared, he could've yanked the lashes out and smeared my makeup all over my damned face.

"That's like trying to finish the *Mona Lisa*. Why mess with what's already perfect?"

Tony took my purse and keys out of my hand before ushering me out the door, but not before caressing my ass.

"Tony!" I slapped his hand away. "Where are we going, anyway?" I laughed as Tony led me blindfolded to his limo.

"That's for me to know and you to find out. But trust me, Bianca, you're going to love every minute of what I have in store for you."

Tony held me close and I was enjoying it.

Once he had me seated in the limo, I heard the cork pop off a bottle. Tony caressed my face and poured champagne. I felt a tickling sensation of the wet bubbles on my nose as Tony held the glass of bubbly in front of me.

"Um, that's delicious . . . Veuve Clicquot?" I marveled as I took a sip of the chilled champagne.

"Yes, your favorite, but it's not as delicious as I remember you to be." Tony leaned in for a kiss and I obliged.

I smiled after our kiss. "Umm, you're going to make us miss our plans if you keep this up."

"They can't start without us." His hand brushed across my erect nipple. "Oh, yes, I can definitely wait. It's been so long since I've held you. You don't realize what it's been like, wondering what you were doing and who you were doing it with." Tony sighed as he pulled me into his arms.

I instantly felt even worse for the decision I'd made. But this was my chance to try to make things right. "Umm, flattery will get you everything and then some." I snuggled closer to him as we continued our ride to wherever.

The car stopped after what seemed like at least thirty minutes. The atmosphere was noisy and airy. It sounded like we were at an airport, but I couldn't be sure. I didn't hear any voices besides Tony's, his driver's. Then I heard two others distinctly, male and female. I was filled with nervous anxiety.

I wanted to take the blindfold off but Tony held me close. "Ah, Tony . . . baby . . . ah, what's going on?"

"Relax, baby. Everything is going to be fine," Tony coaxed me. All of a sudden I was being led up some stairs. I was certain it was a plane.

"Tony, I know we're not boarding a plane?"

"Are you afraid of heights?"

"No, it's just that I'm too swamped with business to be getting away right now." I stopped and attempted to remove the blindfold.

"You know I love it when you're feisty, woman. But if you must know—" Tony gently removed the blindfold. I looked around into the dark night. "If you must know, we are getting on my private jet. Have you ever heard of the mile-high club?" Tony smiled that seductive smile that made me cream.

"Yes, I have but—"

"But nothing. Listen, we're going to see if riding the friendly skies is really all the buzz it's hyped up to be."

Tony gave me a delicious kiss that erased all the doubt I had about boarding the plane. As soon as I entered, I was flabbergasted. The inside was so cozy and breathtaking. It was decorated in tan, gold, and cream. There was a wet bar, a curved couch, two recliners, glass walls, a projection screen for movies, plush carpeting, and farther down, a glass door to a playa's style bedroom fit for a king. I looked at Tony with my mouth hanging wide-open. I was speechless.

What were you thinking by not marrying this man, girl? I wondered again.

"Birthday gift to myself. A better gift would've been you accepting my proposal." Tony's eyes penetrated me, and a golf ball–size lump formed in my throat.

Once we finished eating dinner, it was showtime. Tony had thought of everything. He even had some naughty attire picked out for me. We lounged in a tub full of hot bubbles that smelled of vanilla and talked about what had been going on in our lives since we'd last seen each other.

"I'll be in the room waiting. I'm sure you'll find everything to your liking." Tony kissed me as he disappeared into the bedroom. I couldn't believe I was actually on a plane acting as if I were in a hotel!

Why in the hell did I let this one get away? I asked myself for the umpteenth time.

I dried off and rubbed on some of the vanilla-scented body butter. I felt silky smooth and delightful once I finished. I put on the naughty leather bustier French-maid uniform he bought, complete with stilettos and fishnet, thigh-high stockings.

"Start the music!" I yelled. R. Kelly came on immediately.

When I stepped out, the lights in the room had been dimmed. There was a small dancing stage complete with mirrors and a gold pole that wasn't there before.

I smiled seductively at Tony, then placed my finger in my

mouth, sucking on it like I would his dick later. I walked over to the pole and swung around it like a pro. I even did some upside-down flips and twirls that surprised even me!

I came down into a split, did a flip, stood back up like Prince used to do, and went around the pole again. "Make it clap" was an understatement. My ass had a mind of its own as it showed Tony what it could do. The stripping skills I possessed were immaculate. The music continued to play. I turned around and bent over and peeked between my legs to see what Tony was doing.

He was stroking that big anaconda of his and licking his lips, anticipating my next move. R. Kelly was crooning, wanting to know if I was ready, and I was. I worked Tony over some more as the song progressed before revealing my goodies.

With my back to Tony, I started to slowly undress. First I undid the apron and swung it around my head, then threw it to him. He caught it, never taking his eyes off me. The next song to play was Silk's "Freak Me."

I shook my hips like a belly dancer, dipping low and sexy before my next big reveal. I slowly slid the French-maid dress down, revealing a sexy thong with a bow on the back. I bent over to tease Tony some more before going down into another sexy split. I rolled onto my back and opened my legs as far as they would go. I pleasured one of my juicy breasts by flicking my tongue across my hard-as-a-rock nipple, then I moved the thong to the side and fingered myself.

The chorus played on with Silk telling me they loved the taste of whip cream. They wanted me to spread it on and not be mean. "Umm, this feels . . . *soooo* good! You want some of this pussy, don't you, baby?" I moaned loudly while finger-fucking myself.

Tony was beside himself with lust. He wanted me so badly I could see it in his eyes. The way he bit down on his lip while stroking himself was such a turn-on.

I tasted my fingers and licked my lips. Tony was about to come onstage and join me.

"Unh-unh, baby, I'm coming to you," I purred.

"Damn, you're sexy," Tony said as he watched me crawl over to the circular bed like a sleek black panther hunting her prey. He lay there stroking that king-size monster I was about to enjoy.

The plane hit a bit of turbulence, startling me. "Oh, shit! The plane, it's—"

Tony was at ease the entire time and took control. He laid me down on my back. In one swift motion he moved my thong to the side with his teeth. The first long, sensuous lick made me forget all about the turbulence.

"Umm, just as I remembered, sweet and juicy," Tony commented, then licked some more, savoring my juices. I opened my legs wider, inviting him in to feast on my goodness.

"Aw, yesssss! Ooh, that feels soooo . . . baby . . . oooohhhhh!!!!!!!!"

We hit some more turbulence, but with the way Tony kept going at it, you would never have known.

He somehow got my thong, stilettos, and fishnets completely off without interrupting our flow. He sucked my toes one by one as I grasped the sheets. Tony ran his tongue up the length of my leg and dived right back in. "Hmm, yes, umm . . . you're so damned good," Tony moaned between licking and sucking.

"OohTonyImabouttocum! *Oooooh,* Toooonnny!" I screamed, and trembled, but Tony wasn't finished. He put on his Magnum and pulled me on top of him, entering me at a painfully teasing pace.

"Ooh, baby, come on and give it to me! It's been too long. I need it now, papi!" I begged, and tried to do my own thing, but he held my hips in place, controlling my movements.

Tony continued to stroke me slowly. He was driving me crazy with each thrust. Oh, how I wanted him to pound the fuck out of me, and he knew it. I guess this was his way of punishing me.

"Rope Burn" by Janet Jackson was playing. Tony took a long velvet ribbon from the side of the bed and tied it around each wrist before securing the rope to the bedposts while still lying under me. Although I was trying to get him to fuck me harder, I was puzzled as to what he was about to do. I stopped trying to grind my hips into his pelvis.

"What are you doing?" I asked.

"I know you didn't think that after leaving me the way you did that I was going to make this easy for you. You'll get some of Daddy Long Stroke when I feel it's time."

Tony lifted me off him. I wanted to tighten my vagina lips around his dick in protest.

"Bend your beautiful, sexy ass over." Tony's voice was deep and sultry as hell with his command. I guess I was moving too slowly for him because he popped me on the ass, causing me to jump.

"Now move it before I have to punish you." Tony popped me on the ass again, this time with his rock-hard dick.

"Ooh, papi, I want you to put all nine and a half of those inches in me, please!" I positioned myself and held on to the bedposts. Tony got behind me and teased me some more, then stopped.

I was about to come unraveled with this teasing shit. "Tony!" I whined, my pussy an inferno of burning lava. I was surprised the bed didn't catch fire.

"I'm going to make you regret turning down my proposal. Now you got me cheating on my wife. You know I'm insatiable when it comes to you, don't you?" Tony slapped me on the rear again, then slid back under me. He grabbed my legs, locked his arms around them, and started to fuck me with his tongue again. Tony was the best when it came to eating this good old magna cum laude Mississippi-mud-pie pussy of mine. The tongue-lashing he was giving me should have been considered illegal because I was definitely about to lose my mind!

"Awwwwwwwwbaaaaaaabbbbbbeeee!" Each orgasm was as intense as the one before. If he kept this up, I wouldn't be good for much else. I was already regretting not being able to have this every night, just as he said I would.

"I want . . . I want some of . . . Da . . . Daddy Looong Stroke!"

Tony loved when I begged for it. He held on to my clit through all of my convulsing, never missing a beat.

"OohmiGodTony! *Arrrrrgggghhh!!*"

Janet was now asking someone would they mind.

Tony better have been glad we were thirty thousand feet in the air because I would surely have left his ass for playing so damned much. "TooonnneeeepleaseIcan't . . . can't take . . . any . . . more! Arrrgggghhh!" This time I think I was the one causing the turbulence.

Tony slid from under me and entered me from behind, giving me exactly what I needed. "Oh, yesssss! Just like that, baby! Umm, fuck me real good, papi!"

"You like . . . that, don't . . . you . . . baby? Miss me?"

"Yesss, baby! I miss you sooo much! Ooh!" I hollered.

"Good, because I miss you, too. You like riding the friendly skies?" Tony asked while fucking my brains out.

"Oh, I . . . I love the . . . the friendly skies!" I was fucking on cloud nine, literally, while Janet finished her song.

"How did you enjoy tonight?" Tony asked as we headed down the expressway back to my place.

I couldn't disguise my smile as I took a sip of champagne. "Words can't even begin to express the way I feel, Tony."

Tony stuck his tongue into my mouth. I sucked on it with abandon. "Umm, keep that up and we may have to go for another ride." I was already looking for reasons to prolong the night.

"I thought you were busy with work?" He cupped my breast and toyed with my nipple.

"I am, but I know how to work and play at the same time. You were a much needed distraction." I smiled and used my thumb to remove the lipstick from his lips.

"Well, in that case, I'll let you off easy tonight. I don't want to be the reason for any mishaps." He pulled out a square, velvet box from a secret compartment in the car.

I gasped. My hands automatically went up to my face. "You did—"

"Shh! Let a man do as he pleases when he's trying to woo a beautiful woman back into his life." Tony handed the box to me.

My hands shook as I opened the velvet box. Inside was a beautiful diamond necklace and matching chandelier earrings. "I know this had to have cost a small fortune." I ran my fingers across the glittery diamonds.

"Well, are you going to drool all over it and ask about the price or are you going to allow me to put it on you?"

I turned and raised my hair up so he could place the necklace around my neck. I let my hair down and tears escaped from my eyes. "This is absolutely beautiful." I sniffed.

"Not as beautiful as you are. I love my wife. I mean . . . she's the mother of my kids; but you . . . you are the love of my life, Bianca."

I dabbed at my eyes as I placed the earrings in my ears. Tony placed a mirror in my lap for me to admire my gifts.

"Tony, I swear if I had it to do all over again . . . I'd—"

He stopped me with another tender kiss. The limo stopped in front of my house. I felt like Cinderella minus the two ugly stepsisters.

He cupped my face in his hands before giving me one last kiss. "Let's not dwell on what should have been but what will be . . . until next time." Tony caressed my chin lovingly while staring deep into my emerald green eyes.

The door was opened by the chauffeur. As he helped me out, I glanced back at Tony. The tears continued to fall. "Here's to what will be." I blew a kiss at him and hurriedly went inside my house before I broke down. I couldn't bear to see him being driven away from me into another woman's waiting arms that should have been mine.

"I'm the love of his life," I said, dabbing at my tears and wishing I could go back five years to that day in Paris when Tony had proposed to me. This would be a night I would never forget. I touched the diamond necklace and leaned up against the door, thinking, *If only.*

Three Is Never a Crowd

Lotus Falcon

So call it a midlife crisis or whatever you want to call it, but I like to refer to it as a midlife revolution. I answered an ad for a couple seeking a young single woman who was open to having sex with clean, middle-aged, married swingers. So what if I wasn't young or single, I was open to having sex with clean, middle-aged swingers. Besides, I couldn't really believe everything in an advertisement any more than they could about me. I figured we could check each other out and roll from there.

After calling the secret number on the advertisement, I was given an email address. This exchange of information reminded me of some James Bond 007 movie, and with all the precautions that were being taken to protect everyone's identity, I was soon wondering if I should have embellished my particulars a little more. After emailing Bob and Trish, which seemed like two of the most unoriginal names one could have thought of, I was ready to get it over with. We agreed to meet in public at a well-lit fast-food restaurant. I wanted plenty of people to be around, and I also wanted to be able to make a fast getaway.

I pretty much assumed that Bob and Trish would look like two old has-beens from yesteryear. I envisioned them to look either like Florida and James Evans from *Good Times,* or an older version of Ike and Tina Turner. Almost talking myself out of the meeting, I decided the encounter would probably last every bit of fifteen seconds, at the most. At that point, I simply needed the satisfaction of knowing that I had the guts to actually go through with it. To my astonishment, Bob and Trish were good-looking, ebony people who certainly didn't strike me as the type that would be into threesomes. I didn't look the part either, but that was beside the point.

First, we exchanged small talk and clicked right from the start. For a while, sex never entered the conversation, and I wondered if they had gotten their emails crossed. I did not want to discuss real estate or something else trivial.

Then Bob announced that they wanted to show me something back at their hotel room. They were staying not far from the fast-food joint, one reason why I'd selected the spot.

Ma and Pa Kettle seemed harmless enough so I thought, *What the hell!*

Threesome or no threesome, I was enjoying their company and didn't have anything better to do at the moment.

As soon as we stepped into the room, Bob and Trish seemed more direct. The last thing they wanted was a newbie. Thus, I did what they did and tried to look as if I was down for anything they were down for. I gauged that I could probably knock the shit out of both of them if push came to shove.

They started to neatly take off their clothes and politely told me where I could place mine. I had envisioned this part of the encounter to be a little more dramatic, but I was dealing with a couple of neat freaks. As we undressed, we engaged in the same kind of small talk from the fast-food restaurant, only this time, they were checking me out and I was checking them out.

For an old gal, Trish had rather large breasts. A little saggy, but that only gave them personality and a semblance of realism. For an old geezer, Bob was packing a pretty healthy-size dick. When Trish saw me eyeballing Bob's dick, it was pretty much on! She gave him some sort of eye signal, and the next thing I knew, they had double-teamed me. Each one of them had one of my legs, and I was suddenly lying on my back.

I wanted to say, "Wait a fucking minute," and, "Give me a minute to catch my breath." I wished that I could remember even half the bullshit I had claimed to be down for in my written bio that I had submitted to them. Knowing me, it was probably a bunch of freaky stuff from porn or the erotica I had been into lately. It was now too late and too bad. It was on now and I wasn't going to let those two old geezers "outfuck" me!

To my amazement, the two of them opened my legs as far as they could go, short of snapping me in two, and took turns sniffing my pussy. First Trish took a noseful, and from the way she acted, you would have thought she was smelling sweet-potato pie. She came up out of me with her eyes closed, then it was old Bob's turn to take a whiff. All this sniffing made me glad that I had given myself an extra pussy wash-down in the ladies' room before we left the restaurant. If this was all they were going to do, then I should have charged them to smell my gourmet pussy.

By that time, Bob's dick had pretty much skyrocketed; he was rubbing it all over my pussy, being careful not to penetrate me or have his dick touch my clit. My pussy was getting wetter and wetter, and every time I tried to touch my clit, Trish would pull my hands back. At one point, I was getting ready to tell her "Get the fuck off of me," since my pussy was about to explode.

The area around my pussy was so sensitive that I couldn't fucking stand it, then I felt Trish crawl behind me and cradle me in her lap. My legs were still opened and Bob helped to lift me slightly in her lap. While I leaned back on her, she had her legs wrapped around my legs. My pussy was swollen and wetter than it had ever felt before. Bob obviously enjoyed the view because he was sniffing and rubbing his dick all on me, while he let Trish take charge.

Bob instructed Trish to keep my legs open, but still he wouldn't penetrate me, even after I started begging him to, risking sounding like one of those video hos. I was thinking only, *Somebody better do something before my pussy blows up.* Trish was taking her sweet time, licking her fingers. She told Bob to let her finish and began to lightly stroke the length and width of my pussy from top to bottom. She took long, broad strokes that seemed to stimulate my entire pussy.

Trish placed her middle finger in my pussy and used her index finger to gently clamp my inner lips against her middle finger. She compressed them together and began slightly tugging on them. When she released her grip, waves of pleasure sent a stream of wetness pouring out of me in all directions. Trish realized what her husband liked, because old Bob was between my legs lapping up the rest of his lunch.

For some reason unknown to me, Bob was careful not to touch my clit, but he was darting his tongue in and out of my pussy with such force that I presumed his tongue was a stiff dick. When he *finally* dipped his fingers deep in my pussy and pulled them out, they were covered with fresh drippings, which he kindly shared with his wife. Bob kept feeding Trish from my pussy until both of their lips were glazed. Then my host and hostess took turns sucking my mouth with theirs, so I would not be left out from tasting my pussy from their lips.

Trish went back to her handiwork while Bob leaned back in a close easy chair, taking in everything between Trish and me, yanking on his dick. She was a master at spreading my inner lips open with her index finger while running her middle finger up and down my pussy in long strokes. She fingered me from the bottom of my clit, without touching it, but each time she seemed to get closer and closer, which got me off simply by thinking about it. Bob must have thought the same thing; he looked like he was ready to bust a nut at any moment. Trish started to enter my pussy a little more and was teasing it from the outside and circling around it, exploring the shape of the opening. She kept getting closer and closer to penetrating me, and by that time Bob was taunting her to "go inside."

Trish finally went in, with her thumb at first, then with alternating fingers. As she entered me, she was humping me from the back, and I could feel the fine hairs on her pussy tickling my ass as her wet pussy rubbed up against me. I reached back and rubbed her, and she was wetter than I imagined any woman could be. While I was working her pussy, she was working mine, and old Bob had his dick rocking to the beat as well. Just when I thought Trish could not make me any wetter, she started caressing my asshole with a finger she had dampened in her mouth, making small circles around its opening while she did mini-thrusts inside it. As she fucked my ass with her finger, she pinched my pussy lips and tugged on them a little harder. A stinging sensation started to surface from the pinching, but I followed suit and started working her pussy like she was working mine. Old girl tried to keep up by grinding her wet pussy all up in my ass.

By that time, Bob was about to cum and lifted himself from his fetal position and positioned his dick for easy access for me and Trish to maneuver. With a few more strokes, Bob erupted right in Trish's mouth and fed both of us back and forth, until we were lapping the last remains from each other's mouth. As Trish gapped my legs open, Bob begged Trish if he could fuck me, and Trish calmly said, "Not until I say you can fuck her!"

Maybe it was my imagination, but old girl's tone seemed to change a bit. A little more bass was in her voice and Bob appeared to get more docile. Maybe it was me, but it seemed as though Bob was now more the follower than the leader!

Trish soon signaled for Bob to come and relieve her; he obediently followed her instructions. Bob switched places with Trish and she motioned for him to slide me to the edge of the bed. She then spread my legs open with her hands and gazed at my wet and swollen pussy; my clit had almost doubled in size. As she gazed at my swollen clit, she brought hers so close to mine that they were practically kissing. The sight of her wet pussy all up on mine like that made my pussy begin to bubble over.

As she began to finger me with alternating fingers, she started to finger herself as well. Bob was watching as Trish continued to hold my legs open. Bob began fingering both of us while Trish continued to rub her pussy against mine, just enough for me to feel the soft, wet folds of her slit. Our pussy lips felt both soft and sticky, but the sight of pussy on pussy was visual chocolate! Bob started to rock his iron dick back and forth between my ass and then to the back of my pussy. Without notice, it was "popping" in all directions.

Trish's mouth finally made it down to my glazed pussy. She breathed hard on my clit and then started kissing all around it. She kissed everything but my clit. She kissed my thighs and my belly and continued to tease me until I took her by the hair and held her head captive over my clit and begged her to suck it.

Still teasing me, she looked up and asked, "What do you want me to do?"

Without stuttering, I said, "I want you to suck my clit!"

Finally she began kissing it. She would move away and then come back to it. Move away and then come back to it, and that shit felt so damn good!

She started licking it with nice long strokes, and I could feel her tongue working its way around the lips of my pussy and then dart in and out of it with expert precision. Trish worked her way back to the "bull's-eye" and ran her tongue down each side of my clit and tickled it underneath. She didn't miss a spot and I was enjoying every bit of it. Trish swirled her tongue around the hood of my clit and I started rocking my hips back and forth as she started pushing down harder with her mouth. She didn't come up for air once, and the pressure and rhythm of her tongue on my clit was almost poetic!

I never knew there were so many ways to suck a pussy before hooking up with Trish and her "wonder mouth." Just when I thought it was all over, Trish enclosed her whole mouth around my clit and started sucking it lightly, as she blew on it with her hot breath. There was no doubt this woman had skills. She kept glancing up at my face; I could tell she was getting off by the way I was moaning and driving my pussy into her face.

She started placing deep, French kisses on my clit and sucking on it until I was ready to cum. The stimulation was toe curling, and as I thought I would fly off the bed, Bob anchored me between his legs while he rubbed and sucked on my protruding nipples. This was the first time in my life that my clit was ever given a blow job. Even though Bob wanted a taste, Trish wasn't about to turn the pussy loose.

By this time, Trish was shouting at the top of her lungs, "This is my pussy! This is my pussy! This is my pussy!"

Right when she said that, I erupted all over her face. As I rested my head back onto the bed, Trish finally allowed Bob to join her as she leaned forward and started slurping and feasting on what I can rightly call *her pussy!*

Two Seasons of Dreams

Ahnjel

With a simple "Hello, Kim. How are you?" I knew the hurricane called Us was about to begin again. The man who is and will always be my friend and probable soul mate has carried the label of *My Heart* for years. If only it had been another place and time long, long ago. Strangely enough, circumstances and obligations had kept us apart. But those same circumstances and obligations had drawn us to one another when our lives became overwhelming. For short spans of time we were each other's best time. We might go months with no contact, but when we talked again, it was like knowing that you're home. This particular time it started with an early-morning wake-up call.

Fortunately I had been up for a while, had showered, and was lounging. This conversation led to an invitation for a visit. Once he crossed the doorstep, we settled down to watch a movie and talk. His fingers always had to randomly make contact with my skin. But once our lips touched, I knew the forbidden had begun. I curled my legs across his legs. My head was resting on his chest. His fingers were tangling my hair when he gently pulled my ear to his lips and said, "Can I eat your pussy?"

I was shocked. All I could say was "Okay."

The thought had crossed my mind but I figured I'd keep that fantasy to myself for a later date. You see, this man was so unassuming. No one knew how much of a freak he really was. He told me to lie back, relax, and close my eyes. My legs were still curled around his and I rested my head on the pillow. Leaning forward in one sweep, he had my lounging top up to my neck and my nipples were being suckled as by a newborn baby. I was cradling his head as he was sucking and unbuttoning. He took his time, using his tongue to trail down the line of my stomach, then pausing to dart his warm, wet tongue in that mysterious hole we call a navel.

Meanwhile my lounging pants were being pulled and rolled down all in one motion. He had that one-motion deal down to a science. With my legs spread so one was resting on the back of the sofa and the other was placed on the edge with my foot resting on the floor, I stared at him intently as his kisses around my pussy caused me to overflow with the promise of what was to come.

As I moaned here and there, I suddenly heard him whisper to me, "Breathe!"

Opening my eyes, I asked, "I'm not?"

Evidently I was holding my breath; even before his meal had begun. The next thing I knew my leg had moved from the edge of the sofa and was wrapped around his neck because now his tongue was deep, deep inside me. In between the circular motion his tongue was making, he was sucking lightly and consistently on my clit. And then he was watching me watch him.

Then with one long lick from the bottom of my pussy opening to the hood of my clit, he lingered right there until I came like a fountain. Still with his face buried as though he was searching for treasure, he had to grab me by my waist because I was arching my back and scooting away like I was on the run. Mind you, that was the farthest thing from my mind, because if I could've taken a soldering iron and melded us together until time became endless, I would have. I couldn't even tell you how long this went on. But I knew one thing: after that session right there, he wasn't going anywhere.

So as the spring ended and the summer progressed, our relationship blossomed into what women only wish they could have. How could this possibly go on? It was too good. There were circumstances and obligations other than ourselves, but we were on a runaway train. I'd had this particular dream for a long time: to spend the perfect day with that perfect person who is really feelin' me. And everything I wanted to do within that day goes down as smooth as butter. Not looking for monumental, just the purest of emotional and sexual freedom in my sanctuary of escapism.

Since we were still in constant ecstasy by summer's end, I took the big leap and extended an invitation to him to spend some time with me at the beach house my girls and I rented for a week. We usually tripped from Saturday to Saturday. We had an open house that first Sunday for family and friends. The rest of the week it was only us and we decompressed. All we did was beach, eat, shop, and chill. Oh! You could also import some dick for the day. Only one overnight stay; it was the law.

My baby worked overnight, so we've had the best conversations in the wee hours of the morning. Some of those conversations became my private masturbation pieces. I couldn't be too explicit when he was on the company phone, but if I got him on his cell, *it was on!* His voice late at night got a little deeper, his diction was a little slower, and when he moaned my name, *DAMN!* I was in bed, under the covers, no undies, finger circling my clit, dipping it in every now and then as he described how he was going to eat me so good and so deep that he was going to leave his face print on my pussy. So, all I had to do was feel my way when I thought about him and know that he would always be there with me. Now tell me if that ain't a pussy-eatin' motherfucker! I would be walking around all day with my fingers feelin' my pussy like I was reading braille. Because that was how often I'd been thinking about him lately.

This was the first time our relationship elevated to where all bets were off and we had thrown caution to the wind. Now since we'd taken this leap, the obstacles began to occur, testing us to see how badly we really wanted it. First, getting time off from work and arranging where he was really supposed to be. Then he called to tell me that the transmission conked out on his car the day before his arrival. My disappointment carried through the phone. Then he heard the ladies in the background and began to laugh. He couldn't believe what they were saying.

When it came to one another, we had no shame, no blame, and no judgment. They wanted to make sure my dick got there, that I was well serviced, and all that it entailed. Because when the car obstacle popped up, my girls suggested we go get him, bring him to me, and take him back. Those were the kind of girls I rolled with. That's why I loved those three ladies. I considered them my sisterfriends. They were more sisters than friends.

Everything that my love and I were doing was so out of

character for us. We had really crossed all boundaries. I figured we might as well go all the way. Fuck it!

Lastly, he said, "Don't be so pessimistic. I'll think of something."

After that, my girls and I decided to go to the mall. Guess where we ended up? Victoria's Secret. Not interested in anything in particular, I was led by one of my girls to the thong table. Not impressed; didn't wear them. They all egged me on: "Just try them, you'll love them and so will he." I did pick out these black, sexy ones, and they did look sexy as hell on, so I said, "What the hell," and got three pairs. That picked up my spirit a little bit.

The morning of, with no call during the night, I tried hard to keep the faith. But, I also didn't want to hype myself up so when the call did come in that he couldn't make it, I wouldn't be crushed. The day before, I did buy a beautiful bouquet of baby white carnations and three lavender roses for my room. I figured if I was going to be down, I still had something beautiful to brighten my day. I took my usual 7:00 a.m. walk on the beach with "Get Here" playing over and over in my ear. I was willing the forces to let my dream day happen. By one o'clock, the girls and I were sunning on the beach. My cell phone rang; I held my breath as I heard his voice.

He said, "Hello, what are you doing?" Then he said those magic words: "I'll be there in an hour."

I played it cool as I packed it in and told the girls, "I gotta roll. My baby's on his way!"

Walking back, I was ready to explode. I think I came, just getting a visual. I had my outfit already picked out. I intended on showering quickly so I wouldn't have to rush, but I was thrown off track by that damn handheld shower massager. I felt the need to take the edge off before he got there. When I started to think about how beautiful and big the man's dick was and how he was going to leave his face imprinted on my pussy . . . All I have to say is every woman should go and buy a handheld shower massager, if you don't already have one. If you do have one, then you can feel me. It's a prime-time investment.

I was a little weakened after my escapade in the shower so I took my time to lotion and perfume myself. I chose a casual outfit. A floral, tiny-pleated, sleeveless blouse and an off-white jean skirt. Underneath I wore a black-and-white, floral lace bra that was a little too small. It made me look really boobalicious. And the star of this show was that sexy little black Victoria's Secret thong. This secret weapon was undecorated in the front, but the back held all the artwork. You see, three thin straps led from the front to the back strap that went between your ass. And where each side strap connected to the back strap, there was a small black bow with a tiny crystal in its middle. This man was going to lose his mind. He hadn't been exposed to the kind of freakdom I had on the menu for that night.

I found myself waiting on the porch after everyone had returned from the beach. One of my other girlfriends also had company that day. A whole lot of stuff was jumping off. As I lounged in a chair daydreaming, I heard a motorcycle close by. I take a second look as it parks in front of the house and a man takes off his helmet. It's my baby, looking like Easy Rider.

DAMN! He looked good. He stepped up on the porch, smiled that boyish grin, and said, "Hi, baby."

I wanted to fuck him right there on the porch. You couldn't have told me that he would have used that mode of transportation at such a distance to come see me. We kissed and hugged and felt each other up as much as we could outside on the street, then I brought him inside and introduced him to everyone.

My girls kept whispering to me, "Damn, girl, this man drove his motorcycle all the way down here to come to get to you. Shit!"

We went straight to my room so he could rest his gear and his bag. He had packed as if he was spending the night, but I did not know and did not ask. He could do whatever he wanted, and whatever arrangements he needed to make were not my concern. All I knew and cared about was that he was there and he was going to be there for a while. I guess he felt the family atmosphere, and anyway, whenever he was with me, he knew he was home.

And so my dream day began. We lounged in the living room for an hour or so, watching part of a movie we were not really watching because we couldn't keep our hands and lips off each other. We sat on the porch for a while, deciding what we wanted to do next. There was no need to rush. This was our day. We walked two and a half blocks to the boardwalk and took in the sights. We were like schoolkids, laughing, playing, and holding hands. Every now and then I'd remember that I had virtually no panties on, and it felt strangely delicious.

We ate at my favorite seafood shack because neither of us wanted a big meal. No sense stuffing ourselves since we had some serious homework to do later on. All the while, as I was sitting across from him at the table, his eyes constantly dropped down to my breasts, which were about to explode out of the little-too-small bra. I also had one too many buttons undone. Baby could barely eat, and what he did want to eat wasn't on the menu.

Back at the house we were all having such a good time. After a while we decided to go off by ourselves and just sit on the porch before walking on the beach. All the while I noticed him staring at me. He was staring as I was sitting in the lounge chair, he was staring as I was standing against the banister.

I finally asked, "What's the matter?"

Looking at me with that shit-eating grin, he replied, "I can't keep watching you and not have you."

It took all my strength not to blow the dream and fuck him buck wild until he left. That was what I really wanted to do.

Instead, I said, "Let's compromise. If we go to my room now, we'll never get to take this walk. So if we walk now and not make it as long as I had planned, when we come back, you can have me any way you want me. I promise."

The walk on the beach was idyllic. We walked higher up on the beach so he wouldn't get his clothes wet. He surprised me again when he came down with me in the surf; his pants got damp, and he didn't even care. Every few feet we stopped to look at the horizon and talk about how amazing it was to be together like this. And when we weren't talking, we were kissing. You would've thought we were brand-new lovers. It was like no one existed but us. We were sickening. But I loved every minute of it and so did he. All the while the background to our perfect picture was the sun setting with beautiful oranges, pinks, and purples. The sound of waves crashing nearby. It was so surreal.

Everyone was gone when we got back to the house. The only other place to go was to the bedroom. The scenario was set. I lit candles all over. I had downloaded hours of music for the occasion; all the right stuff. On a corner table there was my beautiful bouquet of baby white carnations and three lavender roses with blooms that were outstanding. I told him the three lavender roses were for the *I love you*s that we couldn't say. I guess we did have boundaries on something. Once I told him to get comfortable, I slowly unbuttoned my blouse for him to get a peek. As he lay down in only his underwear, propped up on a pillow, I slowly walked to the double-door closet. I never turned back to see what he was doing as I started undoing my jean skirt. I had to shimmy a little to get the skirt down, and I was bending over a little bit too much to lift one leg out, then the other. I stood up straight, still facing the inside of the closet with my blouse still on but open. I turned only my head to him and smiled. He had that look of anticipation and surprise as I let my blouse fall off. His visual was clear; so was mine. My baby was completely mesmerized by the most sensuous pair of underwear I'd ever worn. Eyes as big as quarters and his mouth hung open in the cutest little O shape. Made me want to walk right on over to him and sit on his face, but not yet.

Finally he asked me, "What are those underwear you're wearing?" He couldn't even get his words together.

I said, "I told you that I had a gift for you and myself to share, didn't I?"

Before I stepped away from the closet, I stepped into my black heels. As I walked closer to the bed, he was sitting up on the edge of the bed at attention. I didn't stop until I was standing directly in front of him, so close that I could feel his breath on my rib cage. No words were spoken as his head rested between the cups of my bra and his hands were gliding up and down my skin. I was turned around and asked to model this new fascination. Then he brought me back into his arms and held me ever so gently, tracing the straps of my thong as if he were now reading braille himself.

I had prearranged a set of songs to do a lap dance for him.
You couldn't tell me I wasn't a G-string diva. All I needed was a
pole, but the closet door and the bed were good enough. You
must be versatile and improvise when you have to; that I did. I
was making my own self hot. My thong was getting wet with
the thought of what I was going to do to him. I laid him back
down on the bed so that I could straddle him; wet thong, heels,
and all. But instead of straddling him at that moment, I decided
to entertain him from above. Standing directly over his shoulders, I reached into my thong and had him watch me stick my
fingers in my pussy so I could be extra wet when I lowered myself onto his waiting lips. One more extra touch; I crouched
down on bended knee hovering above his face. So close that he
could see the drops of cum dangling from my pussy. I had
pulled the crotch of my thong over in case one of my droplets
fell, then he'd be able to catch it in his mouth.

Right then and there he lifted his head to meet my pussy,
and his face disappeared as I made my touchdown and held on
to the goalpost. I mean, bedpost. And believe me that he said
he was going to go so deep and so good that he would leave his
face print. I would have told anyone to take a mirror and see
whom they saw looking back at them from down there. After
that, the rest of the night was pretty much a blur. I don't remember how or when my bra came off. I do remember riding
his dick and reaching behind myself to massage his balls because that always made his dick harder and larger. I never got
to do my other performance piece involving the sucking of
dick extraordinaire. Unbeknownst to me, the night was supposed to be all about me. My baby had an agenda of his own. It
was my night to be pleasured to the tenth degree. What was
clear was that baby had fucked me so long, hard, and good that

when we came together, he had so much dick in me that my screams and moans became inaudible. Once it was over, we were still shaking and weak from the physical explosion of the love we had just shared. He stayed as long as he could before taking the highway back home in the wee hours of the next morning. I will never ever forget one moment of my dream vacation. I wrote the vision so long ago. And this summer it was realized.

Breath of Love

Teresa Noelle Roberts

Gaston showed up for our first official date at eleven, later than I'd normally start an evening out. I'd been dozing on the couch waiting for him. But if you're going to date a vampire, you have to get used to odd hours.

I could have got up and met him at the door, but it was more fun to buzz him in and then watch him strut, in all his café-au-lait elegance and long legs in black jeans and supernatural hotness. Gaston doesn't walk like mere mortals do. Even when he's not trying to be impressive, he moves like the bastard child of a martial artist and a runway model. When he's trying, he throws in some prowling panther for good measure, and tonight he had his slink on but good.

He's not tall, but he carries himself like a prince. He was never one, just a prosperous free black man in Louisiana back when it was still a French possession. But, in his day, that was enough to make you royalty in a small territory. Tall or not, he was plain gorgeous.

He's also technically dead, animated by a symbiote from another dimension that lives on sexual energy and blood.

A little off-putting at first, sure, but once he explained that the blood-drinking was kind of like a tapas bar—a little here, a little there, not enough to do any harm to the donor—I decided I was all for helping Mr. Friendly Symbiote get its regular hot-sex fix.

Not that we'd gone there yet. We'd met online (in an email group for people interested in African-American history), discovered other interests in common, and hung out a few times. Each time, it had got harder to keep our hands off each other, and each time I'd got more and more intrigued by what lay inside the gorgeous shell, the intelligence and depth that seemed to go way beyond his years. (How was I supposed to know he was over two hundred when he looked younger than me?) The last time we'd seen each other, we'd confessed our mutual attraction and made out like horny teenagers. Then he'd outed himself as a vamp, touching my heart with his trust in me. That was taking a big risk. I mean, I did think he was probably nuts. Until he showed me his fangs, that is, and then I wondered if I was the one who was nuts, because I still wanted him. I was attracted enough—and intrigued enough by the man beyond his good looks—to take the chance.

Then, in one of those frustrating twists of fate, I had to leave because I was off on a crack-of-dawn flight for a weeklong romance writers' conference, then had to work desperately to get a book in for a deadline. That was two-plus weeks ago, and we were finally able to get together in the flesh to consummate the teasing we'd been doing via email ever since.

Okay, I was a little nervous about how I'd actually react in a clinch to the whole lack-of-heartbeat and cold-skin aspect. But

I'm a thirty-plus single woman in New York City. I've dated men with worse issues than a slight case of death. (Impotence? Check. Severe fear of commitment? Check. Criminal record? Check. Over thirty and still living with his mama? Check, and that one made Mr. Criminal Record look good by comparison.) Dead or not, Gaston was dead sexy and, more important, seemed stable and sweet. Plus, he was a primary source for the historical romance I was working on. Research and a boyfriend in one sexy package: now that's efficiency!

"Good evening, my little flower," Gaston said. (The "little flower" thing is absurd, especially since I'm Amazon-size, a tall woman with broad shoulders and childbearing hips, but he could call me his little jar of peanut butter in that slight, adorable accent and I'd still get all swoony.) He drew me into his arms and kissed me.

Ugh!

Bad breath.

Beyond bad breath. I didn't remember it being anything like this horrific before, and we'd done more than enough serious kissing for me to get a good sample.

Stale blood, and death, and rot, all blending together in one putrid mess. Kind of like the way our dog's breath used to smell when it found a nice, overripe deer carcass in the woods upstate.

I pushed him away.

He didn't budge.

Turns out that trashy novels and B movies are right about vampires having exceptional strength. You can't actually push a vamp unless he wants you to.

So I turned my face away instead, muttering, "Brush your teeth, Gaston!"

"But I've missed you so much. I have been saving myself for you since we made our date!"

The words were corny, but what he was doing wasn't corny at all. He ran his hands down my body, grazing the sides of my breasts in the most teasing way possible. Then he gripped my butt with a sure hand, pulled me closer, and ground against me. His symbiote-enhanced little friend, always eager to go, was hitting right where it counted, even through his jeans and my suede skirt, and since I'd been whiling away the early evening writing a particularly racy scene in my new novel and fantasizing about a moment like this—sans the killer breath, of course—parts of me were very happy about this.

If it weren't for the halitosis from Hades, I'd have been all over him.

As it was, my body wasn't sure how to react. On the one hand, a hunky, romantic, intelligent vampire was doing the "forget dinner and a movie; let's make love" dance while hitting a few of my hot spots. And face it, I'd been deep inside book deadlines for a while. I hadn't even been hitting my hot spots myself, let alone having a handsome man do it for me.

On the other hand, that miasma coming from his mouth . . .

I extricated myself from his arms, despite messages to the contrary from several body parts that lacked a sense of smell. "Gaston, baby, your breath . . ."

"I know, *ma chère*. It is not minty-fresh." He gave a shrug, far more French than it should really have been. Under other circumstances, it might have been charming.

"Not minty-fresh?" I meant to be nicer, but as he spoke, he wafted a goat-choking cloud over me. "Baby, if you breathed on Iraq, the UN would be called in to investigate chemical-weapons violations. Toothbrush. Now." I pointed toward my bathroom.

He still moved like a cat as he slunk to the bathroom, but less like a proud panther and more like a housecat who's been smacked after someone caught him on the kitchen table tearing into the chicken. I felt bad about it, but a girl's gotta have her limits.

Unfortunately, when he came back, matters were not much improved. Minty freshness, sure, but underneath was a hint of something darker, something rotten. I could bear to let him kiss me, but it was still more turnoff than turn-on.

I tried to hide it, but I guess I didn't do a good job. He pulled away from the clinch, took my hands, and guided me to the sofa.

"I'm so sorry." He was angled in a strange way, trying to compromise between wanting to look at me and not wanting to breathe on me. "This has not happened in over a century. I was so excited about our date . . ."

I barely suppressed a giggle. He was leading into the same speech one ex used to give about his little personal problem, which had nothing to do with bad breath or immortality, but eventually led to my giving up on the relationship. I can be understanding with an occasional problem with getting a little overexcited, but every damn time we get together? Not so much.

"I understand," I said instinctively. It was what I always said to Steve when his hair trigger kicked in.

Although in this case I really didn't. Gaston was so excited about seeing me that he forgot to brush his teeth for two weeks? That would sound beyond weird from anyone, and especially from someone as fastidious as he was.

"No, I do not believe you do. It is part of being what I am. What animates this body of mine, that so long ago should have been in its grave, is the energy of my symbiote. If the symbiote does not get blood and sex daily, it weakens. And you were away. What you smell is the sorry state of my body. I hunger for you, *ma chère*. My symbiote hungers for you as well. But the result of my hunger is not so attractive, I fear. It will heal itself once I let it have what it needs, but that waits upon you."

"Wait a minute! You haven't seen me in what, seventeen days, and you haven't fed the whole time?"

Another expressive shrug. I'd say he practiced them in the mirror, but he couldn't see his reflection.

"I have fed, a bit. I took blood here and there, though I have not had much appetite. But I have not had sex, and so I weaken. I had not been fully honest with you about my needs when we talked, that I must share sexual pleasure with someone else each day to stay healthy. I had not told you that there were other women in my life, women who are content being . . . what is the modern expression?—a booty call. And when the time came, I couldn't. I thought of you and I couldn't."

"You starved yourself to be faithful to me when we haven't even slept together yet? That . . . that's so sweet."

Forget being a cynical New Yorker. (Okay, I may put on the pose with the best of them, but you notice I'm not writing hard-edged, urban chick lit. I write romances—sexy, mushy, over-the-top romances with happy endings—for a living. How cynical can I really be?)

I felt tears well in my eyes.

He squeezed my hands, started to lean forward toward me. Then he remembered the bad breath and backed off.

He smiled weakly. "I have read the books you write. You believe in true love. I do not think that love has served you well, but you're not like many women I've met lately, unwilling to believe it might happen to you. You may be willing to settle for a good time with a friend, but I think deep down you want more."

I nodded mutely.

"It is perhaps too soon to speak of love, but I care for you, and I think you care for me—and I, too, still believe in romance, even after two centuries of taking pleasure where I can, just to stay alive. When our feelings for each other are so new and fragile, I could not risk them by being with someone else. I care too much for you."

I found my voice again. "But if I'm understanding you right, for you that's like not eating for two weeks because I wasn't around to go out to dinner with you! That's crazy."

"Non, c'est l'amour."

Even my rusty French could translate that.

I admit it, I got all teary.

If he'd showed his usual sweet-breathed, debonair self and told me he loved me, I'd have read him for a player telling a lady what he figured she wanted to hear and just laughed.

But seeing him like this, coming about as close to dying for love, or at least lust, as I ever hope to see someone do, made it different.

Made me trust.

I still wasn't going to kiss him on the lips, but that left a lot of other good places.

I leaned in to him, ran my hands over his chest. I do love a man with sensitive nipples, and he had them, because they puckered under that light touch, making little points inside his silk shirt. I unbuttoned the shirt, planting kisses at each bit of newly bared skin. His skin was cool, but not weirdly so, as if he'd just come in from outside on a winter day and was chilled through. When the shirt was open, I pushed it off his shoulders and sat back for a second to enjoy the view.

Oh, yeah. One hot, technically dead guy.

When I reached for his jeans, though, he pushed me back onto the couch. "Oh, no," he whispered (not too close to my face). "Let me see you."

Inspired, I looked at my less than spacious couch and said, "How about we adjourn to the bedroom?"

I'd never been happy before that I have a typical Manhattan postage-stamp apartment, but it meant the bedroom was just a few steps away.

I'd dressed up a bit, which of course meant there wasn't a whole lot to get off me. The chartreuse silk camisole I insisted on taking off myself—I was afraid he'd rip it—but he slithered my short, black suede skirt off himself, making each movement a caress. I had panties on, but the way he was looking at me, I could tell they wouldn't be for long.

We sat on the edge of the bed, then lay down, his cooler skin starting to warm from contact with my heated body.

Then his lips closed around one of my nipples, drawing it in, drawing it out, making it feel fatter and more sensitive than I think it ever had before. Tongue, lips, teeth—and then he opened his mouth wider, drawing more of my breast into his mouth, and I felt his fangs graze my flesh.

Should have been scary as hell. Instead it was erotic as hell.

"Will you bite me?" I asked. I wasn't sure if I wanted him to say no or yes. On the one hand, being bitten by a vampire sounded pretty scary. On the other hand, I've read some of those sexy vampire books, and if I wasn't the only writer who'd gotten to do some firsthand research, I might be in for a treat.

It took him a while to answer, because his mouth was full, and goodness knows I wasn't complaining about that. My only complaint was that he didn't have two mouths; my other nipple would have loved some of the same Grade A loving.

Finally he looked up and smiled at me, the expression tender, but the fangs a little alarming. "Oh, yes," he said, "but not yet. And not here."

As he began to kiss his way down my belly, I had a feeling what he meant and started to get nervous.

But he stuck with only the lightest of nips and nibbles, the kind any mortal lover might give, as he worked his way to my thighs. There? I knew about the femoral artery . . .

Again, the most delicate and teasing of nips, more like firm kisses, making me squirm and sigh and grow slick with anticipation.

Lips brushing against the damp, silky nothing of my panties, tongue licking at me through the satin until I squirmed, arched, finally begged, "Please. Gaston, please . . ."

He nudged aside my panties, suckled my most tender flesh into his mouth, inserted one finger inside me. A rhythm that matched my deepest needs, making me soar higher and higher until I screamed his name.

Then and only then did he peel off his jeans and pull a condom out of the back pocket. My hands were fumble-fingered, awkward with lust, as I tried to help him put it on.

"I'm not sure my kind can carry human diseases," he said, "but best to be safe, since I've not exactly been monogamous all these years."

He lay over me, and as tears welled in his eyes when he entered me, I felt something inside me break—my last bits of cynicism, crumbling under the onslaught of Gaston.

We moved together, and if you've never really made love as opposed to merely bumping uglies—which is pretty damn fine in its own right—I can't explain what the difference is, but there definitely is one, and it made my heart dance and my body sing.

I felt myself starting to tighten around him, felt my abdominal muscles fluttering in a telltale sign, felt the top of my head getting ready to fly off. Gaston put his mouth on my throat, like a movie vamp, but before he bit down, he asked me, "Are you sure, *chérie?*"

My answer probably wasn't coherent, but it got the "Hell, yeah!" idea across pretty well.

A quick burst of pain, then sweetness like nothing I'd ever felt before. The room got bright, and I was sent into orbit in my own personal Gaston-powered rocket ship. Somewhere along the line, after the bite, probably around the time of the third wave of orgasms, Gaston joined me in outer space.

When we came back down, he kissed me. His breath had a faint coppery taste, as if I were kissing someone who'd just flossed a little too energetically, but other than that, it was back to normal.

"Is it always like that with a vampire?" I asked when we stopped kissing long enough. "Or was this just because . . . you know, you really needed some sex?"

He paused, then laughed. "Oh, *chérie,* I was about to apologize to you for being too abrupt in my weakened state! Oh, no, it's not always like that. Often it's much better."

And he was telling the truth. Was he ever!

Okay, so after a few weeks of getting proof how much better it could be, I was so behind on my work that my publisher and agent were ready to strangle me.

But they say the new book's reached a whole new level of sensuality. And while they hadn't been expecting a paranormal, they're happy with that development, too. Readers just eat up vampire romances, they say, and there haven't been many yet with African-American heroes.

'Til Death Do Us Part

Dangerous Lee

I hadn't seen him in more than ten years. Since he had disappeared after finding out the babies weren't his. Now, here we were at the same bourgeois event; he had a badass chick on his arm and I was dateless. I had never got over him.

I noticed him first, almost as if I were looking for him. Truth be told I had been looking for him since he'd left without saying so much as a "Fuck you." For years I had dreamed of running into him so we could be a family, despite mismatching DNA. My heart sank as I hid around corners, stalking him. He was so damn fine and seemed so confident. His wardrobe was flawless and he looked like a millionaire. I wondered if he had ever made it in the music industry like he had planned. If he had, I wondered why I hadn't heard his name. Maybe he was behind-the-scenes.

All the memories started to flood through my mind and I began to tear up. Someone had been watching me watching him, and when she saw the tears roll, she decided that I needed a drink.

"What's wrong, sweetie? Have a drink," she commanded me.

It was her, Sanad's badass chick. I didn't even notice that she had left his side. I took a quick peek back at Sanad to make sure I wasn't trippin'. There he was, being the people person that I never knew all those years ago. He had really changed. He had definitely moved on. I felt like a damn fool, pining for his ass after all these years. He had no idea that I was in the room. He didn't probably even give a damn that I was alive.

"I'm alright. Thanks for the drink, sista," I said, walking away quickly, taking a huge swig of the champagne. I almost choked on it.

She was beautiful, exactly what he deserved. She was thick, with a nice ass, big legs, cute feet, and I'm not even gonna get into her face. It was a cross between Vanity and, well, hell, I can't think of anyone fine enough, but you get what I'm saying. She was everything I wasn't.

Don't get me wrong. I was fine, too, but she was jaw-droppin', State of Shock, Men All Pause kinda fine. I was an eight but she was a ten! I'm woman enough to admit it. I wanted to see her naked and touch her copper skin because I was sure Sanad had done so. With my recent closely cropped cut, I figured that I could be the man in our relationship.

Before I could get too far, she was after me. I felt her grab my arm. "Listen, I noticed you checking out Sanad, the light-skinned brotha over there. We came in together."

"No, I wasn't looking at him. I have no idea who he is," I lied as I drank the last of the champagne and gave her the glass. "Thanks!"

This time I made sure to run away so she couldn't catch up. My heart was pounding. *Is she gonna check me for checking her man?* I needed to get outta there. I couldn't stay at a party with Sanad and his "10" girlfriend. I didn't really want to be there anyway. I didn't know anyone, but that was the whole point of the party, to network, right? I felt like I was gonna faint and I couldn't find the damn exit. *How the hell did I get in here? Where's the exit?*

I must have looked like a damn fool, darting around, trying to find the way out. I was bumping into people without saying "Excuse me" and stepping on toes. I was starting to draw attention to myself. I felt woozy. *Did that heffa put something in my drink? I'm trippin' but I feel high. What the hell?*

The next person I bumped into was Sanad. We locked eyes and my mouth flew open.

"Lela?" he said.

I couldn't say anything. I turned to go in the opposite direction and there she was, Miss 10! My legs gave way and I blacked out on the floor. That trick did put something in my drink.

As I lay unconscious, it all came back to me. My mind flashed back to ten years ago when I was pregnant. Sanad and I were an on-and-off couple, and when I became pregnant, I wasn't sure if it was his or from this other guy that I pity-fucked because Sanad didn't want to commit. Sanad and I had dated for years, even lived together, but it wasn't working. Though we had broken up, we kept in touch and got together for passionate sex every now and then. When I became pregnant, I assumed it was his, even though I had slept with someone the day after we made love.

He had informed me that he couldn't devote his life to me. He asked if it could be someone else's and I told him the truth. He decided to support me through the pregnancy, but he coldly informed me that if it wasn't his, he would leave me. I should never have settled for that, and neither should he, but I guess love is a hell of a drug and I'm sure he wanted to do the right thing, just in case the baby was his.

It was a fucked-up nine months, and even though he was there as the twins were cut from my womb, as soon as the negative test results came back, he left and I had never heard from him again. It was as if he never existed. There I was with two newborn babies and all these emotions, and the man that I loved and wished were the father of my children had left, as if the past nine months—hell, five years—meant absolutely nothing. The boys' real father had died in a car crash during my sixth month of pregnancy, but I never told him that he could be the father, so there was all this shit I had to go through with his family. I was an emotional wreck and decided to check myself into a mental hospital when my twin boys were three years old because I couldn't handle the mess I had made of my life. Raising twin boys alone was too much for me and I lost it.

As I came to, I was in a dark room. I could hear music and faint voices in the background somewhere; I assumed I was still at the location of the party in someone's bedroom. I slowly began to make my way out of the bed.

"Where are you going?" a voice asked.

I stopped in my tracks. "Who is that?" I asked, still frozen, knowing full well who it was.

The room was pitch-black. I was afraid. I began to wonder if I had been fondled in my unconscious state. If I had, I was pissed that I missed it. Hell, I hadn't been fondled in over two years.

"It's Sanad."

"Turn on the lights," I pleaded, feeling comfortable enough to move again as I made my way out of the bed.

"No, we don't need lights," Sanad said, using his best seductive voice.

I started to walk around, feeling for a light switch or a lamp. You couldn't see a damn thing. I was afraid and pissed off. I hadn't seen this man in years and I was in a dark room with him after passing out. Something was wrong with this picture.

"You won't find a light switch. This room doesn't have one. I made sure of that."

I was frozen again. What was he gonna do? I thought it best to remain still and prepare for some crazy shit to happen. For all I knew, the room was filled with people that I could not see or hear. At the very least, 10 was probably in there as backup.

Sanad continued, "It's been so long since I've seen you. All I want to do is bond with you; use our voices and our bodies to communicate with each other."

"Our bodies?"

"Yes. I saw you out there and you're so beautiful. I had forgotten how beautiful you are."

His voice, it was so powerful. I had forgotten how the sound of his voice excited me. I adored this man. He was the love of my life. Was he playing with me? I could hear him moving toward me. I put my hands up in front of me so that I could feel him coming. As he got closer, I could smell him, then I finally felt him. He grabbed my hands.

"Don't be afraid. You're safe. The drink the woman gave you was spiked, but it was harmless." I tried to move away. "Wait! I know that was harsh, but it's no mistake that we're both here tonight after all these years."

He stroked my face. I was crying. He kissed away the tears. I couldn't resist him, though I wanted to slap the shit out of him and tell him that if he wanted to fuck, all he had to do was ask. This little game was unnecessary.

My hands began to roam his body and I began to unbutton and remove his clothing. I needed him inside me. After all the sorry bastards I had fucked over the years, trying to recapture what we once had, I figured that I could at least have it again, if only for one night. He owed me that much. I felt like this was a game he was playing, one that I didn't deserve. He and I had shared something special, or so I thought, and this in-the-dark bullshit was just plain weird. Yet and still, I wanted him ten years strong.

"I knew you would be here. I set this up so that you and I could be together. I watched you come in. I've been excited all night, thinking about making love to you."

He was stroking me now. I spread my legs to allow him to go as far as my body would allow him. I didn't have any panties on. He let out an evil chuckle. He always liked when I didn't wear panties. He was still talking, but I wasn't listening.

"Talk to me, Lela. I want to hear your voice."

"I love you," I told him as I kissed his lips. It wasn't a lie and it was all I felt I should say.

"I love you, too."

Those were the last words. Now it was all about our bodies communicating.

He was foreign, yet familiar at the same time. His skin was so soft. I wanted to eat him alive, but I decided I should go at his pace. He was being soft and melodic, grabbing my face in the darkness and placing romantic kisses all over me. I held on tight. I had already removed his jacket and unbuttoned his shirt. Damn, he smelled so good. He took the fingers that were in my pussy moments ago and placed them in his mouth and then in mine. I sucked his fingers as if they were four little dicks. I could feel his big dick against me. I missed him so much. Was I still unconscious? I had dreamed of this. Was I dreaming again?

His rough push against the wall made my nervous thoughts disappear. He wanted to get rough. Now that's what I'm talking about! Our tongues danced in a rough rhythm as I ran my fingers through his curly ringlets, and he roughly grabbed my ass.

"Damn, baby, did you lose some of your thickness?" he asked playfully.

I was embarrassed. "Sorry, I'm not a ten," I sassed back, thinking about his new girlfriend.

"You're a twenty, baby."

He pulled my dress up. I removed his shirt and unbuckled his pants and slid them and his drawers down. I was planning to give him head when he eagerly picked me up and smoothly slid his dick in my wet, tight pussy. No one ever got me as wet and excited as Sanad did. Try as they might, they simply didn't have what he had, and I never loved any of them. We had passion.

He fucked and made love to me—something he was skilled at—against the wall as if my pussy were feeding life force into his dick. Maybe it was the other way around. Lord knows I was in need of life force from any source right then. He slid the top of my dress down and removed my bra with his mouth and hungrily sucked, licked, and bit at my breasts. In this position all I could do was smell the sweet scent of his hair and take every inch of his thick manhood. His rock-hard dick felt so good moving in and out. His hands, God, how I loved his hands; they were so big and so perfect.

I removed his hand from my right breast and began to suck his four little dicks again. I could hear him moan in pleasure. I loved to hear how good my pussy was, translated in his moans and groans. I was tired of being fucked on a wall. I wanted to enjoy his entire body. I pushed him off me.

"What are you doing, baby?" he gasped.

I didn't have anything to say. It was all about action.

I grabbed his hand and guided him to the bed. I turned so my pussy was toward his face and I began to suck his dick. I got it all in my mouth against my gag reflex. I needed it all to fit because I knew this would be the last time. He became lost in my mouth. All I could hear was heavy breathing and gasps for air. I was pleased with myself, as I smiled with his dick in my mouth. I started to use one hand to stroke him as I sucked the head. He began to spank me. I liked that shit. I was dripping wet on his chest and face. He began to finger me, and the sound of his fingers mixed with my juices was more than I could handle. I began to lick his balls and I left no pubic hair untouched as I munched at them while smelling my sweet scent in his hair. He put his face in my wet pussy and I worked it against him with a smack. He came in my mouth for the first time. Ten years ago I would have been cautious, but tonight was the last night for me to show out and try things I'd never done before.

His dick was still hard and I was far from being done with him.

"You swallow now, huh?" he asked as he kissed my sloppy mouth.

In between licks, I managed to let escape, "For you."

"Let's see what else you'll do for me." At that moment a piano began to play a familiar song in the darkness. I jumped, but he held me close. "Don't worry, they can't see us."

"I don't care if they can."

I had assumed someone was in the room besides us, but I

didn't really give a damn. After a few moments of the piano, a woman's voice began to sing. I knew it was 10, so I didn't bother to ask.

"This is our song, remember?" he asked.

I did. It was the love theme from *Romeo + Juliet,* "Kissing You" by Des'ree, sung in the key of 10. Over the years I would pop in the CD, listen to that song, and cry like a baby. It was indeed our song, and as I listened to it in the dark with Sanad in my arms, I began to cry again and so did he. He gently laid me down and began to make love to me as we cried and caressed each other tenderly. Homegirl knew the extended mix because it went on for what seemed like an hour; Sanad and I made up for ten years of life without each other.

We lay there together sticky, sweaty, and stinky with each other's juices all over us, tired as hell, but holding on to each other for dear life as 10 continued to play the melody of our song.

"I'm sorry," Sanad whispered into my ear.

I had no words. That's all I needed to hear. The music stopped and I could hear her walking toward us, then I could feel her on the bed. She lay next to me, stroking my hair, and then . . .

. . . I died in their arms.

Nine months earlier, I had been diagnosed with cancer and was given six months to live, so I was on borrowed time. I prayed to see Sanad before I died, and my wish was granted. Now he will pine for me.

Modern Cinderella

Alice Sturdivant

The annual Stepping Onward and Upward charity dinner is a bore to anyone that usually goes, but for me, a first-timer and eager to try out a new black dress, it was a much needed chance to step into a world that I don't usually get to see. Everybody has seen the black elite in our city: rich, glittering, and eager to catch up to and outdo their white counterparts. This evening's dinner was no different, with uniformed waiters hovering discreetly around the numbered tables. As I was led to my table, I was a little disappointed to see that I was the only person being seated there. My disappointment was only lessened by seeing no less than five men discreetly look at me as I passed their tables, ignoring their dinner partners for a second and wondering who the newcomer was. Although the nouveaux riches pride themselves on being fashionably liberal and egalitarian, it was common knowledge that they are mindful of just whom they let in their midst and whom they don't. The Stepping On, Noses Upward, as they were snickeringly called by those not invited to their closed-ranked soirees, believed firmly that society is not about whom you let in, but whom you keep out.

The chair was far enough away from the podium that I wouldn't have to pretend to pay much attention to the speakers, and—more important—I wouldn't seem too terribly rude when I made my early departure. I couldn't be expected to introduce myself as an intruder—a working-class gatecrasher who had the good fortune to have a friend of a friend give her an invitation—could I? Besides, tonight, mystery would be part of the allure, part of the persona. Tonight, I would be another soft, brown-skinned, well-bred, spoiled beauty who walked with ease in shoes that cost a month's rent and a dress that showed off curves without seeming to. The triple-strand pearl necklace I'd pulled from my sister's jewelry box (and sworn never to lose upon pain of death) complemented my caramel skin to perfection and forced me to hold my head high—but the easy smile I lent to the admiring eyes made me out to be friendly, despite my supposed lineage.

I had been seated by the waiter and was waiting for my merlot, half studying the program below my place setting, when he showed up.

"I'm glad to see someone else from the firm is here." He smiled, his gaze lingering a second longer than was merely polite at the expanse of skin below the necklace.

I smiled back, my Chanel-glossed lips turning upward invitingly, and nodded. "It does seem a trifle empty, doesn't it?"

I wasn't going to correct him on his incorrect assumption that we were from the same company. Years of working *for* men such as this made it easy to pretend I'd spent years working *with* them.

When he sat down, his smile widened appreciatively. "Well, I guess it's just us."

He was handsome, with chocolate brown skin, big, dark eyes that seemed to focus only on me, and a dimple in his left cheek. He had a precise haircut that could only have come from a barber who only took referrals, from the right sort of client. In sunlight, his hair would have shown the beginnings of what his assistant would have described as "distinguished salt-and-pepper," but in the dim light of the Whitney dining room, the little whorls of his hair made me wonder what it would feel like against the bare skin of my thighs. He was a little older than I; midforties, perhaps. Experienced.

"I've seen you somewhere before. Did you come to the Hall of Fame induction?"

What a line, but, hey, I'd bite. He was good-looking, and so was I; plus I only had one night to play at this.

"No . . . I don't usually come to these things."

The waiter brought my wine. I caught my tablemate eyeing my hands as I reached for the stem of the glass. I was glad I'd done my own manicure before I left. I looked at his mouth; kissable, definitely.

"Are you from Charlotte? I could have sworn I'd seen you in the office . . . the Durham office, perhaps?" he went on, trying to place me.

While he talked, I studied his eyes, his suit: designer and expertly tailored. The watch that peeked from below his cuff was something French and, while not diamond-studded, had enough flash to let me know it wasn't cheap. He had the air of a high executive, not a mere businessman; usually just the type that I would consider out of my league. But not tonight.

"I don't think we met at the Durham office; perhaps one of

the smaller gallery openings?" I found myself licking my lips, just to see if he would follow the quick movement of my tongue. Something about his cologne was making me pleasantly warm.

His dark eyes caught the pink tip of my tongue against the burgundy shine of my mouth, and I wanted to grin with the knowledge. But even one generation from the farm, I knew better than to show my hand. I sipped my wine.

"What are you drinking?" His eyes were skimming down the wineglass, examining my fingertips, the delicate skin of my wrist. Again, I wanted to squirm in my chair. My clit was quite interested in the firm lines of his mouth and the possibilities it held. I gave him the name of the wine, and he motioned to the waiter and murmured, "I'll have what she's having." His eyes didn't leave me.

The waiter brought his wine, and he reached and took it with his left hand. At first the gleam of the gold band on his ring finger startled me, then I grinned to myself. He'd had practice—we'd been talking for about ten minutes and I hadn't even seen it. So much for discreetly slipping him my number, I thought.

He inquired about my family, still trying to place me, and I lied smoothly that most of my family was in Charleston, by way of Barbados. I saw him imagining years of scandalous interracial relationships that ultimately lent me my deep honey-brown skin and my sandy brown hair, now arranged in a pretty, curly bob. I quirked my mouth at his open study and did not look away. He licked his lips and I could feel the flicker of an imaginary tongue on my right nipple, right below the mole.

"Well, for the next time we meet, why don't I tell you my name," I purred, offering my hand and introducing myself. Let him try to look me up in the city social registers; who cared after tonight, anyway? "Alicia Dwyer."

He took my hand and shook it softly, his eyes still boring into me. "Kenneth. Kenneth Prince."

I didn't know the name and was relieved for a second. His hands were soft but capable, obviously unused to manual labor. Those blunt, long fingers were holding mine a little too gently and a little longer than necessary. Lucky Mrs. Prince, home all by herself, I thought. His thumb rubbed the delicate webbing between my thumb and forefinger. Lucky Mrs. Prince, indeed. I looked into those dark eyes and, for a second, wondered if he was the type to close his eyes when he's deep in a woman's pussy, or if he preferred to watch everything. His eyes stared back into mine, an unmistakable invitation.

He was a looker, in more ways than one. He'd *definitely* watch.

The waiter brought the artfully arranged niçoise salad first course, and we dropped our hands, neither of us having the grace to look guilty. The conversation during the soup course was unfailingly polite: politics, work. I told him about my writing, and he seemed impressed. Apparently writing as a hobby to help out "the masses" is an acceptable pastime for young black rich folks nowadays.

He was the CFO of the company; I had no response for that. We talked about the banquet, whom he knew, what I thought of the dinner. He was charmed that I had issues with people who patted themselves on the back every time an "underprivileged youth" made it to college, not stopping to consider the reasons for the lack of privilege itself. Apparently being a bleeding heart was also fashionable. I was too busy enjoying the low rumble of his voice and the tingling brushes of his superfine wool trousers against my stockinged knee to feel patron-ized. We all but ignored the introductory speaker.

Our seats were right next to each other, and I realized that we'd been leaning together, talking softly, our heads bowed to-ward each other. Almost like conspirators. I imagined that we looked like lovers, and just then, we looked at each other and realized . . .

We could be.

I quickly batted away that thought, but it aroused me, this man, his wife away with their children (two boys, he'd proudly admitted after I'd pointedly looked at his ring and given him an accusing look), the tastefully discreet hotel staff, the immacu-late rooms upstairs, the fact that these things happen all the time at such dinners, that he was still openly flirting with me and I him, in our polite conversation but wondering if the other would, if given the chance, do what we were thinking. . . .

The look he gave me made me realize he was thinking the exact same thing. He was remembering my hands, wondering how they'd felt on his skin, looking at my mouth, wondering if I'd just kiss him or if I'd wrap the glossed lips around his dick, too. I was wondering if he would fuck me against the door of the room, on the bathroom counter, where I'd swipe all the prettily packaged minibottles of shampoo and soap off when I came, if he'd eat me until I begged him to stop, if the thought of his wife would enter his mind when we fucked doggie-style in front of the mirror.

His dimple deepened.

"You have the most delectable mouth, Miss Dwyer." His breath was warm against my collarbone.

"And you have beautiful hands, Mr. Prince." I blushed (pret-tily, mind you—even for us working-class girls, Southern habits die hard) and was terribly grateful for the waiter asking us if we wanted poultry or beef. "The first," I answered, probably too hastily.

Mr. Prince smoothly ordered, then looked at me thoughtfully and whispered, "You're an intriguing woman, Alicia. I'd give anything to kiss you right now. Anywhere. Everywhere."

At first, I wasn't sure if I'd heard him. Then, I wasn't sure if I should slap him. I wasn't sure if he'd seen through my high-class act and made me out for a cheap whore. But when I looked at him, shocked, he drew back, his eyes apologetic. I turned from him quickly, as if offended, then bit my lip as if considering something. But it was an act; I needed to distract myself from my now throbbing clit and my damp pussy, oversensitive mouth, and the fact that I was almost ready to pull up the fine linen tablecloth for him to get down there and have at it. I angled my head as if politely listening to the speaker, but glanced over, catching the want in his eyes. I only half hoped he didn't see my nipples pushing out against the satin of my bra and the thin jersey of the dress.

The salad had disappeared, barely touched, and was replaced by a beautiful-looking quail in some sort of sauce. I'd stopped caring about food fifteen minutes ago; some sort of record. I couldn't resist. I squirmed in my seat, pressing my slick thighs together in vain.

"I'm sorry if I offended you earlier, but please do that again," he murmured.

I hadn't noticed that my squirming had raised my knee-length dress to thigh-high. The huskiness of his voice made me smile. I shifted again, slower this time, letting my weight shift from one hip to the other, rolling as if I were already riding his dick. The skirt shifted upward again, and I thought I heard him groan. I daintily picked up my wineglass and sipped, ignoring the feel of the backs of my thighs against the embroidered chair cushion. My eyes were blankly directed toward the podium.

"My, my . . . stockings." He sounded closer now; when had he moved his chair? Truth was, I couldn't find a pair of panty hose that wasn't already run and had to settle on the stockings and garter I'd bought last Valentine's Day.

"How gauche of you to mention." I was surprised my voice didn't waver. I could have been talking about the weather.

"I'd be happy to make it up to you," he purred, settling his fingertips ever so lightly on my knee. It took significant effort not to jump completely out of my seat. His hand was steady, confident.

"I see," I answered more calmly than I thought I could, and uncrossed my ankles, letting my knees fall away an inch or two.

Let him work for it, I thought, somehow knowing he'd enjoy the challenge. His fingertips spread until his entire palm was over my knee, radiating warmth that spread up my thighs and seemed to radiate right through my belly.

"You haven't touched your dinner," I challenged, and nodded toward his plate.

"There are other things I'd rather eat."

"Greedy, aren't you?"

I spread my legs another inch. He took full advantage, circling his thumb against the mesh of my stocking. His touch seemed to echo throughout points on my body: my nipples, the sensitive hollow below my throat, the aching core of my pussy.

"You have no idea," he promised, his voice conspiratorial.

His fingers inched higher, now at the top of my thigh. If the lights had come up, the sight of his sleeve disappearing beneath the white tablecloth would have been, at best, hard to explain. I inched my legs apart more, finally hooking my feet around the curved feet of the chair. My spine was no longer that of a finishing-school graduate; I'd pushed my back into the cushioned back of the chair. My quivering thighs were giving my anticipation away.

When his hand left my thigh to hover over the heat of my waiting pussy, I thought that I would kill him. When he used his thumb and pinkie to lock my thighs against any thought of them closing against his fingers and flicked my clit delicately with the fingertip of his middle finger through my panties, I could have kissed him. When he pushed aside the light fabric of my panties and did it again, I pushed a forkful of quail into my mouth to keep from crying out.

"Is it good?" he asked, clearly not referring to the well-seasoned poultry.

"Mm, hmm," I answered, chewing thoughtfully.

His fingers were making brushing motions, up and down the folds there, painting the flesh with my arousal.

"I find that when it's good and hot like this, it's really enjoyable." The tip of his ring finger pushed inside me briefly, then returned to brushing the hard, slick bud. "Don't you?"

"Absolutely." I took another bite and eased my hips forward to give him better access. Those dark eyes flickered toward mine, and I met them with a coy smile. "I see you're a connoisseur."

His finger penetrated me again, joined by his middle finger. "Oh, yes," he groaned, a little loudly.

Someone glanced over and nodded approvingly, adding an "Amen!" Apparently Kenneth had just strongly agreed to something the speaker had said. I grinned in the dim light and squeezed his fingers gently.

"Enjoying the speech, are we?" I couldn't resist.

Kenneth answered with a graceful stroke of his fingers, expertly pulling them almost entirely out, then gliding them back in. "The reverend is a brilliant orator," he purred, doing it again, slowly so I could feel the ridges in his fingers. "A master of his craft." He was sluicing in and out now easily, matching his words with his strokes. I imagined his hand must have been soaked. "He enjoys the pleasure of weaving a story, letting the audience's interest build, and ultimately . . ." He paused for effect, his fingers still fucking me slowly and steadily while I tried not to pump my hips against him or beg him for more. "Bringing his tale to a climax." His voice trailed off into a low moan as he felt the beginning flickers of my pussy around his fingers.

"I don't know," I huffed, trying to keep my breathing even. "Sometimes I prefer a more direct route." I shifted again, widening the V of my legs and pushing his manicured fingers deeper, showing him the spot that would push me over.

"True," he agreed, pumping his fingers into me. I could actually hear the soft, wet sounds of his palm slapping against my mound. "A more forceful and direct route . . ." He broke off, concentrating.

"Can be . . . certainly . . . better . . . yes . . . more satisfactory," I panted, not caring that I was giving up my cool, and clutched the arms of the chair, using them for slight leverage to lift my hips up and down on his hand. I could feel the familiar tickle of the beginning of my orgasm, the buzz in my head, the tightening of my muscles around his pumping fingers.

"Yes . . . ," he growled gruffly. Impatient. Wanting to see. I'd been right; his eyes were devouring me—the speaker, the audience, the charity dinner, completely forgotten. "You're so wet, honey, come for me." The words were low, almost slurred, as if he was as drunk from my pleasure as I was.

And I gasped with his request, my body rigid, hands clamped around the arms of my chair as if for dear life as his fingers twisted wetly inside me, his thumb pressing against the side of my clit, wringing every last drop of cream from my pussy. I bit my lip hard, fighting to not scream or cry out. My eyes fluttered shut as the initial shock wore off, and I felt his fingers ease from me after the last of the aftershocks and tremors of my thighs had ended.

At the burst of seemingly thunderous applause, my eyes shot open, fearing that we had been caught. I looked over to Kenneth with wide eyes, but he met mine with searing want. He was clapping along with the other diners, the digits of his right hand still glistening with my juice. His applause, though, was directed at me, along with a deep-dimpled grin.

"Dessert," the waiter announced gently, sliding a dish of a raspberry mousse in front of each of us. He retreated, looking curiously at the high color in my cheeks and the light beads of sweat on Kenneth's upper lip. I shifted in my seat, pulling my dress down discreetly with each wiggle of my hips. My thighs were damp, and my panties soaked. I looked over to see my dinner companion dip the blunt tip of his middle finger into the crest of the pink mousse and bring it to his mouth. I fought not to gape as he brought his tongue out to taste that cream— and my own. He smiled.

"Delicious," he all but sighed. His eyes were locked on mine. "I'd love to taste more." An open invitation. His hand was resting on the tabletop again, and I glanced down at the ring, shiny and forbidding. This had been fun, but Kenneth Prince Charming, lucky Mrs. Prince, and the two little heirs was more of a story than I was willing to take on. Not even with his magical fingers and probably even more magical tongue and dick. I'd be kicking myself tonight, but I didn't want any "ever afters" with him, not even those that involved me riding his fine ass into the sunset. I held my hand out to his. The announcer was back, saying something about the charity auction after dinner. He took my hand as gently as before, his eyes expectant. My honeysweet smile, I hoped, would soften the refusal. "It was nice meeting you, Kenneth," I purred softly, barely audible over the closing remarks.

He nodded, disappointed, but still smiling. His dimple deepened. "And you as well."

I stood up and took my leave, letting my hips sway just a little extra for Kenneth Prince's benefit. I smiled on my way to the coatroom to quickly collect my wrap. A part of me considered leaving a dramatic token—a shoe? A room key? A phone number? But I shook my head and walked out onto the street to hail a cab back to my real life. Sometimes princes were better left in fairy tales.

Daydreamin'

Romeo Walker

Devon sat in class listening to the teacher drone on, his thoughts not on the Shakespeare play that he was supposed to be reading. Rather they were on many different things: music, women, and money.

"Mr. White, what is your opinion of Puck?" the teacher asked.

Devon looked down at his book, drawn back into the play by the question. He searched hurriedly for a passage.

"It's your opinion, Mr. White," the teacher quipped, and walked around the room, coming to a stop beside Devon's desk.

Devon snapped his head up to look at the balding, middle-aged Latino teacher. He stared hard at him. The teacher barely took notice of Devon's hard looks as he again paced around the class.

"Puck, sir, what do you think of him?"

"I don't know—"

"He's a troublemaker!"

Devon turned to see who had interrupted him. His brown eyes fell upon Shantrice Elway. She sat there looking at him with an air of indifference. Shantrice had been in several of his classes. They had spoken on occasion and had even exchanged phone numbers early on, but there was nothing there. She was pretty, Devon thought, but not really a dime.

"Puck seems to like to see comedic things happening in the play," explained Shantrice. She smiled meekly at Devon.

"That's good, Ms. Elway," the teacher said. "When he sprinkles his dust, strange things happen."

Shantrice beamed. Devon glowered. He ran his hand over the waves in his hair. Devon did not like to be discredited or have someone show him up.

"Mr. Devon, maybe you should study a little harder or come to class when you really want to be here."

Devon sighed audibly. He heard snickers and giggles from the back of the classroom.

The class ended a short time later. Devon stalked out of the classroom, determined to get away from the embarrassment. He hurried and shoved his books into his bag.

The movement of the students startled Shantrice. She looked around for Devon. He was angry, she could tell; over what though, she did not know. *That's not good,* Shantrice thought to herself.

Shantrice had harbored a crush on Devon since she had first laid eyes on him. That first time being when she had seen him enter Dr. Green's English 101 class ten minutes late, standing in the doorway looking around.

The latecomer was dressed in a white Dallas Mavericks jersey, black jeans shorts, and white K-Swiss sneakers. All the seats were taken, except for the one next to her. For almost an hour, she had to sit in class inhaling his cologne, becoming more intoxicated with his scent. When he spoke, his gruff voice sounded beautiful to her. Shantrice was so preoccupied that she didn't hear the professor at all during that first class period. Her panties threatened to be overwhelmed. They exchanged smiles throughout the hour. However, when class ended, Devon exited into the waiting arms of some light-skinned cutie. Shantrice surveyed the girl as she walked past. The girl was undeniably beautiful, dressed in a baby blue halter top emblazoned with the UNC logo across the front, a cream-colored miniskirt, and baby blue heels. Her long, curly hair was pulled into a ponytail that flowed down her back. To Shantrice, the girl looked as if she had just stepped out of a music video. Shantrice went back to her dorm room that day and eased her urging with her eight-inch, black dildo. Devon's face, smile, and scent crept into her imagination, spurring her to satisfaction.

Sitting right next to Devon all semester was a torment. He began to appear in her dreams, romancing her, but ultimately leaving her for the nameless beauty in the Tarheels outfit.

Shantrice broke from the daydream, wondering how many times she would let him pass her by. How many times would she wonder what it would be like to have his hands roaming all over her body or to kiss him deeply on his full lips. She fixed her bra, propping up her already ample cleavage and raising her skirt slightly. Shantrice strode from the classroom, intent on her mission to find Devon. She stalked down the hallway purposefully, ignoring the looks from other men and their cat-calls and whispers.

Devon stormed out of the building. He was pissed about class, not just the smart-aleck teacher, but also Shantrice.

"What the hell was her problem?" Devon muttered to himself.

Devon thought back to the first class he had had with Shantrice—English 101. He had searched for a seat and eventually sat down beside the cocoa-brown-skinned female. While not on the scale of Narissa, Shantrice was nonetheless pretty. Narissa had been his girl for more than a year. Shantrice smiled at him invitingly as he walked over to sit down. Throughout the period, Devon noticed Shantrice continually fixing her breasts, causing them to sit up more prominently in her peach-colored, button-down blouse. The twin cocoa-brown mounds of flesh looked tantalizing. Devon's dick sprang to life in response. He began shifting in the chair, trying to hide his growing erection. One time Devon spied Shantrice staring at him longingly. She blushed and turned away.

Devon stifled a laugh. He peered at her again. She was shapely, not model material like Narissa. This girl was more "down-home" thick in all the right places. If he didn't have Narissa, he would holla at her. Right after class, Devon got formally introduced to his pretty "neighbor" as she spoke softly. Devon found out her name was Shantrice; she was from Philly and lived on campus. They exchanged numbers before they exited class. Much to his chagrin, Narissa was waiting for him outside. As he embraced Narissa, he watched Shantrice walk down the hallway, giving the couple a glance before stepping into the elevator.

Devon now headed into the library. Right then he needed someplace to cool down. The library was somewhat empty. He looked around, searching for a secluded, unoccupied study booth. He finally found one, back near the encyclopedias.

Devon had been moving fast, making it difficult to keep up

with him. Shantrice did her best by catching fleeting glimpses of his khaki, one-shouldered bag. She watched him enter the library. She trailed him inside and saw him take a seat at a solitary study booth.

Shantrice stopped right inside the double glass doors of the library. She wondered if she could go through with what she was planning. Her nerves were all jumbled. However, her hormones were working her into a fever pitch. She steadied herself, then glided over to the booth. Devon was completely unaware of her. Shantrice stood back and marveled at him.

"You are so sexy when you're mad," Shantrice breathed into his ear.

Devon moved slightly. He leaned back, his head coming to rest in Shantrice's ample bust. He looked up at her.

"You tried to show me up," he shot at her.

"No, I tried to help you out."

"If you would have let me handle it, I would have came at him with something intelligent," he gruffed.

"Next time I will," Shantrice shot back. She looked at him incredulously. *Arrogant bastard,* she thought to herself. *Even like this he's still sexy.*

Devon's head was still resting on her chest. The scent of his cologne was overpowering. It silently urged her into action. Shantrice laid her hand on the side of Devon's head, slowly massaging his ear.

Devon shifted slightly. He wanted to be angry, but her hand on his head was making it difficult. His ears were sensitive and she was massaging one. Her touch was magical. It was as if she knew exactly where to touch and how much pressure to apply.

Shantrice stood on rubbery legs. The skin-to-skin contact with Devon was powerful. His head resting against her breasts was causing her nipples to harden. Her other hand snaked down to his shoulder.

"You know, I've waited a long time to have you like this," she breathed.

"You have?"

"Yeah, but you've always had someone else," Shantrice whispered in his ear, her lips grazing the tip.

Devon's hand found her leg and slowly slid up her thigh. He wanted to test her. *Let's see how far she'll let me go,* he thought.

Shantrice inhaled sharply. Devon's hand was raising goose bumps, as well as shocking her, as it moved slowly up her thigh. She moaned softly in his ear. His hand eventually found her pussy, which was thoroughly wet. Devon used a finger to play with her and slowly drew it across her lips.

"Ddddaaammmnnn," she moaned. Shantrice grabbed his shoulder to steady herself.

Devon guided her into his lap. Shantrice felt his erect dick poking her ass through his jeans.

"Where did all this come from?" he asked.

Shantrice closed her eyes and leaned into the side of his neck and began planting kisses on it. "I've always wanted you, from the first time I saw you. I found out that you and Narissa weren't talking anymore, so I figured this was my chance."

Her kisses eventually found their way around to his lips. Her hands caressed his body.

"I'm going to take what I want," she breathed heavily. She tugged at his bottom lip playfully.

His lips were as soft as she had imagined them to be. *If this is not heaven,* she thought, *this is the closest thing to it.*

"We've got to stop before someone catches us," Devon said, breathing heavily and breaking the kiss.

"Be bold; let's do this right here," she said, stroking his dick through his pants. "I see someone is ready to get it on."

Devon leaned back. Shantrice's attention was causing his dick to strain to escape from the confines of his boxers and jeans. He was becoming intoxicated with her attention. Somewhere, he thought he heard Maxwell's "Fortunate" playing softly. His mind was ablaze with ideas.

"Right here?"

"Yeah, right here."

Shantrice continued to kiss his neck, weaving a trail of kisses from his neck to the bottom of his earlobe. She placed Devon's finger that had been in her pussy in her mouth. She sucked on his finger, taking delight in watching him squirm in the chair. The taste of her essence and his attention was becoming intoxicating.

Devon's other hand climbed up to her breast and began to rub her nipple. He twirled it between his fingers and looked around. Most of the other people in the library could not see him and Shantrice. However, he was still not satisfied. Shantrice had gotten busy on freeing his straining dick from its confines. When it finally sprang free, surprised by the size, she eagerly began to slurp on it, trying to take it fully in her mouth. Devon moaned loudly. He looked down at Shantrice, who tried to smile with her mouth full of his dick.

"Come on," Devon said, looking around, excited.

Shantrice rose and followed Devon. He led her past the first few rows of encyclopedias, until he was sure that they could not be seen. No sooner had they gone down the aisle than Shantrice attacked his dick again. She was on her knees, her lips wrapped around his engorged dick. Devon spotted a stool and leaned back against it. Shantrice kept sucking.

Devon lolled his head back. He had never experienced something like this.

Shantrice could see that she was having the desired effect on Devon. This was what she had always wanted—to seduce him. Just to take him and fuck him, the way she knew he needed to be fucked. Devon was trying to feel her breasts as she sucked his dick. Finally she felt that familiar trembling in his leg.

"I'ma swallow all of this," she whispered seductively, to Devon's amazement.

He came all in her mouth. Shantrice remembered bragging to her friends that she would never swallow any man's cum. However, right there and then, it felt right. Surprisingly, the taste was not bad. Then she went right back to sucking on his dick, not allowing it to go soft.

"Oh, no, you are not going to get off this easy," Shantrice said. "I've waited a long time for this. I've waited a long time to get ahold of you and I'm going to enjoy every minute I have of this."

She held his dick in her hands. After she was sure it would not go down, she stood up.

Devon eased her back onto the padded stool. Then he began making a trail of kisses from her breasts down to her stomach. At her stomach, Devon stopped to pay attention to her belly ring. He licked the area around the hole as Shantrice whined in delight and her leg trembled slightly. Devon smiled, then resumed his erotic travels. His kisses brought him to her perfectly shaved love box. Devon laid several kisses around her clit, purposefully avoiding it to build up her longing.

"Devon . . . ," Shantrice moaned. "Please, ba-bbbyyyy."

Finally hearing what he wanted, Devon laid kisses on her clit. He eased his tongue around her lips, tracing patterns.

Shantrice squirmed on the stool. Her breath was coming in ragged gasps. Her chest rose and fell quickly, in an increasing crescendo. Devon stuck his tongue all the way into her pussy. He inhaled her scent and savored it. Devon knew she couldn't hold on much longer. Her legs trembled, and then she came, gushing all over his tongue and down onto his face.

Devon rose to his feet, grabbed Shantrice's hips, and bent her over the stool. He pushed her skirt up around her waist. Shantrice wasn't wearing any panties, so that was even less that he had to deal with.

"Since you've been wantin' this, I'm going to give it to you," Devon whispered in her ear.

Shantrice was breathing hard. She was delighted and excited. She knew what was coming; just not when. To her, Devon seemed to be taking a long time. As she was about to turn around, Shantrice felt Devon stuff his engorged dick into her. She inhaled sharply. It felt as if he was trying to push his dick all the way up into her stomach.

"Damn, boy," she groaned. "Yeah, do it like that."

Devon had to control himself; he didn't want to cum too quickly. He wanted to savor this feeling. He wanted to show her all that she had been missing. Devon leaned in and kissed her neck. Gradually he began to build up force, until he was pummeling her from behind. The pain and pleasure was an intoxicating mix, the force of which threatened to tip over the stool. Her pussy tightened around his dick. It felt like a warm, wet vise that threatened to milk him dry. It took all his control not to cum right then and there.

"Come on, fuck me," Shantrice moaned, urging him on. "Hit that shit!"

Devon, spurned on by her urgings, quickened his pace. Finally Devon released.

Shantrice's scream was muffled by her blouse, which covered her mouth, as he came at the same time. He slumped over Shantrice's back. Sweat from his head dripped onto her back.

"Damn," he exclaimed, thoroughly drained but satisfied. Beads of sweat dotted his forehead.

Shantrice rose shakily to her feet. This is what she had dreamed about for so long. Devon made a helluva lover. She didn't know what kind of relationship they could have or if they'd have one, but the sex was definitely the bomb.

"Come on, let's go. Study time is over," she said. "You need to be able to tell the class tomorrow about Oberon and Titania."

A light touch on Shantrice's shoulder brought her back to reality. The teacher smiled at her. She could feel her panties were wet. Shantrice stood up and looked around for Devon. She spied him easing out of the class.

Damn, what a dream, she thought to herself as she hurried and packed her bag and headed out after her target.

An Arresting, Intoxicating Situation

Ms. Lovelie Ladie

Evette had been having a great evening at her friend Karen's birthday party. Evette had had more than a few drinks to celebrate the event and get into the groove.

Evette and Karen were grade-school teachers who became friends while at the same school. Today was Karen's twenty-eighth birthday and the party was on. Evette arrived at the party at 8:00 p.m. and it was now 1:00 a.m. Evette decided it was time to leave because her man, John, was at home waiting for her. Evette said her good-nights to all of her friends and left.

When Evette got into her car, she called John to tell him she was on her way home. He said he'd be ready and waiting, and this excited Evette. She couldn't wait to get to John. Evette looked in her mirror to check if her eyes were red. They were, so she pulled out her eyedrops from her purse and placed a couple in each eye to clear them up.

Evette started the car and pulled off. The club was only a couple of miles from her house. She figured she'd be home in no time. Flying down the highway to get home to John, she was moving so fast she didn't notice she'd passed a police car. She realized it when she saw the flashing lights behind her and heard the sirens blaring. Evette was scared but pulled over on the long, dark highway. There wasn't any traffic tonight. Once she pulled over, she checked her eyes again and they were still a little red, but she thought they should be okay since it was dark. Evette rolled down her windows as the two officers approached her car. One officer came over to her side, and the other officer approached the passenger side.

Evette nervously said, "Good evening, Officers. What's the problem?"

The officer on her side said, "Ma'am, we clocked you doing seventy in a fifty-five zone."

"Oh, Officer, I didn't realize I was going that fast."

"Well, ma'am, you were. Can I see your driver's license, registration, and insurance card, please?"

Evette took her information out of her purse. While she was doing this, the other officer shone his flashlight into her car. He looked around and saw a party favor on the passenger seat.

Evette looked at the first officer's badge. "Yes, Calvin, here is my information."

Calvin took it and went back to his car. The other officer followed, suggesting that they perform a Breathalyzer test. Calvin agreed and they both walked back over to Evette's car.

Calvin said, "Ma'am, we'll need you to take a Breathalyzer test to check your alcohol level."

"What! Why? I'm fine. Can't you tell?"

"We understand, ma'am, but under the circumstances, this is something we need to do," the second officer stated.

"Officer, what's your name?"

"Ma'am, my name is Gregory or Officer Wilson."

"Well, Gregory, I'm just fine. I don't drive drunk!" Evette said in a nasty tone.

"Okay, but we still have to check for ourselves. You'd be surprised at how little alcohol you actually have to consume to raise your blood alcohol level," Gregory stated.

Calvin handed Evette the Breathalyzer. She reluctantly breathed into it. Evette didn't know what to expect, but she hoped it would be alright. She didn't want something like this on her record, and she was extremely nervous as Calvin and Gregory talked at their police car.

She became even more anxious as the two officers approached once again. Her heart dropped as they got closer.

"Ma'am, your level is above the legal limit and we have to take you in," Calvin said, opening Evette's door.

"Make sure it's locked up before you get out, ma'am," Gregory chimed in.

"Officers, please, no! I'm a grade-school teacher and I don't need or want something like this on my record," Evette pleaded as she got out of the car.

"Well, ma'am, you should have thought about that before you got behind the wheel. Driving while intoxicated is against the law. We have no choice but to take you in," Gregory said sharply.

"I promise never to do this ever again. Just please don't take me in."

Standing outside her car, Evette suddenly felt sick. She leaned over and Calvin came over to her to see if she was alright.

"Ma'am, are you okay?"

Evette pulled Calvin to her and began kissing him passionately. Calvin tried to pull away from her, but Evette pulled him back. Gregory walked over to them to intercede. Gregory pulled Evette off Calvin. Evette turned to Gregory and began kissing him while she held on to Calvin with one hand. Gregory kissed Evette back and began to press into her against the car. Evette had placed her hand on Calvin's groin and began massaging it. Calvin leaned back and enjoyed the feel of her hand on him.

Gregory stopped. "Look, we can't do this here. We have to get off the road."

Calvin agreed. "Yes, we don't want anyone to see us. There's a road behind these bushes; we can go back there."

"Yeah, let's do that," Gregory agreed.

The three of them got into the police car and drove to the back of the road where no one would be able to see what was going on. Calvin got out of the car first, then Evette, and lastly Gregory.

Calvin leaned against the car and unzipped his pants as Evette bent over in front of him. Evette began to stroke his hardness with her hands as she blew on his tip. Slowly Evette placed Calvin's stiff dick into her mouth and began to suck it. Gregory got behind Evette and pulled up her skirt and slid her panties to the side. Gregory inserted his rock-hard dick into her juice box.

Evette yelled out, "Oh, shit!"

Gregory was rather large and his entrance hurt Evette. Gregory began to assault Evette's overflowing box with his large tool. Evette began flinching from the pain each time Gregory pierced her hot pot.

Calvin grabbed Evette's head and inserted his hardness

back into her mouth. He was beginning to feel left out. Evette damn near swallowed up Calvin's dick as Gregory hit her pussy so hard she fell forward onto Calvin. This drove Calvin crazy. He began to thrust his stiffness into her mouth. Evette's mouth was soaking wet, and this feeling was so sweet to Calvin. Gregory continued to pummel into Evette's melting pot. Evette's pussy felt as if it were ripping from Gregory's large dick. Gregory pulled his rigidness out, wanting Evette to suck it for him. He came around in front of Evette, and she took a deep breath and inhaled Gregory's long, fat hardness deep into her throat.

Evette almost gagged from Gregory's size.

Gregory laughed. "Take your time. It's okay."

Evette slowed down to allow herself to get used to his size so she wouldn't choke. Calvin went behind Evette and entered her. Evette began to bounce against Calvin as he began hammering into Evette. Her wetness massaged his stiffness and caused him to strike into her harder. This felt good to Evette. She kept in time with Calvin as she continued to suck Gregory's dick. Gregory was holding Evette by the back of her head, keeping her going at a pace that he was enjoying. Calvin slid his dick slowly out of Evette's pussy and slid it across her ass. Calvin rubbed his tip across her opening and prepped her for entry. He inserted his thumb and stretched her opening. Calvin did this until she loosened up enough for him to enter, then he eased his hardness into her ass. Evette loved this feeling. She enjoyed anal sex.

Evette almost forgot where she was; she began to reach back and grab Calvin's ass and pulled him to her. She was yelling. "Yes, fuck me! Fuck me! Damn, I love dick in my ass!"

Calvin did as he was told and started hitting her ass harder.

Gregory was still in Evette's mouth. He said to Evette, "Suck this dick like you love it."

Evette got into sucking Gregory's dick as she enjoyed the pleasure from Calvin being in her hot, tight ass. This was exciting to her, having a dick in her mouth and one in her ass. The three of them were having a great time as all were receiving pleasures that they liked. Evette wanted to try Gregory's big dick in her ass. She wanted to see if she could handle him.

Evette stopped sucking Gregory's dick and said, "Gregory, would you like to fuck me in my ass?"

Before she realized what was happening, Gregory was behind her getting himself ready for entry. Evette said, "Wait, Gregory! You have to go slow. Your dick is too big; take your time."

Gregory listened and began to ease his large member into her tight, bubbling ass. Evette held on to Calvin's legs and she tried to relax as Gregory entered her. She couldn't believe how much pressure and pain she was feeling. Evette tried to breathe slowly and steadily to calm herself as he penetrated deeper into her ass. Then Gregory eased out and went back into her even farther than before. Evette gasped and inhaled as she felt the pressure from his reentering her. Gregory grabbed Evette by her waist and slammed into her.

Evette screamed, "No, not yet! Slow down!"

Gregory wasn't listening; the feeling had overtaken him and he was in the zone. He slammed into her, then out, then bam! Back in. Evette's legs were weakening and she could barely stand up. Calvin was holding her up as Gregory rammed into her.

Evette pleaded, "Gregory! Please cum! I can't handle you! Please cum! Please!"

Gregory answered, "This is what you wanted, remember?"

"Yes, but it's too much!"

"Alright, but to cum I'm gonna have to slam a little harder than I am to get it out."

Evette shouted, "I don't care! Just cum fast! Please!"

Gregory began to beat her ass up harder and faster until he could no longer hold it. "Oh shit! Yes! Damn, I'm cumming! I'm cumming!" Gregory said as he lost all control.

Evette was happy to hear him say those words. Gregory pulled out as he bust his nut all over Evette's ass.

Now Calvin needed relief. Calvin got behind Evette and asked, "Are you ready?"

Evette, still panting from the hurting she'd taken from Gregory, answered, "Yes, I'm ready."

Hearing that, Calvin entered Evette's waiting ass. This gave Evette a little relief. She could handle Calvin's size, although her ass was still hurting from having Gregory inside her. As Evette began to relax, she started pumping back onto Calvin. This caused Calvin to thrust harder into Evette as he slid into her wetness and felt it surrounding him. He was getting into the groove so he could cum. He held on to Evette as he fucked her harder and faster, wanting release and needing to cum.

Evette was helping him by pushing back against him and saying, "Yeah, baby, work this ass! That's right, fuck the shit out of me!"

Calvin did exactly that as he pounded away until he could no longer hold it. Calvin pulled out and banged his dick against Evette's ass, as he was cumming all over it. Calvin released Evette and she fell against the car. Evette was worn-out from the ass whipping she had endured.

Gregory and Calvin fixed their uniforms as Evette straightened her clothes. They were all out of breath and weak.

Evette asked the two officers, "Is everything okay? Am I alright now?"

Calvin and Gregory answered in unison, "Hell, yeah! But don't let it happen again!"

Gregory added, "Yeah, 'cause I don't think you could handle any more of this dick."

They all laughed as they got back into the police car to go back onto the highway to Evette's car.

Evette was on her way again, being careful not to exceed the speed limit. She checked her cell phone and saw that John had called several times. She didn't know what she could tell him, but she knew she had to think of something before she got home. She called her friend Monica, who lived only a couple of blocks from her, to ask if she could come over. She told Monica she needed to get cleaned up before she went home because she was a mess. Monica was okay with that but wanted to know why and from what.

"What did you do? With whom did you do it? Why didn't you get cleaned up where you were?"

"I'll tell you when I get there. It's kind of a long story, Monica. But I'll explain it all to you when I see you," Evette replied.

"Shit, alright, but I want all the details. Don't leave anything out. Hurry up; I'll be waiting."

"Alright, I'll see you in a few. I'm not too far from you."

The two hung up and Monica waited by her door. When Evette arrived, she explained everything to Monica. Monica was surprised, knowing how laid-back Evette had always been.

"Damn, girl, you got a lot of freak in you, but I ain't mad at ya. Shit, you did what you had to do. We all have to make sacrifices in life to get what we want or to keep what we have," Monica stated, rolling her eyes and snapping her fingers.

"Girl, I gotta go. John has been blowing up my phone. I have to think of something to tell him."

"Damn, do I have to help you with everything? Tell John you stopped by here and you lost track of time, listening to me ramble on about my screwed-up relationship. Tell him I needed a friend because I'm fucked up over something that happened between me and Cedric," Monica told Evette as she headed for the door.

"Yeah, that sounds good. But, what about not answering my cell?"

"We were upstairs and you left your phone downstairs when you took off your coat. Okay?"

"Thanks, Monica! I don't know what I would do without you. You're always there when I need you."

Evette rushed out the door to go home to John, hoping that he would believe her. She was so nervous she was shaking as she put her key in the ignition. *Here goes,* she thought as she began driving home.

Head of the Class

B. F. Redd

I had finally accomplished my goal. I had graduated from college summa cum laude, and I had been published in a well-respected journal. I had spent the last four years with my nose to the grindstone, and as a result my social life had suffered. Sad to say, I only counted as my friends my fellow bookish classmates whom I had also been in a type of competition with ever since we had found one another in the same section of the library our freshman year. Yes, it would be safe for anyone to assume that party animals we were not. But full-ride scholarships are not to be squandered, even by "brainiacs" such as myself. So I worked my tail off and made my parents and instructors proud.

This was going to be the beginning of a new chapter in my life, so I thought about the conclusion of the last one. From now on I would be sought after and traveling in more sophisticated circles, so I might not ever have such a moment of freedom again. I would soon be working my way up some career ladder, trying to burst through a glass ceiling or two. After that, or maybe even during, I would do the whole family thing. But to find Mr. Right, I needed to open myself to some new skill sets. I figured this would be my one last chance to do what everyone wanted to do as soon as he or she got to college: have a wild sexcapade!

In anticipation of this goal I came up with a little wager between two of my closer friends and me. These guys, while a bit geeky, were trustworthy and cute as hell; they just didn't realize that they were fine. So, knowing that I had this great thesis in the works, I proposed that whichever of us graduated at the top of our class, that person would have the other two as slaves for a day. Since we would all be moving away, they assumed that I meant as workhorses to help the winner pack up and load trucks. Well, I guess you could say we did move some furniture.

We found out a couple of days before the ceremony that I was indeed the best in class. I realized that word had spread when they tried to turn around when I approached them on the quad.

"Going somewhere, boys?" I called to them sweetly.

Ted and David both stopped in their tracks. With a feigned resignation they turned around and started back toward me. Ted was the taller of the two. His body was thin and kind of sinewy. The best part was his skin, smooth as silk and obsidian in color. He could be the poster boy for the phrase *black is beautiful*. His smile was easy to appear and captivating in its brightness. His long fingers danced over piano keys and computer keyboards with a grace that made me wonder what else they could play well.

Dave was the polar opposite in shades of blackness, yet turned me on equally. He was a tasty Red Bone straight out of

New Orleans. Toffee-colored skin with expressive green eyes and a light sprinkling of freckles across his nose. He wore his clothes kind of big, almost to the point of being sloppy. After being around him all this time, I knew that his body wasn't soft underneath them. Though he worked out regularly, a routine inspired by high school bullies, Dave was almost embarrassed by his physique. He thought people wouldn't take him seriously if they saw how great his body was. It was my plan to let him know that he could be a physicist and a hottie at the same time. They looked as if they were heading to the gallows as they approached. Little did they know that, by the end of the week, they would be grateful that they had lost this bet.

Ted was the first to speak. "Alright, Sue, get your gloating done with."

With a look of false innocence, I asked sweetly, "Would I be the type to boast of my superior intellect?"

"Yes!" came the simultaneous response.

Laughing, I did a little victory dance. "And you know this, man! So, you both will be at my place Saturday night at eight, right?"

"Why so late?" Dave asked with a puzzled expression.

"Because I don't need you until then. You agreed to the terms of the bet. Are you trying to renege now?"

"No, but you said that we only had to be your workhorses for one day, Sue. It's not our fault if you don't want to start packing until the middle of the night."

"Who said anything about packing?" came my sly response.

Now it was Ted's turn to look confused. "So, what do you want us to do then?"

"You'll see. Just be on time."

Happy to be off manual-labor duty, they agreed and I went

off smiling to myself. Thinking of having them both at my sensual mercy was exciting me. I had been watching movies and reading articles on the internet to make the night interesting. It amazed me how many different ways there were to make sure a threesome didn't turn into a boring show for one member. I wanted them both to be satisfied; somehow it had become connected to my fulfillment. I wanted them both to say my name and remember the evening with equal fondness. With my panties positively sodden, I went home to prepare for the festivities.

Anticipation kept me on a high for the next two days. By Saturday I could have bumped into the sofa and had an orgasm right then! I was ready only fifteen minutes early, but in my agitated state, it seemed like hours. It was a relief when they knocked on the door promptly at eight. I called out to be sure that it was my friends, picked up a tray of my fabulous gintinis, and reveled in their expressions when I opened the door. It's best described as somewhere between shock and joy for Ted and plain amazement from Dave. I had been sure to give them no hint of my plan, so my standing there in a sheer black robe over an equally translucent negligee and thong had rendered them temporarily dumb.

I usually keep my appearance pretty plain and hide my attributes for the same reason Dave hides his. But since this was my fantasy, I had splurged on hair extensions, taken special care with dramatic makeup, including long-wearing lipstick, and wore strappy stilettos to accentuate my legs. I'm only 5'5" but about three feet of that is all thick thighs and sexy calves. While they may have had an idea about my legs since they'd seen me in shorts, I think the full jugs I kept up top were a bit of a shock. I usually wore minimizing bras so guys would talk to me and not *them,* but that night I had them pushed up and out for their viewing pleasure.

"Well, don't just stand there, servants. Come in." After they were in, I nodded to the couch. They still hadn't found their voices when they had sat down, so I continued, "If I remember correctly, you are mine to command for the evening. Though I won't have you packing any boxes, you can be assured that you will be working. But let's have a toast first, shall we?"

Dave smiled uncertainly, almost as if he couldn't believe that this was real. "Well, I know I sure as hell could use a drink right now. Are these your usual strength?"

Startling them both, I straddled his lap and fed him an olive, kissing the taste away.

Leaning over, I whispered in his ear, "They, like everything else about this evening, are more potent than ever."

Before Ted could start feeling left out, I took a deep swallow of my drink and leaned over to kiss him long and deep. As I was still astride Dave, I could feel his reaction to this against my mound. Holding the still unspeaking Ted's face in my hands, I turned to him and inquired, "Who's that knocking at my door? Is that you, Dave, baby?"

Thoroughly enjoying myself, I slid off him into Ted's lap so that he was cradling me. He finally managed to pull himself out of his stupor.

"I'm probably going to kick the shit out of myself for this later, but I have to ask: Susanna, are you drunk or high right now? Because even though I'm about to explode in a minute, I won't take advantage of you."

Dave, though his voice was tight with restraining himself, nodded in agreement. "You're our friend, Sue, and if you're not in your right mind, we can still stop this. We may not be able to walk for a few days, but we will stop."

Knowing that I was right about being able to trust them, I said, "The only things I'm high on are the pheromones in the air." Taking their hands, I put Ted's on one of my hardened nipples and Dave's in between my legs to feel the moistness waiting for them. "Does this seem as if I don't want you both? All I ask is that we keep this night to ourselves. Give me your word on this and I'll believe you." When they both assured me that it would always be our secret, I moved on to the next phase. "Now that we've settled that, let's get you two undressed, shall we?"

To lessen any misguided discomfort, I gave my attention to both of them as they stripped down. Soon as they stood before me in their bare glory, I stroked them both, taking turns to taste them with kisses and licks. When I felt them throbbing in my grip, I stepped away and pushed them. Caught off guard, they fell onto the couch. Using the remote, I turned on the stereo to some sexy jazz instrumentals. Staring at them both, I started to pull on the ribbon holding my robe together. It looked as if Dave was about to say something but he just sat back. Ted started to reach for me but I stopped him with the point of my shoe.

"Now we come to the *slave* portion of the evening. You don't touch me without permission. You can't talk without addressing me as 'Professor Susanna' at all times." That brought a grin to both of their faces, as I knew it would. "Do you understand these rules?"

In unison, they replied, "Yes, Professor Susanna."

"Good. Now finish your drinks and don't disturb me as I make myself comfortable."

With that, I continued removing my "clothing" while moving to the intoxicating sounds of the harmonies that seemed to surround us. That was another reason I chose the gintinis. Gin doesn't make you sin; it merely makes sinning all the more fun. It always heightens my sexual awareness, and I wanted them to have that feeling of letting go as well. Closing my eyes, I continued to move to the music, though I was down to my panties and heels. Running my hands over my bronze skin, I only allowed myself to feel the sensations that my touch was generating. Without looking at them, I brought a straight-back chair from my dinette set and placed it in front of them. Knowing they were watching and wanting me, I sat in front of them and licked my forefinger while opening my legs. Sliding my moistened digit into my wetness, I moaned, then with half-lidded eyes I began fingering myself while kneading my full breast with my other hand. Though I was well aware of their presence, it may have seemed as if I were ignoring my friends as my breathing grew more rapid.

Letting my head fall back, I said, "Stroke yourselves. Don't say anything, just look at me and show me that I'm turning you on. When I look at you, your eyes should be fixed on me. Now answer me: do you understand?"

Ted's voice was croaky while Dave's was shaky as they both managed a soft "Yes, Professor Susanna."

"Good, because I want to cum with your eyes on me." With that I slowly raised my head. Inserting three fingers inside myself, I watched Ted as he caressed his thin but lengthy snake. "You like what you see, Teddy?"

Seemingly transfixed, he breathed, "Yes, Professor Susanna."

"I know you do. You want to fuck me, don't you? Don't you?" I asked, my voice rising with my increasing pleasure.

"Yes, Professor."

Ted was pulling on his pole so hard it looked painful to me. Still I stayed in character, though even I admit to wanting to let go soon. But not yet, so I became perfectly still and stared at him.

"Yes, Professor what?"

Realizing his mistake, he stammered, "Yes, Professor Susanna."

"Very good. Since you corrected your mistake, I will not banish you. But you may not touch yourself anymore until I say so. Hands down now!"

The smile in his eyes was the only indication that he was really enjoying himself as he obeyed. Otherwise he looked properly chastised.

"Now, Dave, you be sure you don't make the same mistake."

"Yes, Professor Susanna." I could tell he also was getting off on the role-playing as he was dribbling a bit at the tip of his shorter but much thicker rod.

"Good boy. For your reward, you get one lick."

Before he could move, quick as lightning I leaned over and licked that tasty pre-cum right off him. During all of this I had not removed my hand, and at his shuddering intake of breath, I began to gush anew. Propping my legs up so I had a foot between each of their legs, I brought myself to a trembling orgasm. When I finally stopped bucking against my hand, I saw that Ted was still following my orders, though his dick was jumping with the tension. Dave had on the other hand (literally) blasted his load.

Handing him one of the warm towels I had ready, I told him, "Since you have had some satisfaction, Dave, I believe I'm going to fuck Ted first." Handing Ted one of the colorful condoms I had laid out on the end table, I continued, "While I'm sitting on Ted's dick, I want you to sit in front of me so I can suck yours."

"Yes, Professor Susanna."

Turning my back to Ted, I lowered myself slowly so he could get a good view of my ass descending. With a firm grip, I held his dick just outside of my juicy heat. I began rubbing the tip around and over my clit, wetting him and myself before impaling myself on his mahogany baton. My legs were shaking with the effort, but I kept my movements steady, clinching my inner muscles so that I pulled delightful moans from Ted. Though he was holding me by my breasts and driving me crazy, kneading my chocolate nipples with those magical hands of his, I kept the pace deliberately measured, as I really wanted us all to cum at the same time.

Looking at Dave with sex-lowered eyelids, I crooked my finger at him and asked, "Dave?"

He stepped forward with his throbbing caramel stick and asked, "Yes, Professor Susanna?"

He always was good at following directions. Smirking with the playful power rush, I replied, "Do you want me to suck your dick, Dave? If so, then show me. Make it bounce like it is asking for my lips."

I almost nutted when he complied without a word. Ted had his hands on my hips now and was helping me work it so he could see over my shoulder as I began to suck Dave off. He was so thick I had to put my hand between my lips and his body so he wouldn't choke me. I had read about techniques, but in practice, sucking a wide dick can be as tricky as deep-throating a long one. But after a few minutes, my jaw muscles loosened up and I discovered I had a new talent that really brought me a lot of pleasure. The look on Dave's face was fascinating because I knew I was the one who put it there.

I was nearly drunk with the sexual control I had over them. I pulled off Dave long enough to say, "Dave, don't close your eyes, look at me. Ted, you listen to me. I want us to cum together." Then I got back to work on both of them.

The sounds of our fucking soon mixed intoxicatingly with the music coming from the stereo. Ted was grinding into me and grazing my spot. His noises were more like growls as he tried to hold on until I gave the word. I could tell by the increased thickness and tasty little pearls of liquid that Dave was right there as well, and I was past ready. So I gave Dave a nod as I looked into his eyes, and getting the hint, he grabbed my shoulders firmly and started rocking into my mouth. I let my muscles slacken a bit to accommodate him as I held his muscular thighs and moved my ass like a video ho. Ted got the message and was soon filling me up with his hot load. I sat up at the feeling of him throbbing inside me and got my second nut off. Reaching down and under Dave's balls, I found the male G-spot and had him squirting all over my face and breasts. The salty-sweet smell of his cum was too much to pass up, so just when he thought he was done, I sucked him while still playing with that tender area. Finally he pulled away and fell to his knees.

After a couple of minutes of collapse against Ted, I got up and brought them some more towels. Looking at them as they cleaned off, I felt warmth begin to pool low and tight in my belly again. *Damn! This is a hell of a time to discover I'm an insatiable freak,* I thought to myself. But it appeared to be so because without warning I heard myself say, "Your day of enslavement will be over as soon as you clean me off. So, boys . . . to the bath!"

Running to my bathroom, I giggled like a sex-crazed schoolgirl as they ran behind me with a chorus of "Yes, Professor Susanna!"

Devil's Worship

Rachel Kramer Bussel

"Have you ever had your ass properly worshipped?" I asked, staring at the proud, thick, tight curves before me, the luscious mocha color of Dana's booty straining as she bounced gently up and down. Her bottom was the perfect reward for my months of celibacy, of waiting to kneel down in front of her, to taste and touch and take of her rich, beautiful body. I pinched the tender underside of one cheek, then the other, pulling them apart to see everything in between, a moan escaping my lips as I saw just how wet she was. There's really nothing like a woman's ass spread out before you, waiting to be taken, to humble a man. Girls' butts are so majestic, strong, and powerful, yet so tender. I simply held her there in my hands, letting my thumbs rest along the edges of her lips, pacing myself before diving in for a delicious treat, one that already had my cock hard, strong, and ready.

Before you get the wrong idea, let me tell you that this wasn't our first date, or even our fourth. I'd been courting Dana Thompson for months. Yes, me, Nicky "the Devil" Anderson. I hadn't earned my nickname for nothing, and plenty of women around town wouldn't hesitate to shoot me a dirty look or the finger after the way I'd treated them. I knew what they said about me, and for the most part they were right. For most of my twenties, I'd been a hound dog, a player, a pussy magnet. I'd rarely said no and rarely let women into more than my bedroom. I was young and selfish, greedy and horny, too full of myself to appreciate the true joy a woman could bring me on all levels. Could I help it if women threw themselves at me left and right? Back then, I didn't know any better. Now I do, and I plan to spend my days and nights making up for my reckless ways by worshipping at the altar of Dana's body.

Let me back up a minute. I hadn't started out like that. I'd been a one-woman guy until Melody Kingston broke my heart in college by leaving me for the head of the debate team, a nerdy white guy with glasses and a goatee who looked like he was still a virgin. I would picture his mug as I pumped iron, telling myself that even though she'd left me for his scrawny ass, I'd get back at her by getting as many women as I could, by being the hottest, smoothest, most in-demand brother on campus. And it worked, for a while. I was up to my eyeballs in pussy for most of junior year. I'd roll out of one girl's bed and stumble to class, brushing sleep out of my eyes as my lips still tingled from the taste of her. I pulled many all-nighters sliding between the sheets with one fine woman or another, our bodies and mouths blocking out the loud dorm noise surrounding us. It was an education par excellence, and the confidence I later showed during business school, then striking out on my own to open my PR agency, can all be attributed to the way they guided my cock and my tongue all around their bodies.

I know what people said, that I discarded one girl as soon as another so much as looked my way, but that wasn't really how it felt at the time. When I was with them, sliding hot and nasty against their sweaty bodies, watching them arch and stretch as I pulled my cock almost all the way out of their gorgeous, slick pussies, then slamming it back in and making them scream, I felt like I was in heaven. It wasn't just about the way I felt as my orgasm approached, it was seeing them surrender to bliss, seeing them lose the battle to be anything close to a good girl and just give it up, give in to the lust that had surely been bubbling up inside them for a lifetime. Girls and guys aren't so different that way. Treat a woman right, not by wining and dining her, but by letting her know that you appreciate every little thing about her, from the way she yawns to the curve of her hip to the little noises she makes when you suck on her nipples, and she's an insatiable sex-mad creature like none other.

But even though I do believe that men and women are equal-opportunity fuck sluts, I like a girl who's a bit of a challenge, one who doesn't wear her pussy power on her sleeve. Not church girls exactly, but ones who'll play mouse to my sharp-clawed cat. And Dana was a challenge if ever I'd met one. She'd come to my firm as a struggling actress, making the rounds of auditions, trying to move beyond the black-bitch or white-girl's-best-friend roles being offered to her, teetering just between discovery and disappointment, wanting us to tip her over the edge.

I took a personal interest in her, but knew that if I was to maintain any hopes of getting her into my bed and protecting my professional reputation, I had to build her up in the media and then seduce her. Business first; pleasure later. Otherwise, my judgment might get skewed and I'd be promoting her not on her merits but on my cock's needs. I decided not to date any other women while I waited for Dana, and as I got to know her, she became more and more beautiful to me. I've seen so many flashes in the proverbial pan, girls who want me to get them headlines but then want to retreat from the spotlight the minute they've made it, or who get so full of themselves they forget what got them into the business in the first place.

Dana had hired me because her first love was acting; it was the only thing she'd ever wanted to do, and she was in it for the long haul. She'd turned down some parts that she felt didn't fit whom she wanted to be, hoochie-mama types where she'd have to bare all, which she was willing to do, if the role was right. She took the same care with her interviews, refusing any shoots where the only thing they wanted to know was how big her breasts were or what size cock she preferred. Media hype wasn't something she wanted, but something she needed if she was going to take things to the next level. She wasn't content to simply let me run the show, plugging her name into some equation of "famous rapper plus hot new girl equals instant couple." She wanted to keep it real, a challenge if ever there was one, but as I got to know her, I realized that this wholesomeness made her a delight to work with. I'd find myself grinning when she called, closing the door to my office so my smiles wouldn't give away my true feelings to my staff. What Dana and I had was special, even then, and I savored every minute of it.

I found my thoughts lingering on her pretty face even after I'd gotten home from the office, picturing her standing behind me in the kitchen, arms wrapped around my waist, her face nuzzled into the small of my back. Okay, that wasn't all (I pictured me bending her over, her hands flat on the linoleum floor, while I plunged my cock inside her, making her cum almost instantly. I pictured her losing some of the calm control she exerted over every other aspect of her being, trusting me to be there to catch her as she trembled her way to ecstasy. I knew from our talks that she was single, not a virgin, but close enough. Dana Thompson wasn't the girl who let her pussy leap ahead of her heart; they were one and the same, and the truth was, I didn't want one without the other. I'd have been disappointed if she saw me as one step up on the casting couch, one more person to please to get herself plastered onto every magazine cover around.

Waiting for Dana's star to rise gave me time to check out more than her ass. She was a diligent worker, treating our work like a student who'll do anything to get the A . . . well, almost anything. That she wasn't ready to strip down was so hot, and the more I thought about her, wondering what those breasts looked like, the ones she kept locked away beneath discreet suit jackets, making the rest of us hope we'd be so lucky as to find out what they felt like in our hands, the more I realized that would be her marketing strategy.

"The Good Girl" started to find its way into our pitches, and it seemed as if the media was ready for someone to come along and wipe the smirks off the faces of the "bad girls" like Britney and Paris. Unlike the photos of girls in barely there bikinis we usually shopped around, Dana's photos showed her like a librarian, complete with glasses, an elegant blouse, and a big fat encyclopedia. I did another with her as a doctor, then as an astronaut, in keeping with a role she was gunning for. Maybe the hype could even help her get a few parts, if we played it right.

My brainstorm took off overnight, and we were soon getting calls from magazines we hadn't even contacted. Dana's combination of understated sexiness, sass, and down-home roots seemed to be what everyone wanted, to the point that I had to limit access to her lest she become too ubiquitous before making her mark on the industry. We talked on the phone late into the night, first about strategy, then other things. She told me how homesick she sometimes was, but how she'd walk from her Harlem apartment all the way down to the Village, taking it all in. I wanted to take those walks with her, see everything she saw, hold her hand and remember what it was like to have all of the Big Apple waiting to be discovered. She'd get quiet as the clock ticked into the wee hours and even fell asleep on me once, but I didn't mind. I hoped one day I'd get to tuck her in for real, but until then I had her sweet voice to keep me company.

We started going out after work, first drinks, then real dinners, ones we lingered over, feeding each other delicate bites, lingering long after our plates had been cleaned. Sometimes our hands would touch, but I was always the first to pull away, too fearful of mixing business and pleasure, of losing both if something went awry. I'd never been in a situation where I wasn't in a hurry to get a girl naked, to figure out who she was by the way she writhed, the way she moaned, the way she came. But Dana was different. She didn't talk about sex the way the other girls had, didn't flirt carelessly with anyone who passed. Her eyes didn't flutter at the waiter or the coat-check guy, or even at me, though I sensed something brimming beneath the surface. I, in turn, waited until I got home, alone, naked in bed, to fantasize about her, rather than undressing her there at the dinner table, mentally fondling her nipples, sliding her onto my lap as waiters rushed by all around us.

The day I called to tell her she'd landed the cover of *Rolling*

Stone, hot on the heels of her new deal to star in an action flick alongside Brad Pitt, was a milestone.

"Hello?" Her voice was breathless, and I pictured her standing at the window of her building, looking down on the street twenty-five floors below, cars zooming by, racing to be somewhere important.

"Are you sitting down, Dana?" I asked, having to do so myself. My cock was already half-hard from the sound of her voice, husky without even meaning to be.

"Yes," she said quietly, going solemn as I took a deep breath.

"Good. Because I want to be the first to tell you that you're about to be a cover girl. *Rolling Stone*! All by yourself. They want to profile you and your breakout role," I said, letting my own excitement show in my voice. This was big, even by my standards.

"Oh my God, Nicky. Oh, wow," she said, before I heard the sniffling start.

"Are you crying? Dana, this is good news!" I said, wanting to wrap her in my arms.

"Of course it is! This is great news. They're happy tears."

"Are you alone?" I asked, shifting our conversation to another level. "I hope so. I'm booking you a room at the SoHo Grand. Meet me there in an hour."

"Really?" she asked, taking a deep breath, then sighing. I thought she might refuse and my heart skipped a beat. If she turned me away now, I didn't know what I'd do. "Nicky, you're so sweet. I'll be there. Let me go get ready."

I didn't know if that meant she'd let me stay, but I hoped so. I'd been about to hop in a cab up to her place, but that might be too forward, too much, too soon. I wanted those anonymous walls there to absorb her moans of pleasure. I hopped in the shower, my cock hard as the hot water splashed over me, and I pictured Dana peeling herself out of one of her pin-striped suits. I wondered what else her closet held, whether there were any skimpy dresses or sheer nighties, what kind of underwear she wore. My hand found its way to my dick and I took my time stroking myself. The last girl had been months ago, so far back I could barely remember her name, I'm a little ashamed to say. The only girl's name I'd been whispering to myself had been Dana, Dana, Dana. I said it as I watched my hand pump the cum out of me, picturing Dana in a way that belied everything she'd told me about herself: down on her knees, lapping it up. The forbidden image stayed in my head as I finished myself off. On my way to meet her, I wondered which was the real Dana, the good girl with the heart of gold, or the one who liked to get it from behind . . . or maybe both? Maybe she was just waiting for the right man to unlock her secret doors, find the right combination of trust and lust to allow her to let go.

As it turned out, Dana was the one to come on to me. Well, she started things off with a skintight, red dress and black heels that made every head turn to look at her, though it was her eyes that shone brightest. She gave me a hug that almost made me stagger.

"Nicky!" she said, planting a red-lipsticked kiss on my cheek.

She wasn't pawing me or anything, but this was much more attention than I'd come to expect. My cock got hard immediately and I edged her back.

"Dana, let me look at you," I said, taking in everything from her eyes, sparkling with glitter dust, to her red lips on down. I held her hands until she broke apart to twirl around.

She laughed when she saw the look on my face: pure, dumbfounded lust. "You didn't think I had it in me, did you?" she teased, running a finger down my cheek. "There's a sultry woman beneath all those layers. I just don't like to give it away to those who don't deserve it."

I turned away for a minute, taking a deep breath. The more I saw of this woman, the more she drove me nuts. Crazy as it was, I wished I had a ring, because that's when I knew I wanted her to be my bride.

I turned back to her and smiled. "I know what you're capable of, Dana," I said. The words themselves could mean any number of things, but the dip in tone when I said her name, making it sound like a much dirtier four-letter word, let her know what I was talking about. "I've just been waiting for the right time to unleash it."

Her brown eyes blazed into mine. She stepped closer, tugging on my tie. "Are you sure you're ready for me?" she asked, pulling harder, so I felt the pressure against my neck. Her smile was that of a predator clutching its prey, victory assured. She stepped closer, slipping a leg between mine.

"We should get out of the lobby, lest we ruin your image," I said, though that was only half the reason. I was sporting a full-on erection there was no hiding from anyone. I needed her next to me, on top of me, beneath me, all over me, all at once.

She reached into her purse and pulled out a key card. Never had a boring beige rectangle looked so sexy. Then she turned, her hand resting gently on the swell of her ass, and started prancing away on those heels. I followed, wanting to leap and tackle her, press her beneath me to the ground right there. We walked to the elevator silently, the tension almost unbearable.

"How long have you wanted to fuck me, Nicky?" It was the first time I'd heard her say the word, one I thought she'd banished from her vocabulary. She was the type who said "darn it" and employed other euphemisms when she was upset. Was it all an act? I didn't think so. She was just very selective. She crossed her legs as she stood on the other side of the elevator bank.

When we finally got to the room, I couldn't wait any longer. I grabbed her, pushing up her dress.

"Oh, Nicky," she moaned as I sank to my knees.

There was so much to see and taste and touch, I didn't know where to start. The musky scent of her pussy perfume wafted through the air, but I turned her around. "Put your hands up on the wall." Dana had taught me so much, but I still had a lesson or two to impart. Her ass hovered above me, and I pulled down her panties. I couldn't resist giving each cheek a solid slap, the sound echoing in the room as the sting reverberated in my palm. "Have you ever had your ass properly worshipped?"

"No," came her muffled reply as I spread her open and let my tongue explore her sweet curves. I pressed against her twin globes, giving myself room to taste her sensitive skin, the pucker writhing beneath me as I buried myself between her cheeks. I curled my tongue into a point and dove right in while my fingers moved closer to her sex, stroking the wetness I found there. No one else was in the room, figuratively or otherwise, no cameras, no reporters, no noise except her panting and my grunting as I tasted her essence. My thumbs parted her pussy lips as my tongue dipped in and out of her back door while I wished for more hands so I could touch her everywhere at once. And there on the ground, I did my penance for all the girls I'd mistreated. I worshipped Dana's ass like I'd never get another chance, my tongue savoring her sweetness as more of my fingers found their way into her other hole. I filled her up as best I could, plunging in and out to the beat of her own rocking hips.

"Yes, yes, yes!" I heard her cry, a little louder than before as I pressed three fingers deep into her tight tunnel. I feasted on Dana's bottom, those strikingly soft mounds against my cheeks as I made her cum, felt her sticky syrup coat my fingers. I wasn't done, but I eased out, resting against the back of her thigh as I kissed my way down to her ankle before pulling her on top of me for round two. We spent the rest of the night and most of the next morning worshipping each other, though that first taste of her sweet ass would've been enough. Nowadays, I'm a reformed devil, and Dana, now a bona fide celebrity, has agreed to be my bride. She's turned into a bit of a she-devil, but only in the bedroom. I can't wait to see what happens on our wedding night.

Mr. Everything

(Yes, He Is All That!)

Renee Alexis

I'd heard the rumor, but decided it was absolutely too ridiculous to be true. I even told my girlfriends that they had to be out of their minds to think a man is fine enough for them to want to stand in front of a gym three hours just to see him. Stupid dames.

After relentless attempts on their part to prove the legend was true, I went with them to Powerplus Gym to see for myself. The craziest part of the whole ordeal was waiting for a guy to arrive who probably looked like jack-shit—knowing their taste. What I hadn't truly planned on was seeing almost the entire female population of Troy, Michigan, waiting at the door for the dude. I said to myself, *Damn, maybe he is all that!*

Knowing me, that idea was short-lived. You see, I'm a realist. I don't get hung up on looks and material things. Men are men to me, and that makes them human, which also makes them *not perfect!* I refused to believe that any man looked great

enough to waste an entire day waiting for him to enter a building. What I couldn't get my friends to understand was that after
they wasted the day waiting for him, he would probably go inside and get a good laugh at their expense. That wasn't for me;
no way, no how!

I went with them anyway to prove my point, and we must
have waited two hours or more before I got fed up with the
whole idiocy of it. Hell, he never showed up anyway. I took my
foot and kicked the butt of every girlfriend of mine who'd
dragged me away from my favorite soap opera, *Guiding Light,*
to see some chump bench-press a pretzel. They tried explain-
ing that he always showed up on Wednesdays at 4:00 p.m. and
that they couldn't understand why he wasn't there. I also told
them that maybe the guy had a life and that maybe they needed
one, too. I could hardly speak because the highlight of my
Wednesdays was *Guiding Light.* So what? I taped it anyway.

My friends scuffed off home with their tails between their
legs, and I had nothing to do. Hell, the soaps were off, and all I
had to do was go home and cook—dull city! Instead, I walked
into Powerplus and took out a membership because the flab
around my midsection was too much to bear. Just kidding, it
wasn't that bad, but it was there nonetheless and I hated it!

I took out a one-year membership, had a brief tour of the
facilities, then left on my own to check the place out. I checked
out everything, even the glass window that had four ladies
standing in front of it drooling. That glass window was part of
the tour I hadn't received, so I walked over to see exactly what
they were drunk over.

At first, all I saw were exercise machines, all kinds, walking
machines, leg builders, everything. Then *he* stood up. Suddenly
I turned into one of those trolls staring glassy-eyed at perfec-

tion. He had to be the one the girls were talking about. He fooled them by coming in earlier and missing the devils in heat! Smart man—fine as hell also.

I don't know why I wasn't shown that part of the gym during my tour, so I asked the lady next to me, who had finally gotten a grip on the saliva dripping down her jaw.

"Two reasons," the lady replied. "First, this section is for stockholders; second—him. Everyone who has shown this section to the ladies joining up managed to lose the proverbial 'control of the room.' "

"What do you mean?"

"After getting a dose of Jaylen, who could listen to anything anyone else said? Look at the guy!"

I kept looking at him. He was so fucking sexy that my jaw dropped. Jaylen Matthews definitely was the one my friends were juiced up over. I don't mean juice that you drink, no, the juice that flows from the punany after seeing a man that almost made you pass out from his good looks. That kind of juiced up! Who could blame the heifers? For once, they were on target in the looks department, despite that what they usually brought home from a date was from the insect kingdom.

Jaylen had been bench-pressing weights and I couldn't really see what he looked like until he lowered the weights. Sure, he looked sexy lying flat on his back while lifting almost two hundred pounds over his head, but when he stood, God, was he major eye candy. He was wearing midthigh sweat shorts, tube socks that drooped to his ankles, and a damp sweat top— a killer! His curly, black hair was damp with perspiration; it really set off his caramel complexion.

He returned the weights to their chambers and stood with a bottled water. I could really see how perfect he was. That thick erection he was sporting was an added bonus. All I could see was myself lowering onto it and rocking like crazy. When I returned to reality, I noticed my hands were flat against the window, my jaw dropped, and my tender buds practically clawing out at him. They were so hard that they were hurting, and a dose of his lips pulling on them would have been a dream come true. Then my eyes met his. I swear I thought those big, dark eyes of his could see me. The lady next to me smiled, like she knew what I was going through. She did, that's why she and the others were still there.

Feeling a little foolish about my behavior, I asked her if he could see us or if it was one of those one-way windows.

"He can see us alright, hon. That's why his dick is so big poking through those shorts. He sees something he likes."

When I looked back at him, he smiled a bit at me, then winked before tossing the rest of the water down his throat. I got so nervous and decided it was definitely time to leave. I never told my girls that I saw the living legend, but I went back there the following Wednesday to stare him down at that window again. I purposely went there alone to have him to myself.

I walked into the adjoining women's workout room; yeah, like I could actually bench-press any of the equipment in there. No one told me to leave so I decided to stay in there until security dragged me out.

At nine forty-five exactly, Jaylen pulled open the doors and walked into the men's workout room. He hadn't immediately seen me on the other side since I was in the corner tugging on those power ropes that I couldn't make budge. I didn't really know what to do. If I popped out of nowhere, I'd scare him to death, and he'd be mad. If I let him find me on his own, he'd question what the heck I was doing there since it was supposed to be a restricted area and he'd be mad. Either way, I was screwed, but not the way I'd want to be.

I decided to come out in the open and get it done on my own instead of having him drag me by the hair down to security. I waited until he got into his routine. He started out with a little cross training. I watched from my secluded corner. Next, he pumped a little iron. Watching those muscles flex and bulge like that made me weak in the knees. I liked the feeling. When he lay on his back to do the leg lifts, that's when I lost it in a major way. The weight I had in my hand fell and popped me right on the foot. I screamed out without even knowing it. All I could feel was the pain beginning to throb in my toe, and I sat on the floor to massage it. Unfortunately, at that time Jaylen was the last thing on my mind. What came first and foremost was the pain, then the security guard I knew would be around the bend because of Jaylen alerting him to the perpetrator.

When I got enough nerve to look at the window, Jaylen was pressed against it looking at me. He mouthed to me since it was soundproof, "Are you okay?"

After I figured out his words, I nodded and gave him the okay symbol with my fingers. He stared at me for a few seconds, scanning my frame in that tight-fitting PUMA outfit I'd decided to wear, then moved on to the leg machine again. I knew I'd dodged the bullet since I didn't see him making any plans to go for security. I was in a "stockholders only" area. However, I liked the way he scouted me, and that could be what saved my neck.

Throughout our workouts, we'd peep one another, and he liked the attention I was showering him with. My workout suit was almost see-through and hugging all my curves, and he definitely paid attention because his erection was good and hard, tenting the front of those white workout shorts like wild. I wanted to think it was solely me making those pants tent like that, but working the hell out of those machines may have played a role in it. I'm good, but not that good.

The more I looked at Jaylen, the more I wanted to taste him, feel him pressing into my throat. As usual, I let my mind get the best of me and became nervous over the thought of him.

I looked down at my watch and realized it was minutes to closing time and I was still in my sweats, but I just couldn't leave the window. I hated to leave because he was worth staying and getting caught with. Knowing the kind of man Jaylen Matthews was, he probably got kicks out of the ladies staring his ass down, then going home to his wife. That was the kind of fucking luck I had: finding the juiciest man on the planet, but not being able to land him because of a *wife*.

Then the proverbial lightbulb went on in my head. Yes, I do manage to have a smart idea, occasionally. Jaylen had a passkey to the facilities. My plan was this: purposely get locked in and have to go to him to get out . . . or to get off! Suddenly he made a move I hadn't counted on. He stepped away from the weight trainer and approached the window again. I couldn't move, couldn't speak, all I could do was watch him approach me in that tight, sweaty T-shirt and shorts. Man, the closer he got to me, the hotter I got. In all my orgasmic nonsense it soon dawned on me that he was probably approaching me to tell me to back the fuck off; that maybe he was tired of being stared at as if he were a zoo animal. I got scared and backed up.

Jaylen backed up a bit so I could get a head-to-toe view of him, then he got busy. His eyes stared into mine as he massaged that massive erection up and down through his pants. I could feel my nectar rising within my core. Then it hit me, he was about to give me a live sex show. Was I about to leave the action? Fuck no, I stayed and watched everything that pretty man did.

When his erection got hard and thick within his pants, he let out a damn dazzling smile that made me cum. No man had ever smiled so wickedly at me that my panties got wet; then again, I'd never met Jaylen. His hands slowly took the hem of his shirt and pulled up, exposing a chest I'd have smacked my mother to touch. His pecs were mouthwatering, contours and ripples were everywhere. All my nasty little tongue wanted to do was lick, lick from his collarbone to his tight abs and continue south. My hands clutched my tank-covered breasts and squeezed, feeling my feverish, hard nipples rubbing against my palms. All the while, my eyes never left his.

Bending to remove his socks and shoes was a chore because that delicious cock was in the way, but he managed. His fingers beckoned me to get closer. I knew he was going to slide his pants down next, but I wasn't sure just how and what else he was going to do. After all, the dude was clever with his seduction. Nonetheless I moved back to the window and watched him slide the shorts to his hips. His rod bounced out, sprang to life, and I dropped to my knees, wondering how all that would feel stroking my insides. I watched how he massaged it, making it bigger and bigger within his hand. He stroked that beautiful, thick member until he was about ready to squirt. His muscles tensed, he squeezed it harder, and playfully rubbed it against the glass directly where my mouth was. I swear I could taste him, feel him sliding it between my lips and forcing his inches into me.

He stroked it so hard that I could see the moisture forming on his tip. I couldn't help myself, I had to reach between my thighs and stroke myself to match his tempo. The more he stroked himself, the deeper my finger slid into my valley. When he dropped to the floor, I scrambled to see what he was going to do to *me* next. It was outrageous, let me tell you! That pretty-ass boy got on his back and moved his hips up and down like a lady was on top of him. I screamed in ecstasy over the sight of it. He pumped hard and long, perspiration dripping from him, muscles tensing. I just knew he was going to deliver onto the floor instead of into me. No. He turned over on his stomach and did push-ups, pumping those hips and cock into oblivion. He still hadn't cum for me yet. That was the grand finale, watching him cream into his own hands while staring me down.

He returned to his back and pressed out so much cum that I almost fainted from the orgasm he gave me. When my breathing returned to normal, I looked into my hand, now covered with so much of my own thick moisture that my fingers were sticking together. Then I glanced at him watching me with a sweet smile on his wonderful lips—his erection was still in his hand, and still harder than diamonds.

The windows were nice and steamed by the time he and I finished. I watched as he grabbed the rest of his belongings and headed for the showers. I took off as well, figuring that was all I'd ever get from him. He was cool enough to give me a show without involving the police, so the least I could do was be thankful for the show and go home to watch the stories I'd taped.

While in the shower, I couldn't help but smile in remembrance of the first, and probably last, sex show a man had given me without having touched me. I let the warm water trickle down my aching joints and relaxed. My body mitt delicately encircled my breasts, pretending the sultry touch was Jaylen's fingers. The mind is a tricky and dangerous tool. I could actually feel Jaylen fingering my breasts, sucking on them gently before making a tongue track down to my core. I shuddered in waves of heat. My body trembled, spasmed, taking my mind off the pain from the injured foot. I completely gave in to pleasure and let the most tremendous orgasm hit me like no other one had ever before . . . well, until Jaylen happened on the scene.

Then.

"Damn, girl!"

The words came from nowhere. I assumed they had been in my mind. Nonetheless, my eyes opened and I twirled around to see if anyone had come in. There Jaylen was, standing directly in front of me. I tried reaching for my towel but he snatched it from the railing before I could get it.

His cool, seductive voice melted into my spirit. "Imagine how big this boner would be if I'd been able to see you screw yourself from the front. All I could see was that delicious butt of yours shaking and quivering to some sexual daydream. Was it about me?"

I couldn't speak. All I could do was look down at the towel around his midsection, sporting a killer of an erection. My mouth opened, my voice cracked. "I . . . I, uh . . ."

"It's okay, girl. I know you were thinking about me. How could you not after the show I gave you." He moved toward me, one step away from entering the stall with me. "Did you like my show? Did I get you"—he slapped my fanny—"hot enough to want a repeat performance?" He pulled his towel off and entered the stall.

I tried covering my nakedness with my arms. He pulled them down. "Don't you dare cover up a thing."

"Is . . . is it okay for us to be here—"

"It's okay for me to do any damn thing I please in here." He kissed my cheek. "I'm Jaylen Mat—"

"I know who you are, Mr. Matthews. Every woman within a five-city radius knows who you are."

"Yeah? Who might you be?"

"Carol."

"And as lovely-sounding as one, I might add. Carol who?"

"Barnes; nothing exotic, nothing romantic, just regular old Carol Barnes."

"Not from my standpoint. You're ravishing, and I enjoyed pleasing you. Can I please you again?"

"I'm not a shareholder, just a member. I was actually scared you'd turn me in over being where I shouldn't have been."

"You were exactly where you were supposed to be, Carol Barnes—and I'm supposed to be here with you."

I relaxed, knowing he wasn't going to turn me over to the cops, or even the sex police. Sex police, huh? That sounded good, too!

His hands covered my breasts, much the same way they did in my daydream. He stroked the tight tips with his thumbs, then replaced them with his lips. He sucked them ferociously, licking them like they were candy. My head reared back as he moved from my breasts, licking up and down my neck. My arms wrapped so tightly around him that I thought I'd squeeze him to death; it only made his cock that much harder.

As the water continued to drench us, he lifted me into his arms; my legs hugged his hips. I felt the tip of that delicious cock play with my opening, tease it, rub up and down on it. I faced him, staring into those delicious gray eyes of his. "I want everything from Mr. Everything."

"I've had many names, but that's the best one. So, you want everything, huh?"

"Every single drop."

"I've got a lot to give. You should be careful what you ask for."

"I don't care about anything, just give me what you own, Mr. Everything with gray eyes and beautiful brown skin."

His muscles tightened around me; our bodies pressed against the wall. Within seconds, by body was implanted with the most outstanding cake of dynamite to ever ignite. He pounded away inside of me so expertly and smoothly I thought he was born inside me.

We finished an hour later, but when we tried to leave, the building was locked in every area. I knew Jaylen had a passkey somewhere, but he argued up and down that he'd left it at home; simply an excuse to stay with me the rest of the night. That was exactly what happened, and we made love all night.

The next morning after our shower, he dressed and left while I took an extended shower. After stepping from the nice, hot stall, Jaylen left a message on the steamy mirror. "I left you my passkey. Meet me here later tonight and we'll do it all again. See you soon, my 'not so plain Carol Barnes.'"

I kissed his key, then slipped it into my purse. Yes, the girls would never believe this!

Sure, we had our love affair, and it was a dandy one, too. In fact, it was so scrumptious that he decided a good thing could last forever. We're now engaged and making plans to purchase our own fitness center.

Cougar

Zane

I never heard of the term *cougar* until I became one: a woman in her forties who exclusively craves young dick. I only wish that I had started in my thirties. Then I would have been called a bobcat.

I don't merely crave young dick, I worship it. It has become my mantra: "Young dick! Young dick! Young dick!" I often chant it on my way out to clubs in Charlotte. Now, do not get me wrong. When I say "young dick," I do mean "legal dick." I'm not trying to get locked up for humming on a teenybopper's mic.

Umm, thinking about giving head always drenches my panties. Some women like to go shoe shopping. Some women like to collect antiques. Some women like to play tennis on Saturday afternoons. I like to swallow dicks—whole; young dicks.

Last January, I celebrated my fortieth birthday with a host of family and friends. It was quite a milestone for me but it was also a rude awakening. I realized that men my age could no longer turn me on, rather less turn me out. They were either too worn-out, too stressed-out, or damn near impotent. You would think that a man over forty, with more than likely at least twenty years of fucking experience under his belt, would know how to satisfy a woman. Not! At least not the ones I was getting to know in the biblical sense.

I decided to go older and started dating Alfred. That was my first and last experience with a man in that age range. Shit, he was near sixty and had been fucking since I was born. What a pathetic, lousy fuck he turned out to be. His breath was as foul as a clove of garlic to boot. When he "attempted" to eat my pussy, I had to hold my nose because his breath threatened to make me faint.

Have you ever had a man who spent more time blowing in your pussy than eating it? That was Alfred's ass. One night I was scared shitless that he might actually give me an embolism. I quickly changed positions, sucked him off until he came like a bolt of lightning, and told him to take his raggedy ass home in his raggedy-ass car.

That's another thing. Alfred had to either go Dutch on all our dates or ask to borrow the money from me, which he never repaid. I do not profess to be the wealthiest sister on the planet, not even in Charlotte, but I take care of mine. Speaking of "mine," I have two absolutely beautiful daughters from my one and only marriage. Titus and I were married right after college, and while I can truly say that I loved that man, he disrespected me with another woman. Unlike most women who accept that their men make mistakes and slip up and land in another pussy, I immediately filed for divorce.

Our daughters are seventeen and fourteen and we have joint custody, so I have them every other week. Titus and I only live six miles apart and their school is smack-dab in the middle, so that makes it simple enough for us to manage. I never have men over to my house for sexcapades while my daughters are there. Even though a lot of the teenage boys they bring over from high school consider me a MILF—Mom I'd Like to Fuck—I would never go there. My dicks need to at least be in their early twenties, which is why I love the club scene. In today's age, when clubs are overly nervous when it comes to losing their liquor licenses for serving underage drinkers, I leave it up to them to screen dick for me. The clubs that I go to check the front and back of IDs to make sure they are not phony. Goody, goody for me!

A woman can find men from twenty-one to eighty-one at the Excelsior, my club of choice. Located on Beatties Ford Road, it has been open since 1944, and my parents used to watch Nat King Cole perform there. It is truly a Southern juke joint but I love it. I generally get there shortly after the doors open so I can have my pick of the puppy litter. I want men with a little ruff-ruff in them. Men who want to tear up some pussy and keep it moving. The last thing I need is some young buck catching feelings for me. I could never claim a man that young as my "public dick action."

The first one I ever picked up in there was named Devain. As soon as I spotted him, I wanted to do something deviant to his fine ass. He was only a few inches taller than me, making him around five-nine, but he had the sexiest, sparkling brown eyes and closely cropped, silky black hair. The skin on his face was flawless, and I wondered if the rest of him was a creamy mahogany as well. I was determined to find out.

He stayed on the dance floor for nearly an hour, gyrating up against a young hoochie mama who swore she knew how to handle some dick but could surely not hold a candle to me.

Once they took a break and she headed to the ladies' room to drain her bladder, I made my move.

"I like the way you move," I yelled into his ear over the loud, thumping music.

He grinned, looking me up and down. "Thanks. I enjoy dancing."

I wasted no time. "Do you enjoy fucking also?"

He practically choked on his beer. "Oh, yeah, I like fucking."

"Is that your woman with you?" I asked, gesturing my head toward the restrooms.

"Naw, I met her tonight. I'm here with my homeboy." He quickly scanned the dance floor. "He's around here someplace."

I intertwined my arm with his. "How about we go someplace not around here?"

For a second, I thought I saw intimidation flicker in his eyes. "What's your name?"

"You can call me Imagine."

"Imagine?"

"Yes, you cannot possibly imagine what I'm going to do to you, if you're bold enough to leave here with me."

He laughed uncomfortably.

"What's wrong?" I asked. "Scared of real woman pussy?"

He took another swig of his beer. "What's real woman pussy?"

"You eat ribs?"

"Yeah, I eat ribs. Why?" he asked in confusion.

"The difference between tough ribs that you have to gnaw off the bones and tender ribs that fall off the bones is the amount of time that they have marinated. Real woman pussy has marinated much, much longer than the kind you're probably used to."

"But . . . you're old enough to be my mother. I don't know if I would feel comfortable."

"Is your mother as fine as me?" I lowered the right strap of my dress so he could see my cleavage. Then I grabbed his dick through his pants; it was a brick. "Does your mother make your dick this hard?"

Before he could respond, the hoochie he had been dancing with finally returned from the ladies' room; surely there was a long line as usual.

"Devain, who is this?" she asked, having the nerve to be territorial even though she hardly knew him.

Without letting go my grip on his dick, I responded, "I'm his mommy!"

Her eyes almost popped out of her head as she lowered them and realized I was feeling him up.

"She's not my mother!" he quickly stated, throwing his palms up in the air at the mere hint of incest.

I gazed at him and licked a trail from the center of his neck, over his chin, and drew his bottom lip into my mouth and bit it gently. "Oh, you'll be calling me Mommy by the break of dawn, guaranteed." I let his dick go and took his hand, beginning to lead him toward the exit. "Come on, let's blow this joint so I can blow you."

"Whore!" the young woman yelled out at our backs.

I turned around and marched right back up to her. She cringed like she was expecting a fist in the face. I smiled at her and said, "With enough practice, you might be able to be as good a whore as me. Don't worry. I only want him for tonight. He'll be back next week with his homeboys and you can have a crack at him. After tonight, he might be able to satisfy you better than he could have if he had left here with you instead of me. I'll teach him a thing or two. Then I don't give a shit if you marry him and have ten kids."

With that, I walked away. Devain was waiting at the door, ready to see where my imagination would take us. We ended up at a nearby hotel. I was ready for some action, and besides, since this was my first time doing something of this nature, I had zero intention of letting him know where I lived; rather less my real name. He was "still at home" so that shit was out; nor was I trying to go there in the first place. Neutral ground made me feel more at ease. Even though I was acting like a whore, I was far from one—at that time—and was a bit nervous myself but determined not to let it show.

"So, Imagine, now that you've got me here, what are you going to do to me?" Devain asked. "You talk a good game; now let's see if you can back it up."

I sat down on the bed and motioned for him with my finger. "Come to Mommy."

His cell phone rang. He yanked it out of the holster and glanced at the caller ID. "This is my homeboy. He's probably worried about me."

"Then answer it and tell him that you are in very, very good hands."

"Yo, wassup! I'm straight."

"Your ass better be straight," I said seductively as he stood before me.

"I met a honey and rolled out."

I lifted my right leg onto the bed, reached under my sundress, and fingered myself through the sides of my satin panties. Then I licked my fingertip. "Yes, my pussy is sweeter than honey!"

"I'll get up with you tomorrow."

"But you're going to get it up for me tonight!"

I pulled him by his belt all the way to me and bit his dick gently through his pants. Then I undid his buckle and went to work to free *my dick.*

Devain flipped his phone closed. "Damn, you aren't playing around, huh?"

"I can see that you're still used to baby pussy. I'm about to throw it on you so hard that you will remember tonight fifty years from now, when I'm dead and buried."

"I don't doubt that for one second."

His dick was beautiful, for lack of a better word. Unlike Alfred, who had gray pubic hairs—on top of his jacked-up breath—Devain's dick was as smooth as a baby's ass, with the exception of the big veins pulsating through it.

"Umm, you look so tasty. Can Mommy milk you dry?"

"Mommy can do whatever she wants."

I smirked because I had expected it to take him longer to get into the Mommy thing.

He stepped completely out of his pants and I could see that he had also shaved his pubic hairs off. I loved that shit. "Hmm, you must be used to getting blow jobs since you shave down here."

He chuckled. "I've had a few."

"Then that means I need to step up my game," I stated with conviction. "I'm going to wax it for you."

If you have ever seen those bobble-head dolls on someone's dashboard, then you can imagine my head going back and forth on his dick. It was the perfect size to hit the back of my throat. I had also gargled with salt earlier, before I left home, so my throat could open up even farther. That's a little trick for you young girls; remember that. Salt water is not only good for you when you have a cold.

Devain came almost immediately and I was a bit disappointed but realized that the second nut is always harder to claim than the first one. Now he was ready for me to get down to the nitty-gritty.

"Lie down on the bed, spread your legs like an eagle, and bring your knees to your chest," I commanded.

"What?" he asked, shocked.

"You're supposed to say, 'Yes, Mommy.' Not 'What?' "

"Yes, Mommy."

He looked mighty silly doing what I asked, and I wasn't even quite sure where I was coming from with it. I simply wanted to see if he would do it.

I grabbed his dick and jerked and pulled and tickled his ass with my other hand, and sure enough, he was hard again within minutes.

"Now let Mommy show you how it's really done."

I drew his balls into my mouth first and sucked on them like a couple of gumballs. His dick got harder. I licked the pre-cum out of the head of his dick and then teased him: sucking the head, blowing on it, then sucking it again.

"I'm about to cum," he whispered.

"You better not cum yet or Mommy will spank you!" I chastised him. "You're a bad boy and you better not cum until I tell you to cum. Do you understand me?"

"Yes, Mommy!"

"That's better!"

For nearly three hours, I brought Devain to the brink of ejaculating and then made him stop. I did spank him. He loved it. I bit his dick, and while he seemed shocked at first, he ended up asking for me to do it some more.

I have to be honest. I used to wonder how men could go out

and pick up total strangers and fuck them. Then it dawned on me that the strangers were women who were doing the same damn thing. Now I was "one of them," and in truth being in that hotel room with Devain, a stranger, was the ultimate turn-on.

I eventually gave him some pussy that night, but he was so worn-out from my dick-sucking that he could barely move. I ended up doing all the work by getting on top. That was an empowering experience as well.

After that night, I started hanging out at clubs near local universities to increase my odds of meeting younger men. Livingstone College in Salisbury, Johnson C. Smith in Charlotte, and Barber-Scotia in Concord were all "hot spots." In a graduate dormitory at Johnson C. Smith I decided to test the Big Bang Theory with three men working on their master's. I met them all at the same time and asked them to all work on mastering me. One of them seemed reluctant at first but then fell victim to peer pressure and ended up fucking me harder than the other two put together.

Yes, I am a cougar. All you younger women out there who want to pretend like your pussies are lined with gold, you better watch out. Not only do you have to compete with women your age for men your age, you also have to compete with me. I make no apologies and I take no prisoners, but look at it this way. The more men that I educate on the art of pleasuring women, the more men will be better husbands. You can marry them and birth the babies; I just want to borrow them for a little while. If any young men are out there looking for an older woman to rock your world, hit me up on MySpace. I am easy enough to find, if you look in the right place.

Come See Me

Do not get me wrong. I love money. I love making money. I love spending money. I especially love spending other people's money more than I love spending my own. That was one of the reasons that I decided that I did not mind doing event planning for the large corporation that I had worked for over the past six years. The opening came up and was a chance for me to get out of the office and stop sitting behind a desk. It was a dream job for me, planning meetings, trips, and conventions for top clients. My expense account was practically limitless. All of it was a tax write-off for the corporation.

I rented a pirate ship once in the Baltimore harbor for twelve dinner guests. It had cost a pretty penny but everyone had fun and I got all the praise. I had a wine-tasting at the embassy of Croatia and had the wine critic from the *Washington Post* teach everyone how to tell good wine from bad. I had organized a dinner at a restaurant that served emus, and everyone was so tickled and enjoyed eating the unusual bird. I had done a little bit of this and a little bit of that. However, like all good things, my happiness came to an end.

My job began to get a little stressful. The one thing that I had not counted on was the attitudes from some of the people who were being wined and dined. A lot of them felt like they were better than everyone else. They started talking down to me, like I was their servant. I did not appreciate that shit at all.

The two brothers who owned the corporation decided that they wanted to plan a trip to the Bahamas for ten of their top clients and their respective mates. I was relieved because I hoped to have a little fun in the sun once I got everyone settled. We had a lovely flight over on a private plane—for the most part, the limousines that took us to the hotel were on point, and then all hell broke loose.

The hotel was top-of-the-line but the wife of one of the men on the trip thought she was the queen of Sheba. She had this Southern drawl that drove me crazy every time she spoke my name.

"Mona, can you please get me some aspirin?"

"Mona, I need a pillow for my back. This plane seat is uncomfortable."

"Mona, can you see about getting me a fresh cup of coffee? This tastes stale."

"Mona, can you find out how much longer it is before we land? My head is really killing me."

She had done all that whining on the plane, and her husband, Steven, seemed embarrassed, but he had picked her. Jill, the queen, was a straight-up trophy wife; that much was obvious. She was dumber than a doornail, but her fake boobs stuck out like a bottle of water in the desert. I did notice that the left one was higher than the right and I was dying to make a comment, but somehow managed to control myself.

Steven was a cutie. He was about five-ten, dark-skinned with a goatee and a short, cropped haircut. Actually he was my type, and I had been without sex for a couple of months since an ugly breakup. On the plane, when I had a brief opportunity to sit down between Jill's ridiculous requests, I did embark on an intense sexual fantasy about Steven as I watched him read the *Wall Street Journal.* The two brothers who owned the corporation were single, but I would not have fucked either of them for bone marrow. Their arrogance was beyond belief. Steven, even though he was equally wealthy, was humble and down-to-earth.

Everyone was settled into their rooms and I was lying across the bed in my suite, looking out at the ocean, when my phone rang.

"Hello."

"Mona, it's Jill!"

Shit! Not the queen!

"Mona, this room simply will not do."

I sucked in some air. "What seems to be the issue?"

"It smells . . . funky!"

I wanted to ask, "Are you sure that's not your ass?"

Instead, I said, "What do you mean by 'funky'?"

"It smells like . . . like someone's feet? Someone's stinky feet!"

"Okay, *Jill,* why don't you call the front desk and ask them to have housekeeping come freshen up?"

I could clearly hear the gasp over the phone. I had insulted the bitch. "But isn't that your job? To make sure that we're all comfortable?"

"Yes, that is my job, but I do not own this hotel. I did not pack any air freshener in my suitcase, but I am sure that their housekeeping staff will do whatever they need to do to fix the situation."

"Can't you get us another room, Mona?"

I tapped my finger on the nightstand. "Okay, Jill. I will see what I can do."

"You do that, Mona, but make it snappy. My head still hurts and I need to lie down."

With that, the bitch slammed the phone down in my ear. I took several deep breaths, slipped my manicured toes back into my sandals, took one more long, admiring glance at the ocean, grabbed the pass card to my room, and headed to the front desk.

I was not expecting what I found at that front desk.

"My name is Yemi. How may I help you?"

His name should have been Yummy.

"Yes, I am with the group that checked in about an hour ago, and one of the guests is requesting a room change."

"Which room might that be?" he asked.

"They're in suite 508. Mr. and Mrs. Steven Lewis."

Yemi's fingers sped across the keyboard and then he frowned; not a good sign.

"I'm sorry, Miss . . ."

"I'm Mona Young. Forgive my manners for not mentioning that when I walked up. I'm the organizer of the trip."

"Well, Miss Young, I'm sorry, but we don't have any more oceanfront suites available for tonight. We could possibly move them tomorrow night. What is wrong with the room? Maybe we can fix it."

I giggled. "That's exactly what I told the bitch, I mean, lady."

He laughed. "Rough day, huh?"

"Yeah, you could say that." I paused and stared at him, realizing my panties were getting damp. "The *lady* said that the room smells funky, like someone's feet."

"I apologize. We will send someone up there to take care of it right away."

"Good, but can you do me a huge favor?"

"Sure," he replied with a perfect set of white teeth, attached to a perfectly chiseled caramel face, attached to what I was sure was a perfectly chiseled body.

"Could you call up there and make it clear to Mrs. Lewis that changing rooms is not an option in this hotel? She will not believe me; even though she should recognize that I have nothing to do with it."

"I would be delighted to do that."

I licked my lips, then bit the bottom one. "You are quite accommodating."

He leaned closer to me over the counter and I could smell his cologne. It was enchanting. "I try my best."

"Well, you are doing a bang-up job. You have certainly brightened up my day." *And dampened my drawers.*

"Is there anything else I can do for you, Miss Young?"

I hesitated, then the little voice in my head said, *Fuck it! Go for it, Mona!*

"Actually, there is something else you can do for me, Yemi."

"What's that, Miss Young?"

"Please, call me Mona."

"Sure, Mona. What can I do for you?"

"You can come see me. You can meet me in my room to-night, after this crazy business dinner that I must attend with the bitch, and you can eat my pussy for me and fuck the shit out of me."

I couldn't believe those words had actually left my mouth, but they had.

Yemi stood there, grinning and apparently speechless. Then it hit me.

"You're not gay, are you?" I blurted out. "Not that there's anything wrong with being gay. It's just that, if you are, then I didn't mean to make a fool out of myself." I found myself rambling. "Oh, goodness, are you married? Involved? I am so sorry for making presumptions. You might not even be attracted to me. Do you find me attractive?" Before he could even form a response, I kept going, "Of course, you don't find me attractive. All these beautiful women over here on the island. What was I thinking? I'm so silly. Please forgive me. I didn't mean to . . ."

"Mona, what time?" he asked in the sexiest accent.

Damnnnnnnnnnnnnnnnnnnnnnnnnnnnnnn!!!!!!!!!!!!!!!!!!!!!

"Um, around eleven. Is eleven okay, Yemi?"

"I'll be there."

There was nothing left to add. I started to walk away, then said, "Oh, do you need my room number?"

He chuckled and pointed to his computer screen. "I've got your number."

"And the bitch?"

"I'll take care of her, and then I'll come see you and take care of you."

I do not even remember dinner; the food, the conversation, the people. Even Jill was invisible that night, but Steven was still kind of hot. We ended the evening right around eleven and I rushed back to my room, wanting to take a quick shower before Yemi showed up. When I put my key card in the door, the red light came on instead of green. I tried again. Red. I kept jiggling the handle, as if that would make the light change colors. I hated it when the cards were demagnetized from rubbing up against another card, but that was not the case. I had left everything in my room but the key card and a tube of lipstick. I hoped that whoever was at the desk would replace the key without an ID.

Halfway to the elevator, I heard a door open behind me and Yemi's voice. "Going someplace, Miss Young?"

I grinned and turned around, holding up the key card. "My card wouldn't work."

"That's because I had the double lock on. I didn't want turndown service to show up and turn me in."

He had only his head poked out the room as I approached. When I realized that he was wearing only a pair of red silk boxers, I almost lost it.

"Doesn't turndown service occur earlier?"

"Yes, but why take chances? I do work here, you know."

"What are you doing here?" I asked as I entered, playing dumb and realizing that as an employee, he had easily made his own key card. "I want to hear you say it, in that sexy-ass voice of yours."

"I'm here to eat your pussy and fuck the shit out of you."

"Amen, my brother. *A-men.*"

He dropped his boxers down to his ankles and I dropped to my knees in front of him without a second's hesitation.

"I'm so hungry," I whispered.

"Didn't you just leave dinner?"

"Yes, but they didn't have dick on the menu."

"You like dick."

"I love dick. I cherish dick."

I licked the head of his dick and added, "I adore dick."

I lifted his dick up and licked his balls. "And I worship balls."

"Damn, I think I love you," Yemi stated.

I gave Yemi a blow job that he would never forget, adding in ice and a couple of breath mints for good measure. I told him, "This is what us American sisters call the icy hot."

"It's what Bahamian men call off the fucking chain!" he declared as he fed me his dick for the next thirty minutes or so.

I had him lie on his back on the bed and placed my bikini-waxed pussy on his lips. "Now eat me while I continue to enjoy you," I said as we got comfortable in the sixty-nine position.

His tongue was thick and long, and I could tell that he was one of those men who did not eat pussy so much to please the women as to please themselves. He and I were compatible; we both performed oral sex because we loved it and not as a matter of reciprocity. If a man never ate me out, I would still insist on sucking his dick. Even as a child, I was always sucking on something: lollipops, Creamsicles, dill pickles. Somewhere along the line, in my formative high school years, I graduated to sucking dicks.

Later on that night, we fucked in the Jacuzzi. I let the warm water pulsing through the jets soothe me as I sat on Yemi's dick and cradled back and forth like a mother and child. He was so damn sexy, and I began to regret that I would have to leave. That's the only fucked-up thing about "vacationships." Every once in a while you run across someone that you do not want to be a one-night stand. Yemi was one of those. I craved to take him back to the States with me, but that was not to happen. I realized it, as did he, so we made the most out of the next thirty-six hours.

I still had to work and deal with Jill's bitchy ass, but once I had the chance to get away from the group, Yemi and I were fucking and sucking. We went to town on each other on the sand, right by the ocean late at night. That had always been a fantasy of mine, and Yemi had made it come true. I tried anal for the first time with him and he made it seem easy. It was nothing horrible, as I had imagined, and when his dick entered my ass, I felt like I was giving him a special part of me. He rode me on the sand, with the waves cascading on us. It was such an incredible sensation; one that I will never forget.

I asked Yemi not to tell me good-bye. I promised that I would be back when I got the chance. He promised that he would come see me again, but this time in my hometown. None of that ever happened. I will tell you what did happen though.

Jill got on my last nerve on the plane ride home. I could not wait for her to get the fuck out of my face. When we landed, everyone left except for the pilot and me. I was doing some last-minute paperwork on my laptop, and he said that he did not mind my remaining on board while he performed routine maintenance on the underside of the plane. I jumped when I heard someone get on board. It turned out to be Steven.

"I'm sorry, Mona. I didn't mean to startle you," he said. "Jill left her sunglasses in the cup holder by her seat."

"No problem. I'll get them for you. Is she waiting for you in the car?"

"No, she's already at home. I said that I would come back and get them. She tried to insist on making you bring them. I didn't feel that was appropriate."

I didn't comment as I retrieved the glasses and handed them to him. Our fingers brushed against one another's and it was like lightning.

"I apologize for Jill. My wife has this way of turning people off, and I've tried to explain that to her."

"Well, as long as she turns you on, that's all that matters," I stated sarcastically. "Sorry, I didn't mean it that way."

He stared at me. "Actually, you turn me on."

"I'm flattered, Steven, but—"

Before I could finish my sentence, he was all on me. His kisses were sweet. The way he suckled on my nipples was intense. The way he fingered my pussy with an urgency was invigorating. We crash-landed on the queen-size bed in the quarters in the back of the plane. Then we commenced fucking. We've been fucking ever since; eight months and counting. Do I regret it? Yes and no. I regret that Steven's still married to Jill. He denies sleeping with her but I know he's lying. But I like fucking Steven. It's comfortable, and in a way I like knowing that I am sticking it to Jill. One day, I believe that I can take him, but do I really want him? Once a cheater, always a cheater. That's what they say.

Maybe, just maybe, Yemi will come see me again one day.

Trisexuality

Zane

When I was in my thirties, you could not tell me shit about my sexual prowess. I "assumed" that I had "been there and done that" and that there was nothing new under the sun for me to experience. I was black, beautiful, successful, happily single, and ready to make my first million by the time I was forty. What can I say? Things change.

By the time I hit forty, I was married to a complete asshole, I had put on about twenty pounds, my mortgage company was in bankruptcy because of the shitty-ass economy caused by a president who was more concerned with starting wars than taking care of shit at home, and instead of having my first million, I was struggling to make ends meet.

Carl was wonderful when I first met him over the internet on sisterswhocravebigdicks.com. He seemed to have it all together. Then again, everyone over the internet has their shit together. He claimed to be an up-and-coming music producer with a stable of artists that would put all others to shame, and he boasted about having a lavish home on each coast. I lived in

Seattle and he spent most of the year in Los Angeles. Carl was older than me and knew how to play the ultimate game. He had mastered exactly what women wanted to hear and what women wanted to feel.

On our first date, he flew me to meet him in Chicago. That should have been clue one, that he did not want to show me either of his homes. We stayed in a three-star hotel—I was expecting a five-star—and we went to restaurants like Uno and Applebee's throughout the weekend, which should have been clues two and three. He rented a Toyota Corolla and I was expecting some sort of luxury vehicle. Clue four. Granted, I had heard all the horror stories about women who had met men via the internet and found themselves caught up in some complete bullshit. However, Carl seemed halfway decent at the time, even though everything that he had told me was not adding up.

By the time the weekend was over, I was addicted to the dick and nothing else mattered. We were married less than six weeks later. That's when I began finding out the truth. Carl did not have a home on the East Coast but he did have a grandmother in Brooklyn who lived in one of the last buildings in New York with rent control. He would visit her twice a year, only because she gave him money to come and spend time with her. Carl's home in Los Angeles was a duplex, and he shared it with three other trifling-ass men. Instead of us living there, he moved to Seattle with me since I had my own business—and my own home. Mind you, up until the time we got hitched in a chapel in Vegas, he was insisting that I would have to relocate so that he could build up his music empire. Oh, yeah, the stable of artists. Check this out. He did have some artists, but none of them had a lick of talent. One woman, who called herself Isis, could not sing her way out of a paper bag. This dude Pookie Poo was a rapper who looked like he needed to keep a paper bag over his head at all times. There was not a chance in hell that women would swoon over him. He looked like he had so much sugar in his tank that the only way women would throw their panties at him would be for him to borrow them and put them on his own ass.

Needless to say, my life went downhill after that. Carl would lounge on the couch while I went to my office day after day trying to acquire mortgage loans in a housing environment where prices had fallen an average of 10 percent, foreclosures were at an all-time high, and things were pretty much at a standstill. I finally had to file bankruptcy for my LLC and do something else. But what was something else?

It took me all of two weeks to figure it out. Because of all the stress that my marriage and failing business had put me through, I had put on some weight, but I was still above par in the looks department. One of my friends from college had been urging me to join her in a lucrative business venture. Dawn had always been sex-crazed. I had no idea how far she would take it though . . . until she started dawnsdelight.com and did sex shows over the internet. Dawn had her town house decorated like a brothel, and she—along with a few other women—were making a mint fucking for the voyeuristic people of the world. I had no idea how much they were making until Dawn broke it down for me. She said that if I came there two days a week, I could make six figures a year with ease.

Now, Carl's dick was still good, but he was unappealing to me, lying up on the couch playing video games and eating kettle corn all day and night. There is nothing worse than a man trying to kiss you with remnants of popcorn all up in his grill. That shit is not sexy at all. The prospect of getting back at him for all his lies was intriguing. He had lied about everything that he was about. Why shouldn't I fuck for money? It wasn't like he was paying any bills, and I was nobody's mother so I did not have to worry about my offspring finding out about it.

I called Dawn up and told her that I would accept the position on one condition. I had to wear a mask. She said that shit was out. Men—and women—wanted to see boldness, they wanted to see what true freaks looked like, and I would look plum silly with a mask on while everyone else was "baring their souls." She made it sound like some kind of love story. It was pure fucking.

I had watched them "perform" a few times to try to convince myself to do it. All my life I had fucked one man at a time. Well, I did date two men at once back in the day, but it got confusing because I could not keep my lies straight. I have to give it to men. Keeping up with a pack of lies with various lovers can be a full-time gig. I had spent fourteen hours over this dude's house once, and three weeks later, he asked me when I was going to give him some more pussy because he had not gotten any in months. I was like, "Um, excuse me, but do you not remember me in your bed a few weeks ago?" He replied, "Damn, I had a memory lapse for a second. Of course I remember. That shit was good, too. I was on point that night with my dick action, wasn't I?"

Whatever! He never saw my ass again and I refused his calls.

Anyway, now I was about to embark on some new-frontier madness. I was about to open myself up to fuck strangers for cash. I was about to do things that I had never conceived of doing before. I was about to become a "trisexual."

• • •

On my first day "at the office" Dawn introduced me to a brother named Adonis. He was already naked and chilling on a sofa when I walked into the room. I had never met a man while he was nude, with his dick sticking straight up in the air, while he was smoking a joint. I started trembling. His dick was fourteen inches if it was a centimeter, and I had never experienced more than nine. I had never broken out a ruler but I was comfortable with those figures. What I was not comfortable with was the thought of having to limp back to my car at the end of the day.

Cornelia, one of the "worker bees," came in the room wearing a nightie. Before I could even say, "Girl, what's up? I haven't seen you in a minute," she was on her knees slobbering all over Adonis's dick like it was her life force. Dawn had taken her position behind a camcorder and was moving around like she was an award-winning director, catching the action from various angles. I stood there in amazement, wondering how in the hell Cornelia could get so much dick in her mouth.

This went on for a good fifteen minutes, until Adonis shot off a load that would have impressed even the biggest porn star.

Dawn looked at me and said, "Your turn. Take off your clothes and get jiggy with it."

"Get jiggy with it?" I asked, appalled. "What do you mean?"

Cornelia, who had a faceful of semen, gawked at me. "Oh, so now you're gonna play dumb?"

I pointed at Adonis. "You expect me to suck dick after her?"

All three of them answered in unison, "Yes!"

"But I can't suck that dick!" I stated in shock. "Look at the size of that thing!"

Cornelia stood up and put her hands on her hips. "I just sucked it. What, you think you're better than me?"

Adonis smirked. "Look, if you didn't come here to get fucked, take your dead ass home." He was imitating the Parliament/Funkadelic phrase that people chanted at concerts: "If you didn't come here to P-Funk, take your dead ass home."

Before I knew it, another half dozen people were in the room, chanting, "If you didn't come here to get fucked, take your dead ass home!" Apparently this was a regular routine because they really got into it. It was like when someone is celebrating a birthday at a restaurant and the entire wait staff comes over to sing "Happy Birthday"; except they were mocking me, daring me.

That shit worked like a charm. Next thing you know, I was naked, sitting in between Adonis's legs with a toss pillow under my knees, and doing my best to suck the skin off his elephantine dick. I never even liked to drink after other people; now I was sucking dick after other people. I gagged, I choked, I had trouble breathing, but I kept going. He told me to play with his balls; I nearly yanked them off his body. He told me to finger his ass; I stuck two fingers up there and tried to give him a prostate exam.

By the end of that day, I had "discovered myself." I now knew my true calling. I was a freak by nature, a woman of greatness when it came to throwing down. I was the one who would be dubbed the Trisexual.

For months, it went on. I had my pussy eaten. I ate pussy. I had my ass eaten. I ate ass. I rode more dicks than every other woman there. I loved dick. I even loved pussy, and before then, I had hated to even look at my own pussy. I never realized that every dick and pussy had its own individuality. I used to buy into the premise that dick was dick and pussy was pussy, but nothing could be further from the truth. Each one has its own special look, special taste, and special ability to give pleasure to another.

Poor Carl didn't have a clue. I would still break him off once or twice a week for good measure, but things were not the same. Instead of working at Dawn's two days, I was over there all the time, waiting for some action. I was ripping off men's clothes the second they walked in the door, making sure that I got to the dick first. I became so popular on the website that men—and a few women—emailed Dawn trying to set up private sessions with me. They did not want to be plastered all over the internet with a webcam, but they wanted to fuck me nonetheless. They wanted a try at the Trisexual, and if they looked even halfway decent, I was down.

I started flying to them, as long as they paid for it. One man, Ronald, emailed Dawn and said that his wife could not fuck him right with a strap-on dick. He asked if I was capable of doing it right. When Dawn approached me about his offer, I stated, "If he wants to be fucked up the ass, I will fuck the living daylights out of him!"

Four days later I was landing at JFK Airport and taking a cab to Queens. I was a little taken aback when his wife answered the door, proclaiming, "Thank goodness you're here! Ronald's driving me nuts! I have the strap-on all ready for you!"

Sure enough, when I walked into the upstairs bedroom, Ronald was lying on his stomach tied to the bedposts with nylons, and a gigantic strap-on dick was sitting at the end of the bed waiting for me to put it on. That shit turned me on like nothing else in my life. For years, men had fucked over women, and now I had the opportunity to fuck them back—with no grease!

Ronald was so excited as I mounted him that he came before I even stuck the strap-on in his ass. I stuck it in slowly at first and told him, "You're gonna be my bitch by the end of the night!" I made him my bitch, too. He screamed with delight. He praised my good deed. He paid me ten thousand dollars for giving him the fuck of the century. Then I left.

I stayed the night in New York City, on Ronald's tab of course. I chose the most expensive hotel I could find and ordered almost everything on the room service menu. I got bored halfway through the night and decided to "peruse" Times Square. Okay, I admit it. I wanted some dick, and dick is never hard to find anywhere but it is extremely accessible in the Big Apple. I found a lively bar, took a seat on a bar stool, and searched for what was appealing to me for the night. Instead of one appetizer, I found two. They were an attractive couple, obviously tourists because they looked scared. I was not from there either but I wasn't scared of a damn thing. I approached their booth and asked if I could sit down. It did not take much convincing to lure them back to my room. They were engaged and from Texas. I turned both of them out and wished them a long, happy life together.

The next day I flew back home. Carl was waiting for me at the door, so angry that smoke was damn near coming out of his ears. My secret was out. One of his friends had seen me on the internet. Now all his friends knew about me fucking on Dawn's site. His parents knew. His grandmother in the rent-controlled apartment in Brooklyn knew and had declared that he was not getting another penny of her money since his wife was making a bundle "selling ass."

What amazed me about the entire thing was that Carl cussed me out like he had some kind of leverage in our situation. He threatened to leave me. I asked him, "How long will it take you to get your shit packed?" He announced that it was already packed. I said, "Good, then don't let the doorknob hit you on the ass on the way out." He stood there, shocked, realizing something that most men never see coming. I did not need him. I did not want him. I could make it without him. I could do badly all by myself and he was not contributing shit.

Carl did leave and returned to his musical pipe dreams. I stayed with Dawn's enterprise for another year and decided to move to Vegas after my divorce was finalized. I became a high-class hooker and made more money than Dawn was providing me by starting my own stable. What's the name of my company? That should be obvious. It's called Trisexuality.

About the Contributors

After meeting both Zane and Allison Hobbs in Philadelphia, **Ahnjel** decided to appreciate life and indulge her sensuality by taking a leap of faith. Having recently turned fifty, she is excited about this story, her first publication.

Renee Alexis is the author of many short stories published with Kensington's Aphrodisia line. When she's not writing spicy stories, she's engaging in her other ventures: teaching school and making gemstone jewelry. Born and raised in Detroit, Michigan, she loves the excitement and activity of urban living. She loves hearing from fans: reneealexis.net.

Anthony Beal: This thirty-two-year-old horror erotica writer with aged tequila for blood devotes his scribblings as well as his leisure time to varying degrees of sacrilege and libertinage and is believed to exist in more than one universe. Between attempts to take over the world, he hangs his hat at theofficialanthonybeal.com.

Been (bēn) is a make-believe name for a real sista who writes stuff: real stuff about make-believe people, make-believe stuff about real people, and make-believe stuff about make-believe people. Occasionally, she writes real stuff about real people, but she changes the names so they won't sue her for real and stuff. She lives in Cali.

Camille Blue is a writer, a book reviewer, and a librarian living in Milwaukee, Wisconsin. She is currently working on a novel. Ms. Blue may be contacted at camilleblue2007@yahoo .com.

Rachel Kramer Bussel (rachelkramerbussel.com) is senior editor at *Penthouse Variations,* hosts In the Flesh Erotic Reading Series, and wrote the popular *Lusty Lady* column for the *Village Voice.* Her work has been published in over one hundred anthologies, including *Best American Erotica 2004* and *2006,* and her books include *Caught Looking, She's on Top, He's on Top,* and *Naughty Spanking Stories from A to Z 1* and *2.*

Dina lives in Michigan and is a gifted spiritualist and writer. She is currently writing her first erotic novel. She can be reached at dinawritesbooks@yahoo.com.

Lotus Falcon is a native of Washington, D.C., who holds a BS in education and an MPA in public administration. She is an educator in the D.C. public schools system who also leads women empowerment/sexuality workshops and sells adult toys and products. She is currently working on several writing products for children and adults and is married with seven children.

Samantha J. Green is an eighteen-year-old native of Shreveport, Louisiana, and the self-proclaimed number one FAN of Zane. She began writing at the age of twelve and is currently attending Centenary College of Louisiana, where she majors in communication with an emphasis on professional writing. She can be reached at dal8ydestiny@aol.com.

Lesley E. Hal is the author of *Blind Temptations: The Seduction of Sex, Lies & Betrayal,* which is her first book. You can visit her website at pleasureprinciplepublishing.com. Her first novel is available at barnesandnoble.com and amazon.com.

Chris Hayden is a native of St. Louis, Missouri. Door of Kush Multimedia publishes his novel, *A Vampyre Blues: The Passion of Varnado.* His story "Selena the Sexual Healer" (under the name Victor DeVanardo) appeared in *Chocolate Flava.*

Tigress Healy is one of many pseudonyms for this flourishing writer. Originally from New York, she now resides in Georgia with her family. She is currently working on several erotica and cultural fiction projects. She can be reached at tigresshealy @yahoo.com.

Linda "Sunshine" Herman is a thirty-one-year-old wife and mother residing in Cordele, Georgia. She has been employed as an emergency dispatcher for more than twelve years. Her passion is entertaining others through her creative writing.

Wanda D. Hudson is the author of *Wait for Love: A Black Girl's Story.* She is currently working on her second novel titled,

A Sheltered Life. Ms. Hudson can be reached at www.wanda dhudson.com.

Ms. Lovelie Ladie: I have an AAS. I have always written poetry. My first book should be out by March, titled, *Love Sweet Love,* a book of erotic poetry. I also plan to publish my book of erotic tales, which is where "An Arresting, Intoxicating Situation" came from. This will be my first story published, but definitely not my last. I love writing and this is a dream come true for me. Thanks, Zane.

Dangerous Lee is the writer of the monthly humor advice column *Ask Dangerous Lee* and an internet radio personality on nghosi.com. When she's not writing, she's starring in B horror movies such as *The Executioner's Tale* and raising her daughter. Visit her at myspace.com/dangerouslee.

B. F. Redd currently lives in the Birmingham, Alabama, area with her husband and three boys. She started writing as an emotional outlet and, on the urging of friends, began posting her poems and stories on the internet. They caught the attention of another author, and she is now working on her book of short stories called *Ridin' Dirty.*

Teresa Noelle Roberts writes romantic erotica and erotic romance, both under her own name and as one-half of the writing team known as Sophie Mouette. Her stories have appeared in *Best Women's Erotica 2004, 2005,* and *2007,* numerous *Wicked Words* anthologies from Virgin Black Lace books, fishnetmag .com, and many other publications. Sophie Mouette's first novel, *Cat Scratch Fever,* was published in 2006 by Virgin Black Lace.

Michelle J. Robinson resides in New York City, is the mother of identical twin boys, and studied journalism at New York University. Her short story "Mi Destino" was included in Zane's *New York Times* bestseller *Caramel Flava,* and she has recently completed two novels—*Color Me Grey* and *Serial Typical.* Michelle can be reached at Robinson_201@hotmail.com or at myspace.com/justef.

Alice Sturdivant is the pseudonym of a freelance writer who lives and writes in Hopkins, South Carolina.

Tyanna graduated from the University of Connecticut (UCONN) in May 2006, with a BFA from the School of Fine Arts. She looks forward to exploring her possibilities and achieving much success throughout her journey in life. She is a Contemporary Artist and samples of her work can be found on myspace.com/ty_madyson.

Memphis Vaughn Jr. is the editor of TimBookTu, the premier African-American online poetry and writing website. He edited *Journey to TimBookTu: An African-American Poetic Odyssey,* a collection of poetry, short stories, and essays published in 2002, and was a contributor to *Chocolate Flava* under the pen name blk_man4u. He resides in Mobile, Alabama, and is currently completing his collection of erotic short stories in 2008.

Randy Walker is a native of Mississippi, where he is licensed to practice law. He recently completed his first novel, *The Keys of My Soul,* and currently serves on the English faculty of Lane College in Jackson, Tennessee. Randy can be reached through his website, randybandit.com.

Romeo Walker is an aspiring writer, originally from Baltimore, Maryland. He is a proud graduate of Alabama State University and a member of Iota Phi Theta Fraternity Inc. Thanks to Shantel, Romeka, Tiana, Portia, Courtney, Ronica, Demetrius, Todd, Cameron, Temica, Anna, Dawn, and Hermelyn.

Zane is the publisher of Strebor Books, a division of Atria Books/Simon & Schuster. She is the *New York Times* bestselling author of more than ten titles and the executive producer of *Zane's Sex Chronicles,* a Cinemax Original Series. She resides in the Washington, D.C., metropolitan area.